IF YOU

LOOK AWAY

Prologue

Snow fell in brittle flakes, whispering against the windows, but Brynlee didn't care. She kicked her blankets off and glared at the red digits of her clock. Midnight. *Too early. Too late.*

The house looked perfect, as always—garland across the banister, the tree downstairs glowing like a magazine cover—but none of it mattered if the presents weren't right.

Last year, the stacks had nearly touched the ceiling. It had taken her hours to open everything. She should've been dreaming of what else she'd get this year, but all she could think about was the sour ache in her chest.

Three days left. *What if it wasn't enough this time? What if they forgot the list?*

She shoved the covers away and marched for the stairs.

The tree glittered, mocking. The garland shimmered like it knew a secret.

And underneath—

Her breath caught hot in her throat. *Three? That was it? They'd given her three?*

Heat rose sharp in her face. *This was wrong. Unfair. Pathetic.*

The snow outside pressed harder against the windows, like it wanted in.

The First Crack

Brynlee froze at the sight, fists clenching at her sides. *Maybe it was a trick. Maybe her parents hadn't set everything out yet.* But the pit in her stomach knew better.

She crept closer. One box was large, but thin. Another was small enough to fit in her hand. The third was a cube, heavy-looking. All of them wrapped perfectly.

The words jammed, barbed in her throat. *Three gifts. That wasn't Christmas.*

She sank to her knees on the rug, pressing her palms flat against the wrapping paper as if by sheer will, it might summon more. Nothing.

The fury rose like fire.

They had the money. They always had the money. Why would they do this to me?

All the kids houses looked like gift shop explosions—mountains of wrapped boxes spilling across the floor. Brynlee's Instagram feed was clogged with photos of towers of ribbon and glitter, proof that other parents cared enough to buy their kids twenty, thirty, sometimes fifty things.

The hiss of the heater clicked on, but the warmth didn't reach her.

"Bryn?"

She flinched. Her dad stood in the archway, rubbing his eyes, his plaid pajama pants wrinkled.

"What are you doing up?" he asked softly, then followed her gaze to the tree.

"This is it?" Her voice cracked, sharp as broken glass. Panic burst out before she could stop it. "Oh my God—we're broke, aren't we? That's what this is? Your way of telling me? Or—or maybe UPS and FedEx are just late with the rest?"

The second the words left her, her hand flew to her mouth. Her chest dropped like she'd missed a stair in the dark. Too much. Too cruel. She wanted to drag them back down her throat, but her dad's face had already shifted—creased, tired in a way she'd never meant to see.

Her stomach twisted, shame burning under her skin, but pride rose quicker.

His voice was steady, gentler than she deserved. "Love, I know it's not what you were expecting, but—"

"But what?" she snapped, leaning into anger to drown the regret. "What would possibly make you think this is enough? Everyone gets more. Everyone!"

His sigh was heavy, lined with something she didn't care to name. "We chose quality over quantity this year. You'll understand—"

"I don't want excuses."

She shoved past him, heat blazing up her throat, and slammed her door hard enough to rattle the frame.

Brynlee threw herself onto the bed, clutched her pillow, and squeezed her eyes shut.

Her phone buzzed on the nightstand. A group chat blew up with pictures of stacked presents and captions dripping with fake modesty. *Look what my parents did this year*

Brynlee dropped the phone, face hot, throat tight. Her fists twisted the sheets.

Three.

She squeezed her eyes shut, Proof she wasn't worth more.

Sleep dragged her under fast, hard, merciless.

And in the dark behind her eyelids, something shifted.

The air turned sharp and cold.

And she wasn't alone anymore.

The Ache That Eats

The corner of her room breathed.

Brynlee's eyes flew open to colors wrong and heavy—tree light smeared across her walls like bruises. The air thinned, metallic. A slow, wet inhale uncoiled from the dark.

Shadows peeled upward and took shape. Skin too clear, stretched over edges of bone. Bruises bloomed and slid beneath its forearms like ink finding new places to hide. Raw tracks carved down its cheeks where tears had burned and kept burning. Its breath leaked in damp gasps that smelled of iron and mildew.

And the hands—split nails, knuckles cracked and weeping, the meat of the palms torn as if it had clawed through concrete to get here.

"Brynlee," it said, her name dragging over broken glass.

She shoved back against the headboard. No sound came out.

It leaned close, hollow eyes widening as if they could swallow her.

"I am the Spirit of Pain." The words dropped flat, no performance in them — just a sentence that had always been true.

Its fingers closed around her wrist—ice that wasn't cold so much as the absence of anything warm. The floor beneath her bed fissured, a hairline crack spidering fast, then splitting wide.

The room fell away like a trap door.

She hit hard on cracked pavement slick with frozen spill. The Spirit still clamped her wrist. Night air bit clean through her thin pajama top.

"Watch," it rasped.

A small house hunched ahead, paint peeling like brittle paper. One window held a weak square of yellow.

Brynlee stumbled forward *because the hand on her arm made her.* Her face pressed to the icy glass.

Inside: a round table. Four paper plates. Four people.

A father with work-split knuckles bowed so long his lips kept moving after everyone else lifted their heads. A mother smiled too big as she slid part of her portion onto the girl's plate when she thought no one watched. A boy and a girl—pulled careful pieces of chicken, chewing slow as if every bite might be the last for a while.

No one spoke. The room breathed with the sound of forks against paper.

Her face burned, hotter than the glass she was breathing on. *She wiped a clear patch with the heel of her palm and couldn't stop looking.* The hollows in their cheeks. The way the mother's throat bobbed when she pretended, she wasn't hungry. The father's hands—those hands—red and cracked, a map of ache.

Behind her, the Spirit shifted.

It wasn't the same shape anymore. Ribs showed sharper. Lips whitened from being pressed together too long. Its hands mirrored the father's—split, raw, bleeding in the same places. The bruises re-bloomed in new constellations across its arms.

Brynlee squeezed her eyes shut. "Stop." The word came out thin, torn.

The Spirit leaned until its ruined mouth hovered near her ear. It didn't explain. It didn't soothe.

"See."

She opened her eyes *because not opening them hurt worse.*

Breath rasped against her ribs, too sharp to pull in clean. Swallowing was like dragging glass down.

Her fist hit the glass before she could stop it, the sound too loud, too alive. The words ripped free with it—*there has to be more, somebody has to have more*—because she couldn't stand what she was seeing, couldn't breathe through it.

The Spirit's grip pulsed. Pain radiated up her arm, old and borrowed and familiar all at once.

"Enough," she whispered, not sure who she meant it for.

The window spidered. Thin fractures raced across her reflection until her face broke into pieces she couldn't line up.

The Spirit's voice came from everywhere at once, soft as frost: "You will not unsee."

The world cracked like bone.

Darkness took her again.

Echoes in Empty Places

The blackness folded in on itself. Brynlee's body pitched forward, weightless, like she was being swallowed and spat back out in the same breath.

She hit concrete this time—knees scraping, palms raw from the impact. The air stank of rot and exhaust, damp seeping up through her thin pajama pants.

When she blinked, the dark lifted just enough to reveal brick walls rising crooked on either side. A rusted dumpster squatted at the far end, plastic bags spilling sour milk and grease.

And on the dumpster sat another figure.

Carved. Too thin, shoulders sharp under a ragged coat. Eye pits darker than the alley, deep enough to swallow echoes. A mouth curved in something almost a smile, but nothing human touched it.

"Brynlee."

"I am the Spirit of Loneliness." The words clung to her skin like damp, not spoken so much as soaked into her.

A sharp pressure banded her windpipe. He slid down from the dumpster, boots hitting water with a hollow splash, and stretched out a hand. His fingers were long, brittle things, the nails split and curling as though they had been gnawed by hunger itself.

She hesitated, chest pounding, *but the alley tilted, her balance spilling away from her until her palm slapped into his.* The skin was dry, papery, the grip both fragile and impossible to escape.

He led her toward the far corner.

There, collapsed inside a cardboard box, was a girl.

Brynlee's breath hitched.

The girl couldn't have been more than sixteen, maybe her own age. Hair matted and damp from the drizzle. Cheeks streaked with grime. She hugged a photograph to her chest, clutching it like it was her only heartbeat.

Brynlee crouched, pulse hammering. *The photo showed the girl as a child—six, maybe seven—grinning between a mom and dad whose faces were younger, softer, untouched by grief.*

The girl's lips moved. A sob hiccupped out, and she stared at the Christmas lights strung across the market on the next street over. The glow reflected in her eyes, wide and glassy.

The Spirit leaned close, whispering as if the words came from inside Brynlee's ribs:

"No hands to hold. No voices to call her name. Just cold. Just empty. Just the lights she can't touch."

Something clawed up Brynlee's throat, raw and splintering, like it would rip her open if she held it in. The words broke loose anyway, ragged, pleading. "Somebody has to see you. Somebody has to care."

The girl wiped her nose with the back of her sleeve, sniffled, and pulled the picture tighter. A small sound escaped her, not even a word, just need shaped into noise.

Her chest hollowed, as if the air had slipped through a crack in her ribs.

For a split second, *Brynlee saw herself in that box—knees to her chest, arms locked around nothing but air.*

The memory of waiting outside school too long, convinced her parents had forgotten her, surged up like a bruise she thought had healed.

What if the world looked away and forgot she existed too?

The Spirit of Loneliness grinned wider now, though his teeth were too small, too sharp. "You feel it," he said. "You wear it. Because loneliness is never only theirs. It finds you too."

The alley buckled. The market lights winked out one by one until the cardboard box was swallowed whole.

The Spirit's voice dissolved with the last thread of light:

"You cannot unknow her face."

Full But Empty

Light hit like a slap.

Brynlee stumbled into a room too bright, too clean—white marble, glass everywhere, a ceiling so high the chandelier looked like a frozen explosion. A tree rose beside a wall of windows, monstrous in its perfection, its needles glittering with frost-spray. The floor beneath it drowned in wrapped boxes, a hundred tiny monuments to having more.

She wasn't alone.

A woman-shaped outline stood at the window—already there, not arriving, not hiding. Just present, the way an empty chair waited in a room. Her edges blurred every time Brynlee tried to hold focus, *like memory refused to keep her shape.* If there were eyes, they slid past her and kept going. *Being unseen pressed against her skin, real as touch.*

"I am the Spirit of Rejection," the blurred outline said, flat as a verdict, as if the title had already been written across her chest.

A tinny chime cut the room. A video call ringing. The glass wall bloomed into a screen.

A girl sat alone on a white couch that could have seated ten. Sixteen, raven hair glossy, sweater crisp. Behind her, another tree climbed higher than this one; the gifts under it stacked into a small skyline. Everything gleamed as if afraid to be caught dull.

"Mom?" the girl said, voice catching. "Dad?"

The screen split. Two hotel rooms, two parents. Night outside both windows. Their smiles looked professional, the kind people wore for strangers.

"Sweetheart," the mother said, glancing off to the side at something else. "Look at all that. Isn't it wonderful?"

"Come home." The girl swallowed. "Please. Just for Christmas morning."

Her father's laugh was polite, the kind that closed a door while sounding friendly. "Sixteen hours for gifts we already paid for? Baby, be reasonable? We'll FaceTime. We'll be there that way."

"It's not the same."

"Don't be dramatic," her mother said. "You have everything you asked for."

The girl flinched. "I didn't ask for you to be gone."

Acid lurched in her gut. She'd never had to beg for her parents' time—but hadn't she already measured their love in boxes anyway?

Brynlee dragged breath hard enough to burn, shoved the words out raw. "Can't you see her? Can't you see how much she needs you? She's your child—yours—and she's dying inside without you!"

The force of it left her throat scraped hollow, chest trembling as if she'd torn the plea straight from her lungs. But on the screen, the parents didn't shift. Their eyes slid past, blank, as if her voice had never touched them at all.

Silence stretched. The father checked his watch. "We have meetings. We love you."

The call ended itself.

The room swallowed the echo. The girl folded in, palms over her eyes, shoulders shaking without sound. A ribbon slipped from a box and crept across the marble like a thin vein.

The Spirit didn't move toward Brynlee. Didn't turn her way. Her voice came as if to the room, not to her.

"Provision is not presence."

The words landed heavier than a shout.

Brynlee's chest tightened until it hurt. *She knew the shape of wanting to be looked at and having eyes slide off. She knew the quietness of measuring love in what arrived instead of who did.*

"Look how full," the Spirit said, still not looking at her. "Listen how empty."

The tree's lights pulsed harder, then too bright, then out—burning an afterimage into Brynlee's vision: a mountain of gifts, and a girl who might as well have none.

Her throat closed on the word *Stop* before it left, but the plea throbbed in her chest.

The Spirit's head tilted, almost curious, almost bored. "You asked for more," she said, voice as even as a line on a graph. "It would not have kept anyone."

The marble under Brynlee's feet cracked, hairlines racing like frost. The chandelier hissed, glass straining.

She fell before the lights went dark.

False Dawn

She woke choking on a sob.

The ceiling was hers again—hairline crack, glow of morning through frost. Her room. Her house. The smell of coffee rising from downstairs, cinnamon ghosts clinging to the air.

"Mom!" she croaked, voice breaking on the single syllable.

Footsteps, fast. The door flung open. Her mother's face appeared first—sleep-tangled hair, confusion turning to alarm—then her father behind her.

Brynlee was already moving, stumbling out of bed, crossing the cold floor on bare feet to slam into both of them at once. She clung *like something was trying to pull her backward into the dark.*

"Hey," her dad said softly, arms wrapping around her, voice careful. "Hey, Bryn. What happened?"

She didn't have words. She had *the taste of iron in her mouth and a bruise burning on her wrist and three faces carved into her mind—pain, loneliness, rejection—that wouldn't blink away.* Tears came hot and miserable. She let them.

Her mother smoothed her hair. "Nightmare?"

Brynlee nodded against her shoulder. *It felt like a lie. It felt like the only thing she could say.* But the bruise burning on her wrist argued otherwise.

Her father pressed his cheek to the top of her head. "You're safe," he said. "You're home."

They held her until the shaking eased. When she pulled back, her mother's thumb traced under her eyes, gentle. Her father searched her face like he was reading a language he used to know.

"Can we… not do gifts this morning?" Brynlee's voice rasped, small. "Not yet."

Both parents blinked. *If she weren't still raw, their faces might've made her laugh.*

"What do you want to do?" her mom asked carefully.

The question hung in the air. She didn't answer. Couldn't.

Silence pressed close, thick as the dark she'd just clawed out of. The room still smelled like sleep—warm sheets, her mother's perfume faint on her skin—but underneath it all was the tang of sweat cooling down her spine. Her hands wouldn't stay still. She curled her fingers tight, uncurled them again, like she could wring the dream out through her palms.

Her wrist throbbed, phantom-deep, right where the bruise had burned in the nightmare. The echo of it crawled up her arm until she tucked it under her shirt, hiding it. Hiding herself.

Her parents watched, waiting, but their faces blurred at the edges. The girl's face was sharper—hollow, folded in on itself under the weight of everything that didn't matter. Brynlee swallowed hard, throat raw from a scream she hadn't really made.

"Can we go out? To the children's home? The one by the church. There were wish lists. I—" The words snagged, splintering in her throat before she could force them out.

The thought of ripping paper, pretending joy lived in boxes, twisted her stomach. She saw the girl again, folded on herself under a mountain of things that didn't matter. She couldn't—she wouldn't—be that. "I want to use my money. The savings. I want to help."

Her father's brows knit, a question he didn't voice.

"Please." *She said it like a plea and a vow.*

He and her mother looked at each other over her shoulder, some quiet communication passing. Then they both nodded.

"Okay," her mom said. "Okay."

By late morning they were standing in a fluorescent lobby that smelled like lemon cleaner and crayons. Paper snowflakes hung crooked from the ceiling. A bulletin board held a blizzard of index cards with children's names and scrawled wishes: *Soccer ball. Warm socks. Jasmine-scented shampoo. Any book about horses. Something that sparkles.*

Brynlee's throat tightened at the smallness of it all. *Warm socks. A soccer ball. Things lighter than lies, smaller than excuses. And she had demanded more, like enough could ever mean full.*

A woman with a clipboard smiled and thanked them and didn't ask questions when Brynlee kept plucking cards until her hands were full. They spent the afternoon chasing cheap miracles—a ball from the sporting goods store, a plastic tiara, a paperback horse series boxed set, shampoo that promised jasmine twice on the label.

Her parents laughed in the aisles, short bursts that sounded like relief wearing a costume.

On the way home, cocoa steamed in cardboard cups between them. The sky sank purple toward evening. Brynlee stared out at the thin winter sun and felt a strange lightness in her chest—like she'd set something down she hadn't known she was carrying.

Back at the house, her mom said, "We could do a movie. Apple Cider?"

"Hallmark?" her dad said, mock horror.

"Something with a town gazebo," Brynlee said, and the way her parents laughed probably meant *this was what a normal family sounded like.*

They set the three gifts beside the coffee table. They stayed wrapped. No one mentioned them.

The tree blinked its slow colors. The movie murmured. Her father's arm lay heavy along the back of the couch. Her mother's socks didn't match. *It felt too good. Fragile. Like a snow globe she didn't dare shake.*

When she finally drifted, her last thought was grateful and small: *Maybe her mind had made monsters just to scare her straight.*

The shadow in the corner stayed still. Waiting.

Distant Light

Christmas Eve tasted like cinnamon and ordinary.

Brynlee woke to the muffled thud of her dad bumping a cabinet and her mom humming something off-key that wanted to be a carol. The house smelled warm—coffee, butter, the faint pine of the tree. *No iron. No damp.* Her wrist ached when she flexed it and then didn't. *She let herself believe the quiet.*

"Morning, B," her dad said when she shuffled in, hair wild. He lifted a spatula like it was the start of a magic trick. "Pancakes shaped like reindeer or pancakes that accidentally look like roadkill? Your choice."

"Surprise me," she said, and it came out *almost light.*

They ate too much. Syrup ran into butter, and her mom told the story about the time Grandma burned the ham so badly the smoke alarm sang for an hour. Brynlee laughed in the right places and some wrong ones, and when her mom kissed the top of her head just because, she didn't flinch.

They went outside, sledding until their faces burned, then came in for cookies that stuck to the pan and a terrible movie about a gazebo. Cocoa steamed in their hands. For a few hours, it was simple. Safe. The kind of day she'd thought only lived in pictures.

She looked at the three boxes. The paper gleamed. *She could try to want them. She didn't.*

"Tomorrow," her dad said quietly, catching her looking. "Or not. Your call."

"Later," she said. *"I like them like this."*

He nodded as if that made perfect sense.

———

Christmas Day was gentle. Breakfast lasted an hour because no one wanted to move. They FaceTimed Aunt Jess. When they finally did open one gift—just one—her parents handed her a small envelope with a card inside: a donation receipt for the children's home, but the name line read *In honor of Brynlee.*

Heat climbed up her throat in a good way.

"Your idea," her mom said. "We just… liked it."

"Yeah," her dad added, scratching at the side of his neck like he did when he was trying not to make a big deal of something. "Felt better than buying you more stuff we'll trip over."

Brynlee traced the letters with her thumb. "Thank you," she said, and *meant it so hard it almost hurt.*

They left the other boxes wrapped. *It didn't feel like deprivation. It felt like putting a bookmark in a chapter she didn't need right now.*

———

On the twenty-sixth, Harper dragged her out for "emergency returns and celebratory fries."

The mall sagged under its post-holiday hangover—garlands drooping, SALE signs with their smiles slipping. Harper was impossible to miss copper curls frizzing from a loose braid, wrists stacked with jangling bracelets, today's hoodie splattered with silver paint from some art project she swore she'd finish eventually. Her eyeliner never quite matched, but her grin could light a room enough that no one cared.

"You're quiet," Harper said around a fry, not unkind. "Like… content. Is this growth? Are you growing? Should I water you?"

"New Brynlee," Brynlee said, because it was easier than telling the truth. "Limited edition. No returns."

"Bold," Harper said. "But you're keeping me."

"I'm keeping you."

On the way home, Brynlee rolled the window down two inches and *let the air bite her. It felt clean.*

At night she slept heavy. *Dreams flickered at the edges sometimes—colors wrong, a feeling like she was being watched by something patient—but when she turned onto her other side and dragged the blanket to her chin, they slid away.* Morning always came. She woke to coffee and radio news and her mom humming while the dog barked at nothing in the yard next door. The days stacked neatly.

***

New Year's Eve passed soft and ordinary—pizza on paper plates, countdown on TV, her parents' laughter filling the gaps. Midnight fireworks rattled the windows. Brynlee whispered her resolution to the dark: *Be better. Stop counting. Start seeing.*

When she crawled into bed, the house was quiet in the right way.

It was over.

It had been a dream.

A lesson.

And she had learned it.

She pulled the blanket to her chin and let herself believe that—*fully, finally, without question.*

Downstairs, the three wrapped gifts waited in silence.

Bleed-Through

The mirror was honest, but Brynlee knew how to outwit it.

She smoothed her brand-new sweater over her ribs, tugged the sleeve. The jeans had cost too much, the sneakers gleamed white-bright, laces crisp like they'd never known dirt. *She wanted it that way.*

First week back — people noticed. And she wanted them to.

Her hair, dark blond with streaks cut sharp by salon lights, curled just right around her shoulders. She tilted her chin higher, practicing that look she'd perfected: half-bored, half-above it all. A look that said, *Of course I'm worth watching.*

Her gray-blue eyes caught the light, cool as glass. She leaned closer, mascara wand steady, painting them sharp. *The girl in the mirror looked untouchable. Exactly how she was supposed to look.*

Until her mouth tugged wrong for half a heartbeat—too sad, too bare. Brynlee froze, blinked, and it was gone. Just light, glass, angles. Just her. She told herself that, anyway.

She ignored Harper's texts buzzing against the counter, let them stack unanswered. *Harper would still be there, always was. Brynlee's reflection, though — that had to stay flawless. People remembered the version you put in front of them, not the one that flinched at her own reflection.*

She pressed her lips together, one last test of indifference, then slung her bag across her shoulder.

The mirror girl stared back, sharp and polished, like she'd already won the day.

Brynlee didn't blink until she flicked off the light and left the room, shadows stretching long in the glass behind her.

***

January made everything look thinner.

Salt chewed the curb, the air hurt to breathe, and the school's front doors yawned open like a mouth that wasn't happy to see anyone.

Inside: lockers slamming, announcements coughing static from the ceiling, kids dragging themselves through the first week back.

Brynlee slid into homeroom beside Harper. Harper's bracelets clattered while she told some story about her cousin's disastrous ski trip. Brynlee even laughed once. Math was dull, history duller, teachers droning like bees against glass.

Normal. *The right kind of normal.*

By lunch, the hum in her mind had eased. She joined the line, eyes glazed on the gray scoop of potatoes slumping onto her tray.

And then—

"Excuse me."

A voice. Small. Careful. Right through her.

She turned.

Two kids. Thin coats, thin wrists. The girl's braid was crooked, her cheeks winter-raw. The boy's hands were split at the knuckles, skin red and rough. Forgettable faces—*except Brynlee had pressed her forehead to their window.*

Her pulse jumped.

"Go ahead," she said, stepping aside *though she hadn't decided to.*

They nodded, eyes down, trays clutched too tight. Paid with coins that clinked too light. Slid to the far end of a table, just the two of them.

And bowed their heads.

The cafeteria noise dulled. Trays clattered, laughter spiked— but it all sounded far away, muffled, like cotton stuffed in her ears. Their lips moved. And suddenly she could hear.

Thank You for this food. Thank You for today. Please help us stretch what we have. Please help Dad's hands stop cracking. Please help Mom not feel so tired. Amen.

The prayer cut straight into her bones, same cadence, same words *she had already lived.*

Heat spiked under her sleeve, the exact spot the Spirit's hand had clamped down. Her chest cinched tight, ribs refusing to open. Then the air shifted—oily, sour, like old takeout left too long in the dark. The smell hit so sharp it dragged her straight back to cardboard and cold grease. *Wrong. It shouldn't be here.*

Her hands rattles the tray, noise sharp enough to make kids glance over.

The girl lifted her head. Eyes too bright, too tired. She looked straight at Brynlee.

And the boy leaned in, voice low, audible through the roar that had returned around them.

Mara.

The name detonated inside her.

Not new. Not stranger. *A name she had already known— whispered in the dark, in a dream that wasn't a dream.* Hearing it now, spoken aloud, in a cafeteria full of people who didn't hear anything unusual—

Her body swayed like the floor had tilted.

"Bryn?" Harper was at her elbow, tray balanced on one hip. "You alive? You're ghosting."

Brynlee tore her gaze away, throat locked. "Yeah. Fine."

They sat. Brynlee's gaze on her lump of gray potatoes. Harper launched into a story about her aunt and a disastrous Santa costume. Brynlee nodded at the right places, but the words washed useless against her.

Her eyes kept dragging back. *To Mara tearing her roll into tiny pieces. To Jacob cracking some quiet joke, making her smile without smiling himself. To the prayer still pounding in her ribs.*

Her stomach twisted like it was wringing a washcloth.

Coincidence didn't stretch this far.

Not a lesson.

Not a dream.

Real.

And it had found her.

Slipping Normal

By Wednesday, the noise in her head had thinned to a faint buzz. Not silence.

Almost.

Ashwood High was the same as ever—gum stuck to desks, teachers with voices like background static. Around her, the room buzzed with catch-ups—new phones passed hand to hand, stories about uncles getting drunk at Christmas dinner, ski trips that ended in sprains and bad souvenirs. Harper filled the gaps at their table with bracelets clattering as she talked, weaving herself right into the noise. Brynlee even laughed once, sharp and too quick, like maybe if she hit the right note everything would click back into place.

But the quiet never lasted.

In the hallway between classes, the lights hummed too loud. One bulb stuttered in time with her pulse, white-hot on, black-out off, on again until the lockers around it stretched too long. For a blink it felt like she'd stepped into a tunnel.

"Bryn?" Harper's hand landed warm on her shoulder. "You good?"

She forced a shrug. "Didn't sleep."

"Join the club," Harper said, rolling her eyes, but her smile faltered.

Brynlee adjusted the strap of her new bag, chin high, *like that could fix the crawling unease under her skin.* When she glanced at the mirror strip on the trophy case, *her reflection lagged half a step behind.* Not a trick of light. Not her imagination.

At lunch, she sat across from Harper, stabbing mystery meat with her fork. Normal noise surrounded them—clatter, laughter, trays slamming. But then the overhead speakers coughed static, spitting half a sentence before dying. For a second, clear as breath on her ear, she heard it:

"*See.*"

She dropped her fork.

"Okay, seriously," Harper said. "You're starting to freak me out, Bryn."

"Nothing." *Too fast.* She snatched the fork, forced a bite. She forced a bite. It tasted like wet paper.

That night she dreamed of Jacob Williams. *His father's cracked hands folded over grace at a table too bare. The same hands reached for hers across the dark.*

She woke with her own knuckles red, skin splitting in thin white lines.

Harper's Anchor

By Friday afternoon Brynlee was starving for normal, for something that didn't flicker or echo or scrape at her ribs.

Harper delivered in spades, dragging her downtown with the promise of fries and distraction.

They sat in the back booth of a greasy diner where the vinyl seats clung to skin and the ketchup bottles never fully closed.

Harper talked with her whole body—hands flying.

She told a story about bombing a chemistry quiz because she got distracted by a moth on the ceiling, and Brynlee laughed, too loud, fries catching in her throat until she coughed soda bubbles up her nose.

It felt almost right.

Harper smacked her napkin at her, eyes shining. "You're so dramatic. I should start charging admission." Brynlee rolled her eyes, but *warmth pooled somewhere low in her chest.*

After fries came thrift shopping, Harper's favorite game. She pulled a sequined jacket from the rack and spun into it, sleeves swallowing her arms, grinning like she'd just reinvented herself. "Behold," she said, "the ghost of eighties prom past." Brynlee snapped a photo before Harper could duck, and the flash caught Harper's smile in a way that *hurt*. Not the forced kind, not the filtered kind—*just joy, uncurated and unbothered.* Brynlee envied how easy she made it look. She tried on nothing, content to watch Harper pile on absurd scarves and a pair of purple boots three sizes too big. *For an hour the world stayed ordinary.*

In the mirror behind Harper's shoulder, something shifted. For a second, *Brynlee saw her best friend alone, sequins dim, smile gone.* The outline of the Spirit of Loneliness bled into the glass, its hollow grin cutting through the shimmer. She blinked hard, heart dropping into her stomach, but the mirror only showed Harper again, laughing as she tried to moonwalk in the boots. Brynlee forced a laugh back, *too loud, too sharp.*

Later, when Harper dropped her at home, she caught Brynlee's hand before she could pull away. "Hey. You're…different lately. Don't tell me it's just midterms. What's really going on?"

Brynlee stared at her, throat closing. *The bruise on her wrist burned under Harper's touch, heat flooding up her arm like a warning.* Over Harper's shoulder, the front window warped—the Spirit of Loneliness there again, too close, its voice like damp paper: *Say it, and she is ours too.*

Brynlee yanked her hand free. "Drop it," Brynlee said, the words heavier than she meant them to be.

Harper didn't believe her. Brynlee saw it in the pinch of her mouth, the shadow in her eyes. But Harper let it go, waving as she backed down the driveway, bracelets clinking like chains dragged over tile.

Inside, Brynlee pressed her wrist to her chest until the skin throbbed. *She hadn't realized how tightly she'd been holding onto Harper until the Spirit made it clear: she couldn't keep her anchor without dragging her under.*

Second Encounter

The house slept like it had learned how to breathe without her. Pipes ticked, the heater coughed itself warm, and somewhere downstairs the fridge kicked on with a low hum.

Brynlee lay flat and watched the red digits on her clock bleed into each other.

She told herself if she could keep the seconds in order—twelve-thirty, thirty-one, thirty-two—the night would behave.

The air thinned the way it did before a storm. The corner by her dresser darkened, not more shadow but less light, as if something had drunk it. She didn't say please. *She'd learned that saying anything invited the wrong kind of answer.* The Spirit of Pain unfolded out of the dark with the same sound wet paper makes when it tears. Skin too tight, eyes not eyes, breath like rust. It didn't need to tell her its name. *Her bones already knew it.*

"Get out," she said, and it sounded small. The Spirit tilted its head as if studying a word, it didn't recognize, then reached. Its fingers were colder than cold, the absence of heat, closing around her wrist exactly where the bruise lived. The floor split without cracking, the way a dream unhinged its jaw. She dropped.

The church basement smelled like coffee that had burned hours ago and cheap soap. Folding tables made two crooked rows; a cardboard sign read COMMUNITY BOX in a scrawl that wanted to be hopeful.

The Williams family's house from that first night hung in her mind, hovering above this place like a memory with a roof. Down here, the father—map-red knuckles split wide—stacked cans into a box: beans, tomatoes, corn. Around him people moved quiet, heads bent, lips moving as they counted without thinking. A volunteer read numbers from a clipboard, forcing a smile every time someone said "thank you" like it was a challenge. Their daughter—Mara—ducked down to tie her shoe, hiding the wet shine in her eyes.

Brynlee's mouth filled with metal. She pressed her palms to the table edge to stay upright and felt splinters bite. The Spirit stood too close. "We cannot lift," it said, not a confession so much. "We make you see."

"I already see." *Her voice shredded.* "I saw. Isn't that enough?"

"If it were enough," Pain said, "you would be asleep."

The room flickered, same place but not. Now the volunteer's voice blurred into the radio in the corner. The radio bled into the room: *Community Vigil this Friday, seven p.m., Ashwood High gym—* The words clanged off the concrete walls and kept ringing long after the station changed.

They moved without walking. A grocery aisle at closing time gleamed too bright under exhausted lights. The father's hands again, pushed white around a jar lid that wouldn't give. Jacob reached up without being asked, teenage fingers trying to be a man's; the skin at his knuckles split in a clean, thin line. He didn't make a sound. The cashier watched everything and nothing at once, *her eyes sliding away like oil.*

Pain leaned close enough that its breath cooled her ear. "There are aches made by hunger and aches made by looking away. Yours is the second. It will teach you the first."

"No." *She tried to pull back.* The Spirit didn't tighten its grip. It didn't have to. The ache in her own hands bloomed like a bruise thawing from the inside. Heat climbed her wrists; her fingers went stiff and bright with pain. She swallowed a sound.

They fell sideways into a kitchen with no paint on the cabinets, a clock that ticked loud enough to bruise. The mother wrapped the father's palms with a strip of torn sheet while Mara pretended to do homework at the table, her pencil making no marks. Jacob rinsed a plate that didn't need rinsing. The whole room held its breath around *not enough*. When the mother finished, she kissed the father's knuckles like they were something holy. He flinched and told her he didn't, *she said I know, and that was worse.*

Brynlee tried to touch the edge of the counter to *prove she could touch anything in this place, that she wasn't only a pair of eyes the Spirit had rented.* Her fingers slid through wood and came back empty, colder. Pain didn't look at her.

"I'm trying," she said, and *hated how it sounded. Like the apology you spit out when you've already decided not to change.*

"You are watching." The Spirit's head bent as if it were listening to something she couldn't hear. "It is a start."

Cracks webbed across the kitchen window. They split her reflection first—her face splintering, her mouth tugged into pieces—before crawling into the glass itself. When it gave, it didn't burst outward. It caved, folding in on itself. The room folded with it.

Brynlee woke with her heart punching at her ribs like it had hands. The house was hers again: the slice of porch light at the bottom of her door where her dad always closed it too soft to latch. She flexed her fingers and choked back a curse. The skin at her knuckles had split in three neat places, everything angry and raw as if she'd been punching winter. *She pressed her hands to her mouth and tasted blood through skin.*

In the bathroom, cold water hissed against porcelain, then bit into her skin. Pink bled off her fingers, curling lazy into the drain, like it had nowhere else to be. The mirror threw back a face she barely recognized—creased, used-up, older than it had any right to be. She pressed tissue to the splits; it soaked through fast, blooming red. Bandages would show. She didn't own gloves.

Her hands shook as she dug through the drawer until tape and gauze scraped against her knuckles. She wound it like she remembered the mother doing—too tight at first, panic making her squeeze until her fingertips went white, then looser, just enough to bring the feeling back.

Her wrist throbbed beneath the wrap, heavy, alive. Not just a bruise anymore. *Something breathing under her skin.*

Downstairs, her mother looked up from her mug and stilled. "What happened?"

"Door," Brynlee said without thinking. "Caught it."

Her father frowned like he wanted to believe her and couldn't quite make the leap. "We should—if it hurts—"

"It doesn't." It did. She lifted the bowl of cereal like it weighed nothing. Milk sloshed. *Her fingers burned where the condensation kissed the gauze.*

At school, she kept her hands under her desk and her sleeves pulled down. The heater hummed a flat note. The announcement speaker coughed and cleared its throat and coughed again. *Vigil for Missing Youths—this Friday—Ashwood gym at seven—* The words echoed the radio's, voice different, meaning the same. Harper shot her a look across the room, eyebrows up. *Are you going?* shaped with no sound. Brynlee looked away. The gauze itched. *She could feel Jacob two rows over, the way you feel cold through glass; when he raised his hand to answer, the band of skin across his knuckles was a thin, healing red.* Mara passed him a pen with a cap chewed to ruin. Neither of them glanced her way. *She wouldn't have, either.*

By lunch, the gauze had bled through in spots the color of old roses. She shoved her hands into her pockets and ate with her head down and still felt watched. *Not by the room. By whatever measured how long she could pretend.* On the way out, Harper bumped her shoulder hard enough to make her hiss. "Jesus. Sorry, I didn't—what did you do?"

"Nothing," Brynlee snapped, the word cutting sharp.

Harper blinked. The pause between them felt like a floorboard you found soft under your foot.

In last period, the principal's voice came thin through the intercom. He talked about community and unity and how darkness didn't get the final word, and Brynlee thought about the Williams kitchen, the way the darkness there wasn't dramatic enough to preach about. It was the kind that showed up every day and sat down and ate.

When the bell finally dismissed them, she walked to her locker and pretended she didn't have to use her elbow to work the combination. Pain had been right about one thing. Watching wasn't enough. *It didn't make anything stop hurting. It only taught you how to recognize the shape of the hurt when it came for you, too.*

Fracture at Ashwood High

By Monday the gauze had loosened and the splits on her knuckles sealed to thin red seams. She could flex her fingers without flinching, but the skin tugged *like it remembered*. She kept her hands hidden anyway. People stared at the smallest things at Ashwood High, and Brynlee couldn't stand the questions.

The cafeteria reeked of ketchup and bleach, the line barely crawling. Harper was ahead of her, balancing her tray. Brynlee felt heavy, *like she was moving through water*.

Two spots ahead, Mara Williams stood with a tray that looked *too light*. A roll, half a pear, milk. Jacob stood at her shoulder, his tray the same, knuckles split just like hers had been. They didn't notice her, but she noticed them—every careful motion, every small laugh they carved out of the air between them *like survival depended on it*.

She should've looked away. *She didn't.*

When they slid into their seats at the far edge of the cafeteria, alone as always, Brynlee's throat tightened. She saw them bow their heads, lips moving in the same cadence as the prayer that still lived in her bones.

The noise around her dulled. Laughter thinned, trays clattered far away.

Her tray slipped in her grip.

"Bryn?" Harper turned, catching her shoulder. "Earth to you. You almost dropped your tray—what's up with you?"

Brynlee blinked hard, the sound of forks and chatter crashing back in. "Nothing. Just—tired."

Harper frowned, unconvinced, but moved forward when the line jolted ahead.

They sat at their usual table, Harper spinning a story about her cat who fell in the bathtub trying to join her. Brynlee tried to laugh in the right places, but her eyes kept pulling back to the Williams table.

Brynlee's chest ached *like it had been rented out without asking.*

The Spirit's voice crawled along her ribs, softer than a whisper, closer than breath: *Speak, and she won't exist.*

Her gaze snapped to Harper, who was still laughing, still unaware, still hers. A shadow bled into the wall behind her— long, thin, the shape of Loneliness, its grin cut too deep, splitting past where a mouth should end.

Brynlee's breath caught.

She forced her tray aside and stood so fast her chair shrieked against the floor. "Bathroom," she muttered. Harper blinked, startled, then turned as if to follow.

"No," Brynlee said, *clipped.* "Stay. Don't follow me."

The urge to confess surged, jagged and raw, but the Spirit's words coiled tighter: speak, and she won't exist. Brynlee swallowed it down like poison and ran, *her hand burning like it had been thousands of fires running under it.*

The Warning

That night the house refused to settle. The heater hissed too long, the rafters ticked like a metronome she couldn't shut off, her parents' voices drifting in low fragments through the floorboards.

Brynlee lay awake until the clock smeared itself past one a.m. *She closed her eyes, counting her breath, telling herself sleep would come if she just pretended hard enough.*

The air changed first. It thickened, sharp and metallic, until *her tongue felt cut.* Then the bed shuddered once, not enough to rattle the frame, just enough to say *we are here.* She kept her eyes closed as long as she could. She was dragged under by sleep.

She stood in the gym at Ashwood High. The bleachers rose like black teeth, the polished floor shining too bright, wrong-bright, like no janitor could ever scrub it clean.

A voice brushed her ear, low and female, not close enough to belong to a person. "You count by things."

Brynlee turned. The Spirit of Rejection waited near the half-court line, her body blurred, edges humming like static on a dead channel. When Brynlee tried to pin her down, she slipped sideways, unfocused. The gym lights flickered, one by one, as if the bulbs themselves didn't want to look at her.

"What do you want from me?" Brynlee's throat ached with the words.

The Spirit didn't answer. Instead, names bled across the floorboards in chalk strokes, crooked, uneven, as if written by children's hands. Mara. Jacob. Then more. Dozens. Hundreds. They sprawled across the polished wood, scrawling outward in frantic lines until the court was swallowed in names—some she knew, some she didn't. Classmates. Neighbors. Faces she'd walked past without seeing.

Her chest tightened. "Why me?"

Rejection's head tilted, the movement too casual, too bored. "Things are not bodies. Love without a face is absence."

The gym lights snapped off, plunging her into black. Only the pulse in her wrist glowed, throbbing against the bruise like a warning beacon. She tried to step forward, but the chalk names shifted beneath her, slick and alive, smearing, tangling around her shoes like they meant to hold her in place.

The Spirit leaned closer without moving. Her outline bent, deciding to be nearer. "You hide behind things—shoes, lashes, polish. You think if they see enough shine, they won't notice what's missing."

Brynlee's voice cracked into the dark. "You can't make me like you."

The blur shimmered, tilting as if she might laugh but couldn't remember how. "We do not make. We remind. Refuse us, and you are still claimed. Accept us, and you are still claimed."

The court splintered under Brynlee's feet, hairline cracks running to the walls. Chalk dust burst upward, erasing names as the floor gave way. The sound was deafening—screech of wood, names shredded into dust.

She screamed back, raw and scraped out of her chest. "I'm not yours!"

The Spirit's reply dragged soft as chalk on slate. "Not yet."

And the floor dropped.

Harper Doubts

By Thursday the halls of Ashwood felt tighter. *Too many bodies, too much noise, all of it pressing in.* Brynlee kept her head high, her clothes sharp, her voice steady when she answered teachers, but inside *she was splintering.*

Harper didn't miss it.

They sat on the steps outside between classes, a pocket of cold air where breath hung visible. Harper shoved a bag of trail mix between them, her bracelets clinking as she dug out the chocolate pieces. She chewed slow, watching Brynlee instead of the crowd.

"You've been weird," she said finally, quiet enough that it almost sounded like she didn't want to hear the answer.

Brynlee forced a laugh. "Weird how? You're the one eating only M&Ms and leaving me with peanuts."

"Don't deflect." Harper's grin twitched, but it didn't last. She picked at the cuff of her sleeve until a thread unraveled. "Seriously, B. You ghost out half the time. And you're…different."

The word landed heavy. Harper wasn't one for careful phrasing. Usually, she just said what she thought, unfiltered.

"Different how?" Brynlee asked, *sharper than she meant to.*

Harper's eyes softened, not defensive but almost scared. "Like you're carrying something I don't get to see. And you don't trust me with it."

Brynlee looked away. Her chest tightened, but not from the Spirits this time. From Harper's voice, frayed at the edges like she'd been losing more than sleep.

When Brynlee finally turned back, Harper's smile had slipped entirely. "I'm not saying tell me everything. Just…" She shrugged, curls frizzing free. "Don't shut me out, okay? You've been my person since before we could spell our names. I don't know what I'd do if you—"

She cut herself off, but the silence finished it. *If you left. If you broke. If you weren't here.*

Brynlee's throat ached. *She wanted to say everything, to spill the shadows and the spirits and the truth pressing behind her ribs.* But the air shifted, colder, heavier. Over Harper's shoulder, the glass door darkened. But the reflection wasn't what shifted—her own skin was. Thin red welts raised across Brynlee's forearm, one after another, blooming as if invisible claws traced them in slow, deliberate strokes. The Spirit of Loneliness lingered at the edge of sight, smile stretching too far, savoring each mark as it surfaced.

The voice pressed inside her chest, heavy, intimate.

She doesn't feel it yet, does she? We could let her. We could carve her name right beside yours.

Brynlee jerked to her feet, too fast. "Drop it," she snapped. "You're making it bigger than it is."

Harper blinked up at her, hurt flashing across her face before she masked it with a roll of her eyes. "Right. Classic Brynlee— perfect, untouchable. Should've known better."

Brynlee *wanted to take it back, to grab Harper's hand and make her understand.* But she couldn't risk the Spirit sliding closer.

The bell rang. The steps emptied. Harper slung her bag over her shoulder without another word and walked inside.

Brynlee stood in the cold too long after she left, *trail mix untouched at her feet.*

The Vigil

The gym at Ashwood smelled like wax and paper snowflakes. Candles lined the bleachers in uneven rows, their flames bending every time the doors opened to admit another wave of people.

Posters of the missing hung along the walls, taped crooked, corners curling.

Too many faces. Too many names.

Brynlee sat with Harper near the middle, the flicker of light turning everyone around them into moving shadows. The microphone at half-court squealed as the principal welcomed parents, students, neighbors. His voice carried that careful tone adults used when they wanted to sound steady.

"…tonight is about unity. About remembering the ones we've lost, and the ones still out there waiting to be found."

Brynlee gripped her program, the paper damp under her fingers. She forced her eyes down, but the black-and-white photo on the front cover met her anyway. *Lydia Grace Turner. Sixteen. Missing for ten almost eleven years. A face she already knew, not from flyers, but from a cardboard box in the dark.*

She felt Harper watching her, ready to crack a joke to soften the mood, but Harper didn't. She sat still, serious, her bracelets silent. *The weight of her silence scared Brynlee more than anything.*

Speakers took turns at the microphone—parents, siblings, classmates who wanted to read poems they'd written or light candles for friends who hadn't come home. Their voices braided together, trembling, too human. Brynlee's stomach turned with every story. She didn't need candles or poems. She had seen.

A draft pulled through the gym when the side doors opened again. Brynlee's head turned before she could stop it.

That was when she saw her.

A girl she didn't recognize at first glance, standing stiff at the edge of the crowd. Polished coat, pressed skirt, hair pinned neat—but the candle in her hands trembled as if it wanted to fall. Her face was pale, her mouth set *like she'd rehearsed not to cry.*

Something about her didn't belong here, but she was here anyway.

Brynlee couldn't stop staring.

Vivienne LeClair. She didn't know the name yet, but she would.

The Spirit of Rejection brushed close, its blurred outline shifting in the corner of Brynlee's sight. Its voice dragged like glass across tile: *Rejection wears silk too.*

For one heartbeat, the girl's face rippled, flickering into Lydia's. *Same candle, same eyes wide in the dark.* Then it was gone, only the stranger again, steady in her stillness.

Brynlee's throat constricted. *She wanted to tell Harper, to whisper what she saw, but Harper's hands were folded tight in her lap, her eyes glossy in a way Brynlee had never seen. She wasn't Brynlee's anchor tonight. She was adrift too.*

Someone read a list of names. The candles wavered. *Brynlee swore she heard each name whispered twice—once by the speaker, once by the Spirits.*

Her knees trembled. *She thought she might stand, might scream Lydia's name into the microphone, might rip the silence open wide enough that everyone could see what she saw.* But then Rejection leaned closer, voice crawling under her ribs: *Your words will damn them.*

Her hands stayed locked on the program, nails biting the paper until it tore.

When it was over, the crowd thinned into the winter dark. The girl with the trembling candle slipped out the side door without looking back. Brynlee lost sight of her in the crush of coats and smoke.

Harper bumped her shoulder, softer than usual. "You okay?"

Brynlee nodded. The torn program stuck to her palm, damp with sweat, as if it wanted to brand her with every name she hadn't spoken.

Fallout

The house had that after-church quiet. Coats on hooks, shoes left crooked by the door, the faint smell of candle smoke in the air.

Brynlee shut the door behind her like the cold might follow if she didn't.

Her parents looked up from the kitchen table, two mugs between them, a deck of cards spread in clumsy stacks as if they'd been trying to keep their hands busy while they waited.

"How was it?" her mom asked, voice shaped around care like it could keep anything from breaking.

Brynlee could still see the candles in the gym, the faces on the posters, the girl with the perfect coat gripping wax as if it might anchor her. She could still hear the names, *each one said twice—once by the principal and once by whatever lived in the rafters.* She swallowed. "Long."

Her dad's fingers stopped worrying the edge of a card. "Do you…want to talk about it?"

She didn't. She wanted to peel her skin off and see if the noise underneath got any quieter. She wanted to stand in the shower until the hot water tank went empty and listen to the pipes shake so she didn't have to listen to herself. She shrugged instead, the version of okay they all understood. "Tired."

Her mom read the lie but didn't press. "There's soup," she said gently. "Or cocoa. Or we can just…sit."

"Cocoa," Brynlee said, because *saying no to anything soft felt like spitting at a hand offered to steady her.* She sat at the counter while her mother warmed milk in the dented saucepan and her father pretended not to watch her. When the mug slid in front of her, steam ribboned up, sweet and ordinary. She wrapped both hands around it and waited for the heat to move into her. It didn't. *The warmth stayed in the mug like it didn't trust her to keep it.*

Her dad cleared his throat. "They said the news might cover it at ten." He looked at the stove clock and then away. "If you want."

She pictured a camera panning too slowly over faces that had already been missing too long. She pictured someone's voiceover calling it community while the air in the gym had felt like grief you could drown in. "Maybe," she said, which meant no.

They tried a few more neutral things—weather, a neighbor's new dog, something about the pothole at the end of the street that was going to swallow someone's tire if the city didn't deal with it. She let their conversation wash over her, *the way you let a movie play when you don't care how it ends.* When the cocoa was gone and the silence around the three of them started to feel like an animal learning the room, she kissed their cheeks, said goodnight, and climbed the stairs.

Her room remembered her. The dent in the pillow, the sweatshirt she'd left slung over her chair, the string of fairy lights that had burned out in one spot and made the rest look tired. She set her phone on the desk and stood a long time with the lamp on and the overhead off, as if *the angle of light might decide what kind of night it was going to be.* Then she went to the bathroom and turned the shower as hot as it would go.

Water beat at her shoulders. She braced her forearms against the tile and watched steam muscle the mirror into a blind square. For a minute, it worked—just water, just heat, just the small clever lie that she could scrub a feeling off. Then the spray started to sound wrong, a flicker in the pressure, a stutter like static. *Between the beats of water, a whisper in the pipe: remember.* It could have been a trick of old plumbing. It could have been the Spirits turning the smallest thing into a message. *She closed her eyes and let her forehead rest against her wrist until the skin there went numb.*

In bed, she didn't turn the lights all the way off. The lamp stayed low, casting a weak circle over the comforter, enough light to make the corners stay corners. She scrolled without reading, thumb moving by muscle memory. The vigil already had a hashtag. Some classmates had taken a picture of the bleachers laced with candles, a caption that said *light pushes back the dark* with three heart emojis. Another post zoomed tight on Lydia Grace Turner's flyer, the grain of the photocopy making her eyes look older. Comments stacked under both about *how beautiful, how sad, how tragic.* The words looked like daisies laid on concrete and left to weather.

She searched Lydia's name anyway. Links to old articles, the same school photo everyone used from Kindergarten, the age rendered photo, a clip from a news segment where the lower third called her *BRIGHT, KIND, MISSING.* Brynlee clicked and watched the anchor say what anchors said, the mouth moving like a metronome while b-roll of volunteers stapling posters played. *None of it knew about the cardboard box in the alley or the way the Christmas market lights had smeared themselves in the girl's eyes. None of it knew anything that mattered.*

She typed and erased in the search bar: *market with lights downtown*—delete—*cardboard box alley Christmas*—delete—*I saw her.* The last hung on the screen, blinking its cursor like it might become a sentence if she looked away long enough. She closed the browser before she could become the kind of person who left evidence of the truth where anyone could find it.

Her phone buzzed. Harper: *You home?* Another: *You okay?* Then: *I didn't know it would hit like that.* Brynlee stared at the dots when Harper started to type and stopped, then started, then stopped again. She pictured the way Harper had held her candle, both hands around the paper collar to keep the wax off her fingers. She pictured the way Harper's mouth had turned down at the corners, small and helpless. *She thought about typing I saw something and felt the air in her room shift, the same cold patience that had pressed against her in the gym, waiting to see which way she would break.* She sent *yeah. just tired.* The reply came quick: *Same. Night, B.* A second later, and she could hear the grin even without seeing it:

Don't get all saintly on me tomorrow and make me look bad in homeroom.
Brynlee smiled in spite of herself and then stared at the shape of
it on her face in the black window and let it go.

She killed the lamp. Dark pushed up against the glass, thick
as if someone had hung blankets over the world. For once, the
Spirits didn't come with a tear in the air or a smell that didn't
belong. They didn't peel themselves out of the corners. They
didn't speak. *They sat with her the way something heavy sits on a shelf it
knows won't hold if it chooses to fall.* It should have been a relief, the
not-speaking. *It wasn't. Their silence had its own edges.*

She lay there and let the after-image of the gym play itself on
the underside of her eyelids—the candles, the voices, the girl by
the door whose hands trembled around light she couldn't keep.
Brynlee thought about standing up in front of everyone and
saying Lydia's name and the way the Spirit's voice had slid in
under the bone of her sternum and said *your words will damn them.*
She thought about not standing, about how she had swallowed
the name like it was hers to keep. *Either way, someone bled.*

Downstairs, a pipe knocked. The house exhaled. Somewhere
in the dark, a car passed, the headlights dragging a slow white
rectangle across her ceiling. When it faded, nothing moved for a
long time.

"*If I say nothing, they win,*" she said into the room, barely a
sound. "*If I say something, they win too.*"

No answer came. She didn't expect one. She stared at the
place where the door didn't quite close and waited for morning,
which felt less and less like rescue and more like another kind of test.

Harper Unmasked

Saturday made the neighborhood look like someone had turned the volume down on everything. Salt rings on the asphalt, bare branches against a sky that couldn't decide if it was blue or bone.

Brynlee was halfway through pretending her homework mattered when Harper texted *come over* and then, a breath later, *please.*

The second word did what the first never could. Brynlee pulled on her coat and walked.

Harper's garage door was up halfway, a crooked mouth with cold teeth. Inside smelled like sawdust and old rain. The space had turned itself into a studio without asking anyone's permission—drop cloths taped crooked, canvases stacked along the wall like sleeping doors, every surface spattered with the metallic sneeze of that silver paint Harper loved. Music from somebody's playlist bled thin out of her phone, more rhythm than melody.

Harper stood hunched over a canvas spread flat on the folding table, hair twisted into a messy bun and pinned with two paint-smeared pencils. Her forearms carried streaks of silver, black, white, and grey—shadows she wore like second skin—but here and there brighter flecks of yellow and green still clung, old layers breaking through the way light sometimes cuts into storm clouds. A swipe of pale grey streaked her cheekbone, sharp as a slash, the rest of her bent wholly into the work..

"You didn't knock," Harper said without looking, and then she did, and the relief that flashed across her face hurt to see. "Good. I was going to start singing to fill the silence and you don't deserve that."

"What are you making?" Brynlee asked, because *that was easier than asking if the please meant panic.*

Harper stepped aside. The canvas was mostly shadow, a window sketched in with chalk lines, light suggested more than painted. In the lower right corner, a chair waited for someone who hadn't decided to sit down yet. It was simple and it wasn't. *Brynlee felt something lean toward it in her chest.*

"It's nothing," Harper said too fast, then softer. "It's my mom's break room at the hospital. She sends pictures on her overnight shifts sometimes. Says it keeps her from thinking about time." She wiped her hands on her jeans and left a comet of silver across her thigh. "She's got three overnights this week. It's…loud when she's gone."

"Loud?" Brynlee glanced at the empty driveway, the quiet street, the thin ribs of trees.

"In here." Harper tapped two fingers against the side of her head. "Like a radio stuck between stations. I do the bracelets, the music, the paint—you know." She rattled her wrist, and then realized she was without her armor, she shrugged. "Fakes it quiet."

Brynlee stood with her hands shoved in her pockets, the cold finding skin anyway. Harper kept talking, the words dragging a little now that they'd started moving. "Last night after the vigil I thought I was fine. Then I got in bed, and my chest did this—" She made a fist over her sternum, opened it, made it again. "Like when you miss a step in the dark. It passed. I don't…like saying panic attack because it makes it a thing that might come back if you name it. But I couldn't make it shut up. I came out here and painted the chair because it felt like a thing I could fill if I needed to."

Brynlee looked at the chair and at Harper's hands, paint under the nails, the moons of her cuticles bitten. Harper never let herself be still long enough for anyone to see the edges; she kept the room laughing so no one asked questions. *The chair was a question.*

"I'm fine," Harper added a beat too late, and then she laughed like she could file the word down until it fit. "I'm always fine."

"You don't have to be," Brynlee said, and heard how little practice she had with that sentence.

Harper watched her for a long second, the smile easing off her face like a coat she didn't need. "Then don't make me do this alone, okay?" She flicked her gaze over Brynlee's shoulder toward the open mouth of the garage, the clean winter light beyond it. "I know you're…somewhere else lately. Just—be here right now. With me. Tell me the true thing."

The air thinned, subtle, the way it did before the Spirits decided to be real. Something stood just outside the garage's half-open door where the light couldn't decide to fall, a long smear of waiting that had learned how to look like nothing. Loneliness smiled from the reflection in a pane leaning against the wall; if Brynlee stared, the grin widened. *Say it,* it breathed—not words, but an understanding pressed into her skin. *Say it, and we will find you, wherever you hide.*

The truth clawed up anyway. *I see things. They make me see them. The girl in the paper. The box. The names in the gym.* It pressed against her teeth like a flood.

She swallowed hard enough to hurt. "The vigil…" she tried and had to start again. "The vigil's still buzzing. Like a radio that won't tune. It'll fade."

Harper stared at her, disappointment moving under her face like a shadow changing positions. "You always do," she said. *It wasn't praise.*

Brynlee took a step toward the canvas because moving felt like surviving. "The chair's good," she said, and meant it. "It makes me want to sit."

"That's the point." Harper nudged a second stool with her foot until it kissed Brynlee's ankle. "Stay. Paint something ugly with me so I don't have to call it a night yet."

The shape at the door leaned in, patient, almost tender. *Brynlee pictured silver paint on her fingers, pictured laughter knocking around the garage until it scared whatever waited into letting go. She pictured sleep later, clean and unvisited. Then she pictured a mouth at her ear whispering yours, too, and saw Harper's chair empty for real.*

"I can't," Brynlee said. "Dad needs the car early."

"You walked," Harper said, blinking. The hurt wasn't big; it was precise. "You could have said you didn't want to."

"I do." *She didn't know if she meant it in the present tense or as a memory.* "Tomorrow?"

"If you answer." Harper dragged the heel of her palm across her cheek, left a comet there to match her thigh. "I'm not auditioning for a new best friend, B. I'm just asking you to show up."

"I'm here." *It sounded like a rumor of a promise.*

"For five minutes at a time," Harper said, but she nodded toward the street anyway. "Go. Tell your dad you're a good kid. I'll be here trying to make a window look like a window."

Brynlee hesitated long enough that the hesitation became its own answer. She backed into the bright and pulled the garage door down by its cold metal handle until the space snapped shut with a hollow clatter. On the sidewalk, the air bit clean. She jammed her hands deeper into her pockets and didn't look back because *she didn't trust what she'd see—Harper, small in the new dark, or the Spirit smiling in the glass.*

At the corner, a neighborhood cat launched itself off a snowbank and vanished, soundless. A car passed, bass low, a rumble that made the curb vibrate. Brynlee walked faster, and the walking didn't change anything, but *it gave her something to do with her body while the rest of her argued itself to pieces.*

By the time she got home, the house lights were out except for the lamp her mother always left burning in the living room. Brynlee slipped upstairs, shut her bedroom door, and leaned against it until her legs stopped shaking. When she finally peeled off her coat, pain flared sharp along her side. She hissed, tugged her sweater up, and froze.

Three welts rose across her ribs, thin and angry, *like someone had dragged a heated wire just under the skin.* They hadn't been there an hour ago. They stung worse when she touched them, as if her body knew she'd chosen wrong.

The chair had stayed empty. The Spirits never did.

In the mirror above her dresser, her reflection looked back, pale and wide-eyed, but alone. No Harper. No silver paint comets. No laughter. Just her. *And for a blink, over her shoulder, Loneliness grinned.*

She yanked her sweater back down and turned off the light.

Vivienne's Transfer

Sunday's quiet had edges. Brynlee sat at her desk staring at a blinking cursor long enough that the shape of it burned her eyes. The essay prompt—*Compare two communities and how they manage scarcity*—might as well have been a dare.

She typed three lines about cooperation and resource-sharing, deleted two, left the last.

Her phone buzzed twice from Harper—memes, a photo of the garage window at dusk captioned *the chair looks smug now*—and once from an unknown number that turned out to be a mass text reminding families about the district's food drive.

She put the phone face down and it still pressed on her, a small square of light insisting it knew what she owed.

When darkness slicked the window, she told herself she felt better.

She didn't.

She felt arranged.

Monday morning the announcements crackled to life with the forced cheer of a snow day that wouldn't come. "Good morning, Ashwood High," the secretary said. "Please join me in welcoming a new student who'll be starting today—Vivienne LeClair."

The name walked down the rows ahead of her, heads tilting, whispers pocketing and passing it along.

Money. Private school.

LeClair like the hospital wing.

Brynlee didn't move.

She knew the face before she saw it: a candle trembling between careful hands.

Second period, the door opened, and she was there.

Vivienne stood straighter than the desks deserved, the kind of posture taught, not natural.

Coat folded over her arm, hair pinned so clean it made other girls' ponytails look like apologies.

Her eyes did a quick inventory of the room and then did nothing with the information, not reaching for anyone.

The teacher said a few things about welcoming her, offered the seat near the window.

Vivienne nodded once and went quiet in a way that made the quiet around her real.

At lunch, curiosity moved the cafeteria like weather.

Brynlee took her place in line and watched without admitting she watched.

Vivienne hovered with her tray half a beat too long, measuring the topography of tables, and then angled toward the far edge where two seats always stayed open because they belonged to people who didn't push.

Mara looked up first—surprised, not starstruck—and slid over without the choreography most tables required. Jacob made room with his knee.

Vivienne set her tray down like it might break the table if she didn't place it right.

The three of them did the simple work of being human to each other: passing napkins, shifting milk cartons so elbows had space, finding small sentences that didn't ask for too much.

Vivienne smiled once, small and brittle. Brynlee felt something in her chest tilt.

Rejection wears silk too, the soft drag of a voice reminded from somewhere that couldn't be pointed to.

Brynlee didn't look for the Spirit.

She stared at Vivienne instead and felt heat rise in her face, an anger with no clean name.

She'd promised herself she'd protect the Williams kids. Vivienne orbiting close felt like a test she wasn't ready for.

She told herself she was above gossip, then opened her phone under the table and typed anyway. *Did you see her? LeClair moved to cafeteria Siberia.* She didn't send it. The unsent thought sat there, a slick coin in her palm, and made her feel exactly like herself. She erased it letter by letter and the erasing did not absolve her.

After a class where the clock dragged its feet in wet shoes, she ducked into the girls' bathroom and let the door hush shut behind her. The fluorescent light hummed a flat, unfriendly note.

She ran water over her hands, pretending she'd touched something that needed washing off, and looked up.

Her reflection did not look back.

For a breath, the mirror gave her the room without her in it—three sinks, a paper towel dispenser hanging crooked, the far stall door where a scratch spelled *hope* as if the person ran out of space before they ran out of need. Where Brynlee should have been, there was nothing.

When her face bled in, it arrived wrong: eyes sliding past themselves, mouth too wide and then too thin, the edges of her blurring like glass breathed on. She blinked and the mirror didn't blink with her. Panic rose, quick and electric, the kind that makes your fingers feel far away from your hands.

"Stop," she said, and heard how small the word was against tile.

The world behind the glass flexed. The sinks fell back like a set rolled on tracks. In their place, a room she knew without recognition unfolded: long table set immaculately, plates blank, chairs empty, candles that would not catch. Names etched on the backs of the chairs—Mara, Jacob, Lydia, Harper, and hers—and a thin layer of frost on all of it. Doors lined the walls with handles only on the outside. The Spirit of Rejection did not step into the frame. It didn't have to. Its voice laid itself over everything like a transparent sheet: *To everyone who looks at you, you will be enough of a shape until you are not. Then you will not exist at all.*

"I get it," Brynlee said, which was both a lie and an admission. Her hands gripped the lip of the sink and found it real enough to bite her palms. "You can't make me help her." She didn't know which her she meant—Vivienne with her careful smile, Lydia with her printed face on a flyer, Mara with her roll torn into coins. *She meant all of them.*

We cannot lift, Rejection said, amused and bored at once, echoing an earlier verdict. *We can only peel away everything you hide behind until there is nothing left but the choice.*

The room in the glass swung closed, a lid on a box. Her reflection reassembled with a shudder, suddenly too bright, colors all a fraction off as if someone had leaned on contrast. For a second the mirror stretched her face long and thin, a funhouse cruelty, then snapped back to ordinary. The hum of the light found its pitch. A stall flushed. A girl she didn't know shouldered past her without seeing her at all.

Brynlee turned the tap off and the silence after the water felt like judgment. She dried her hands too hard and tore the paper towel. When she stepped into the hallway, second lunch was already pulling itself back into classrooms, the noise changing shape. At the far end, Vivienne walked between Mara and Jacob—close but not touching, like three magnets agreeing which poles they were—and the sight of it hurt in a place that didn't have a name in any anatomy chart.

She texted Harper without thinking: *New girl sits with the Williams.* The dots bubbled. *Be nice,* Harper sent back. Then: *You okay?*

Brynlee stared at the question until the screen dimmed and took her face with it. She typed *sure* and *later* and erased both. In the trophy case glass, her reflection stood crisp, obedient, exactly where she put her. *The mirror gave her back a version of herself she could use. She didn't trust it to stay.*

The bell tripped the next period into motion. She flowed with the hall and pretended it was a choice. The Spirits didn't touch the back of her neck; they didn't need to. They had already shown her what not-helping looked like. The punishment for pretending she could stay above it had been simple: erase her and see if anyone noticed.

She kept walking. She did not look into the next sheet of glass she passed.

Harper Confrontation

By Wednesday, Harper had stopped waiting for Brynlee to volunteer the truth. She cornered her after last bell, right outside the side doors where the smokers pretended the rules didn't exist.

"You're gonna tell me," Harper said flatly, dropping her bag against the wall with a thud, "what's going on."

Brynlee glanced at the parking lot, half-empty, slush chewing the edges of the asphalt. "Nothing's going on."

"Don't." Harper's bracelets clattered as she folded her arms. "You're twitchy. You disappear. You text like you're writing grocery lists. And when I look at you, you look like you're already leaving."

Brynlee forced a laugh. "That's dramatic, even for you."

"Don't turn it into a joke." Harper's voice cracked on the edge of the word. She pressed her sleeve to her eyes like she'd just remembered the wind could sting, but her shoulders stayed squared. "Do you know how terrifying it is watching my best friend turn into a stranger and not know if it's me, or you, or—" She broke off, breath hard. "I'm scared, B."

The honesty hit harder than any Spirit ever had. Harper didn't do scared. She did loud, messy, too-much. *Never scared.*

Brynlee wanted to blurt it all—about the Spirits, the punishments, Lydia's face on the flyer that wasn't just a flyer. She opened her mouth. The air shifted, sharp and metallic. Behind Harper's shoulder, the brick wall darkened, shimmered—like oil slicking across stone. Shapes pulsed under it, bruises surfacing and fading in restless waves. Pain lingered there, not with a body but with weight, its hollow gaze pressing into her until the ache took root in her bones. The message carried straight through her marrow: *Speak, and you'll wear it.*

Her throat closed like iron. She forced out one syllable: *"Don't."*

Harper flinched like the words had slapped her. "No, you're not."

"I can handle it."

Harper let out a short, bitter laugh. "Handle it? You can't even look me in the eye anymore."

Brynlee forced herself to. Harper's curls had frizzed free of her braid, her eyeliner smudged under one eye. She looked tired in a way Brynlee had never noticed before—like someone who'd been holding a light up too long and was burning at the edges.

"I don't want to lose you," Harper said softly. "But you're making it really easy."

Brynlee opened her mouth and closed it again.

"Go home," she said finally. "Please, Harp. Just—go home."

Harper's face shuttered. She picked up her bag without another word, the clink of her bracelets muted now, a sound that landed heavy instead of bright.

Brynlee waited until she was gone. Only then did pain radiate in her wrist, and spread outward like black water—her shoulder, her ribs, her thighs. She gasped, staggering into the wall. When it let go, she dragged herself to the bathroom and locked the stall.

Under her jeans, a constellation of bruises was already forming. Dark, raw, blooming in fingerprints she didn't remember earning.

She pressed her forehead to the metal partition until it stung. *She couldn't tell Harper. She couldn't protect her and keep her too. And now her body bore the proof.*

First Contact

Thursday's cafeteria buzzed louder than usual, the kind of restless noise that came when snow threatened but hadn't yet delivered. Brynlee moved through the lunch line on autopilot, tray in her hands, ears half-turned to Harper at her side. Harper was still talking—something about her aunt's new boyfriend and a karaoke machine—but the words felt far away. Since yesterday's confrontation, every sound between them rang brittle.

At the edge of the room, Mara and Jacob sat in their usual corner. Today, they weren't alone, *again*.

Vivienne LeClair sat across from them, posture precise even on a cafeteria bench. She cut her apple into deliberate wedges, sliding one across to Mara without comment, as if sharing food was something she'd practiced. Jacob said something under his breath, and for a flash Vivienne's mouth softened—not a smile, exactly, but a crack in the surface.

Brynlee's stomach lurched. *She didn't know if it was hunger, envy, or both.*

She took her usual spot with Harper, but her eyes kept drifting to that table. Vivienne leaned in, listening closely to whatever Mara was saying. The three of them looked like they'd been orbiting each other for years instead of hours.

"You're staring," Harper said, spearing a fry.

"I'm not."

"You are. And don't say you're studying her outfit." Harper chewed, eyes narrowing. "What's the deal? You mad she didn't sit with you?"

Brynlee rolled her eyes, but her pulse was sharp in her throat. "I don't care where she sits."

"Liar." Harper smirked, but it didn't last. She pushed her fries toward Brynlee, bracelets clinking softer than usual. "Girls like that don't show up without a reason, B. Don't let her make you the reason."

Brynlee didn't answer.

Later, in history, Vivienne ended up in the seat next to her. The teacher droned about colonial trade routes while Vivienne took notes in looping, controlled handwriting. Her perfume was faint, something expensive Brynlee couldn't name, *like flowers pressed into glass.*

Brynlee's bruise throbbed under her sleeve, a dark reminder of yesterday. She caught herself staring at the neat line of Vivienne's knuckles. Without thinking, she whispered, "You don't have to sit with them, you know. People will..." She trailed off, not sure what she'd meant—judge her? Assume things? Leave her alone?

Vivienne turned, pen stilled, eyes cool and unreadable. "People will always say something. Easier if you stop listening." Her voice was calm, practiced, like she'd already rehearsed this defense too many times.

Brynlee blinked, caught off guard. She expected sharpness, not philosophy. *I guess.*

Vivienne studied her a moment longer, then added, "They're kind. Mara and Jacob. That's enough."

Before Brynlee could respond, the teacher called for attention. Vivienne turned back to her notes, wall built again, no crack showing.

But Brynlee had seen it—the way Vivienne's eyes lingered on Mara like someone watching a door to make sure it stayed open.

When the bell rang, Brynlee stuffed her books into her bag. She glanced at the reflection in the classroom's window as she passed. Her own face flickered, stretched thin for half a second

before snapping back into place. Rejection's warning lingered:
You will not keep both worlds.

She walked faster.

Blurred Boundaries

By noon the building had that over-warm, over-crowded feel that made the air taste like pencil shavings. The library's heaters clicked like they were counting to something and the computers hummed in a way that lined up wrong with Brynlee's pulse. She opened a blank doc for the essay she still didn't write—*Compare two communities and how they manage scarcity*—and stared at the cursor until it felt like it was staring back. A bulletin board by the printer held a new flyer: OLD TOWN WINTER MARKET—SUNDAYS, DUSK—string lights sketched along the border, a cartoon mug steaming. The font was cheerful and wrong. The alley from her nightmare breathed behind her eyes; cardboard, drizzle, the thin sound of someone swallowing a sob. She looked away fast and the edges of the paper still seemed wet.

She made herself type three sentences about cooperation and mutual aid and then hated them for sounding like the kind of answer teachers liked and nobody lived. The room shifted—no one moved, but the light dipped and then recovered, the hum of the computers finding a harsher note. In the quiet, the intercom coughed, then exhaled a breath that wasn't a voice so much as a decision. *See*, it said, or she made it say, and her chest cinched.

She closed the doc and pulled up the district archive to pretend she had a purpose. The screen populated with headlines that didn't matter. When she clicked one, the article loaded and then drained to blank, as if the words had walked themselves off the page. The white reflected her face back at her—only not quite. The eyes didn't hold; the mouth didn't shape to her thoughts. For a second the glass held a room that wasn't the library at all: A corridor unfolded behind her reflection, mirrors lining both sides, hundreds of them. Each one carried a version of her, slightly delayed, stacked into shrinking perspective. None of them met her eyes. One by one, the reflections turned their heads away, synchronized like puppets on the same string. The sound of glass bones creaked through the room, the noise of something looking and refusing. She blinked and the archive reappeared, bland and helpful. The cursor waited like it had all the time in the world.

Across the room, someone whispered and laughed. Mara's voice, low, followed by Jacob's careful joke. Brynlee turned reflexively and watched through the stacks as Vivienne leaned over a Chromebook between them. Vivienne pointed at something on the screen and Mara nodded, that small grateful tilt of the head she did when kindness didn't cost the person giving it. It should have been ordinary. It wasn't. The three of them were quiet in a way that made quiet look like a choice. Brynlee's palms went damp. *She told herself she could walk over, say something neutral about the assignment, insert herself. She stayed put. The decision sat in her bones heavy as a coin she refused to spend.*

The bell spat everyone into the hall. She caught sight of Jacob at his locker, wrestling a stack of textbooks against a door that never shut right. One slid, smacked his wrist, tumbled to the floor. The thud echoed like it wanted attention no one gave. He didn't swear; he just winced, jaw tight, and bent for it. Brynlee met his eyes for a second that lasted too long and then looked past him like she hadn't been looking at all. *She told herself he didn't need help, told herself it would be weird, told herself anything.* By the time she reached the corner stairwell, a dull ache had started deep in her hip, spreading like spilled ink under skin.

Her phone buzzed in her pocket, two messages stacked. Harper: *Trying to forgive you in advance if you ditch me for new royalty.*

Meet after last bell anyway? Then a photo—Harper's garage window, late afternoon light turned to silver, the canvas chair waiting. Brynlee typed *can't* and erased it, typed *later* and erased that too, typed nothing and let the unsent words weight her hand.

In English the teacher diagrammed sentences until the board looked like a map to a place language had never visited. Brynlee watched and thought about carving names into the backs of chairs. She thought about the flyer for the market and the way the cartoon steam had looked like it was breathing. She thought about Lydia's photo, the grain of it making her eyes older. Her hip throbbed in time with the clock. When the class laughed at something the teacher said, the sound lagged a half second behind the movement of mouths, and for the length of that half second the room wasn't the room—it was a gym with unlit candles and a table set for no one.

The final bell scattered everyone. She cut down the back hall to avoid the crush at the main doors and ended up by the old science wing where the lights always hummed a little meaner. The stairwell there split the building into a pocket of its own—a landing, a turn, a shadow. At the bottom step, tucked under the angle where light didn't reach, sat a cardboard box. Not new. Not crushed. Waiting. She stopped so hard her breath stumbled. *It could have been for recycling. It could have been nothing. She knew it wasn't.*

She stood there long enough that the cold from the stairwell concrete reached her ankles. The box sat quiet. A paper scrap lifted at the edge as if someone had breathed near it and fallen asleep mid-sigh. She made herself walk down two steps and look in. Empty. Except not. A photograph lay face down, the back mottled with damp. She didn't turn it over; she didn't need to see the image to know it would have a girl between parents, younger faces uncracked by time. She reached anyway and the paper lifted, lighter than it should be. Underneath, someone had scraped a word into the cardboard with something dull. *ENOUGH.* The letters cut shallow, like whoever carved them had run out of strength before they ran out of the word.

Her throat closed. On the landing above, sneakers squeaked, and a laugh ricocheted off tile. She dropped the photo back into the box like it might burn her and backed up the steps. When she reached the top, she looked down again. The box was gone. Bare concrete, a scuff where it had not been and now wasn't. A draft lifted the hair at her neck.

On impulse, she pulled out her phone and typed *Old Town Winter Market* into a notes app, not a search bar, like writing the name where it couldn't answer back would keep it from being real. The words sat there, small and black, and made a shape in her day they hadn't had five minutes ago.

At the front doors the glass gave her a clean, easy version of herself—hair in place, mouth steady, eyes a color you could name. She didn't trust it. Outside, the sky had flattened to that pre-snow blank. The air smelled like pennies. Somewhere far off a siren wound itself thin.

She told herself she would meet Harper. She told herself she would go straight home. She told herself she would delete the note. She told herself a rotation of things that sounded like plans. Then, without deciding, she looked again at the flyer she remembered too clearly— *SUNDAYS, DUSK*—and knew where her feet were going to take her soon whether she said the words out loud or not.

Behind her, a door shut gentle. In the reflection, for a breath, Lydia stood at the far end of the hall, she had traced an L on the glass. The condensation dripping. A body passed between them and the picture broke. When the space cleared, the hallway held only its usual ghosts: lockers, posters, the stain on the floor no janitor could kill.

Brynlee didn't turn around. She pushed outside into the flat light and let it have her.

The Pull

The week thinned into a blur—gray hallways, gray sky, gray slush chewing at the edges of everything. Brynlee told herself she was holding steady, that if she went through the motions hard enough the Spirits would lose interest. Get bored. Leave her the way they'd found her.

By Friday night the lie broke.

She woke with her pulse hammering, sweat cooling under the edge of her shirt. The lamp on her nightstand was still on, weak gold against the frost at the window. She told herself she'd only dreamed, that the ache in her hip from earlier would fade if she stopped prodding at it.

Then the dresser warped.

Not the mirror—wood itself, lacquer bubbling, surface buckling like something alive pressed from the inside.

She sat up, breath snagging.

The grain rippled outward, stretched, and then split. Rows of lockers shoved themselves into the world, running forever in both directions. Each one bore her name stenciled black and sharp.

A single door rattled open. Inside: a slip of paper, edges damp, one word clawed across it in crooked ink—*Never Enough*.

Metal slammed. Every locker door snapped shut at once, the sound rolling like thunder through her chest.

Her reflection leaned out of the nearest door. Lips moved. No sound, only the words in her bones: *You are not enough to keep them.*

Brynlee slammed her hand against the dresser. The corridor shattered, wood snapping back into ordinary shape. Only her face stared back now—pale, trembling, too wide-eyed to belong to her.

A knock on her door made her jolt. Her mother's voice muffled: "Lights out, Bryn. Try to sleep."

"Yeah," she croaked, too fast.

The hallway carpet muffled footsteps retreating. Alone again, Brynlee gripped the dresser edge until her knuckles ached. The reflection held steady but looked wrong—colors too sharp, outlines too obedient.

She shut the lamp off. Darkness pressed close, waiting.

When she finally closed her eyes, the dream was already there:

Tile underfoot. Fluorescents burning too bright.

A mall. Too clean. Too loud.

Glass storefronts in rows.

And Lydia Grace behind one, hands flat, mouth forming *help*.

Brynlee woke gasping, pulse already knowing where her feet would take her next.

The Mall

Late January made the mall feel like a greenhouse for the bored. Coats puffed on chairs like deflated bodies. Salt-scabbed boots squeaked on the polished tile. Air carried a permanent syrup of burnt sugar and pretzel salt. SALE signs sagged in every window, percentages shouting from red posters—since New Year's and would keep on until someone took the tape down.

Harper claimed the second-floor railing like it was a stage, hips hitched, chin up. "You owe me for the last week," she said, already halfway into a story about her aunt, karaoke, and a cordless mic that picked up the neighbor's police scanner. Brynlee laughed in the right place, then forgot how to keep laughing. The dream from the night before sat under her breastbone like a compass needle still refusing to budge. Her eyes kept catching on glass—storefronts, phone screens, mirrored columns—checking for a distortion that didn't come.

Harper nudged her. "Earth to—" She followed Brynlee's gaze down the escalators to the main concourse. "What?"

Brynlee didn't answer. She had already seen her.

At the far end of the atrium, just beyond the frozen fountain that hadn't run since December, a girl stood alone. Too-thin hoodie, sleeves tugged over knuckles, hair hacked ragged and tied back like someone tried to tame it with fingers and gave up. She stared at the directory sign with the big YOU ARE HERE star and flinched when anyone brushed close. The kind of flinch you learned from practice. She clutched something small in her fist—paper, maybe a photo—thumb working the edge until it softened.

Lydia Grace Turner.

Not the grainy photo from flyers. Alive. Breathing. Right there.

Brynlee said her name without meaning to, a breath turned sound. "Lydia."

Harper blinked. "Who?"

"Lydia." Louder now, the syllables cracking. Heads nearby turned. The girl did too.

Their eyes caught and held. Recognition hit like a blow. The same face from the news, from the box in the nightmare, only present-tense. Lydia's mouth opened soundlessly, then shaped the word Brynlee already knew it would: *help*.

Brynlee moved. Harper grabbed her sleeve, missing the cuff by an inch. "Bryn—"

Two men slid in from the edges of the crowd as if the mall had made them from the air. Nothing theatrical: puffy jackets, ball caps, the camouflage of the ordinary. One angled in from Lydia's right, hand soft and practiced on her elbow. The other stepped behind, close enough to block the directory from view. "There you are," the first said, voice gentle for strangers' ears. To anyone else it looked like shepherding. To Brynlee it looked like a door being closed.

Lydia jerked away, fast as a sparrow. The paper in her fist crumpled. She lifted her free hand toward Brynlee—palm out, fingers spread, a signal from a burning building—and tried to run. The second man caught her by the hood, not yanking, just hauling her momentum back into his pull. "Hey," he said, kinder, the word shaped for bystanders. "She's with us. She gets turned around."

"She's not," Brynlee shouted, voice too big, echoing off the tile. Conversations hiccupped and then hurried themselves back to normal. A woman with a stroller frowned without stopping. A kiosk guy glanced up from his phone and went back to scrolling. Security, two stores down, looked over and then looked away when the first man lifted a hand in a relaxed wave and a not-smile that read we've got it.

Harper's fingers found the meat of Brynlee's arm and held. "What are you doing?"

"That's Lydia." Brynlee's voice broke on the name. "Lydia Grace Turner."

Harper's mouth opened, shut. "No. That's—a fight, or a custody thing, or—Bryn, you don't know what you're—"

Lydia twisted, a clean, desperate motion. For one second her face cleared the man's shoulder and locked on Brynlee again, eyes wide, raw. The word on her mouth this time wasn't help. It was *please*.

Brynlee tore free of Harper's grip and ran.

She flew down the escalator wrong, skipping steps, catching the rubber rail with a slap that left her palm slick. The men were already moving, steering Lydia toward the dark mouth of a service corridor between a shoe store and a tea place. The sign above it said EMPLOYEES ONLY in letters that had stopped deterring anyone years ago. One man glanced back, quick, eyes skimming the crowd, and met Brynlee's. The look he gave her wasn't a threat, not exactly. It was recognition. He had seen her see.

"Hey!" Brynlee shouted, raw. "Stop!"

The second man shifted, not enough to look like a block, just enough that when she reached the corridor mouth her body found the space occupied. The first man's hand tightened on Lydia's elbow. "It's okay," he said to the world, the kind of okay that ends things. "She's confused." To Brynlee, without moving his lips: "Go home."

Lydia twisted again, the hood choking her forward. The paper in her fist broke, half of it fluttering to the tile like a dead moth. Brynlee reached without seeing and came up with nothing but air and the smell of old mop water.

A door inside the corridor clicked, then thudded. Silence swallowed the sound a second too late.

Brynlee lunged. Harper grabbed her from behind, yanking her back just enough to keep her from hitting the cinderblock wall with her face. "Stop," Harper hissed into her ear, voice shaking. "What are you doing? Do you want to die?"

"She was—" Brynlee's breath went thin. The corridor smelled like hot dust and chlorine and something else that wore a human name when it needed one. She pressed forward again; Harper held her harder. "Let me go."

"Security," Harper said. "We'll get security."

The guard who had glanced over before was already talking into his radio, posture slow with the calculus of who gets helped first and how much. By the time he reached them, the corridor had become only a corridor again. He listened to Brynlee's words with the trained patience of someone who had heard too many. "A girl," he repeated. "You think she mouthed help." He glanced at Harper for corroboration. Harper's eyes went to the floor and then to Brynlee's face. "I saw two guys with their...niece?" she said and flinched at her own question mark. "It looked like—" She stopped.

"It's her," Brynlee said. "It's Lydia Grace Turner."

The guard's mouth flattened. "We'll review the cameras," he said, which sounded helpful and already late. "If you want to file a statement, we can do that." He gestured toward a small office with a glass door and a dead plant. A line had already formed: a shoplifter with a red face, a man arguing about a parking ticket the mall couldn't have written. "Or you can call the police," he added, a suggestion that moved responsibility neatly from his hands to someone else's.

Brynlee's own hands shook. Her phone felt slick. She thumbed 9-1 and stopped, heart beating so hard she heard it over everything else. The men were gone. The door they'd gone through had no window. The camera pointed the wrong way. She had nothing to give but her voice and a name that would make people look at her like she'd swallowed a headline.

Harper pulled at her sleeve. "B," she said, soft, urgent. "Please. Come on. We can't fix this here."

Brynlee stared into the dark mouth of the corridor until her eyes invented movement they couldn't have seen. The air from inside breathed out cold, then stopped, like a lung deciding not to.

On the tile near her shoe lay the other half of the paper from Lydia's hand. Wet, chewed soft at the edges. She crouched and picked it up without meaning to. The image on the soaked side had bled, but she could still make it out: a girl younger by years, pinned between two smiling parents, summer sun flattening the shadows on their faces. A crease ran through the girl's mouth like a cut.

She folded the scrap into her palm before she could think better of it.

Harper tugged again. The guard had already turned away, radio at his mouth, eyes sliding over their reflection in the store glass like it had learned not to keep what it saw. "Please," Harper whispered. "Please."

Brynlee let herself be pulled back into the current, away from EMPLOYEES ONLY, away from the smell of bleach and breath. The mall reasserted itself with bright lights and music from three stores at once. People carried bags and babies and soft pretzels. Someone laughed too hard. Someone else said *We should go* and meant it about nothing that mattered.

On the second floor, by the railing where they'd started, Brynlee's legs went unsteady. Harper stood close enough their coats touched. "Tell me you're not going back there," she said, not a dare, a plea.

Brynlee closed her fist around the paper until the wet bled into her skin. "I can't promise that."

Harper made a sound that wanted to be a sigh and wasn't. "Then don't make me follow you."

They stood a long time, both of them facing the fountain that didn't run. The overhead lights threw their shadows side by side across the marble. Harper's moved when she shifted her weight. Brynlee's stumbled a beat late, then snapped to catch up—as if it had to be reminded she still belonged to it. For that blink, she had no shadow at all..

Proof in Pieces

The ride home was a silence Harper couldn't fill. She tried—half-hearted jokes about kiosk perfume, about fries in the food court, about anything—but her words slipped off Brynlee like rain off glass. Brynlee sat pressed against the passenger door, one hand buried in her coat pocket, fist closed around the damp scrap of photo until it cut into her palm.

Every red light felt like a delay designed to smother her. The mall kept replaying in her head: Lydia's mouth shaping *please*, the men's calm grip, and the way the crowd had seen nothing. Not nothing—they had chosen nothing. She rubbed her thumb across the crease in the paper like it could open a door.

"B," Harper said finally, voice fraying. "Say something. Please."

Brynlee turned her head, slow, like it weighed too much. Harper's face looked pale in the passing streetlights, her curls frizzed from the static of her coat hood. She looked... scared. Not the bright, loud Harper who mocked teachers and sang off-key to the radio. Scared Harper.

Her throat closed like a fist. She pressed her lips together until the words broke on the inside.

"Bryn," Harper said, voice unsteady. "Give me something true, even if it's small."

The honesty hit harder than any Spirit ever had. Harper didn't do scared. She did loud, messy, too-much. Never scared.

Brynlee wanted to blurt it all—about the Spirits, the punishments, Lydia's face on the flyer that wasn't just a flyer. She opened her mouth. The bruise on her hip pulsed, as if Pain itself had pressed a hand there. A warning. Her words died in her throat.

Harper pulled into Brynlee's driveway, headlights sweeping the front porch. She put the car in park but didn't move to kill the engine. "I don't want to lose you," she said softly. "But you're making it impossible."

Brynlee opened the door, the cold slapping her bare ankles where her jeans rode up. She got out without answering. Harper's voice followed, small through the crack of the open car: "Please don't make me your enemy."

The car door shut. The engine carried Harper away.

Inside, the house hummed with its usual warmth—heater cycling, her parents' voices drifting from the kitchen, a laugh-track on TV. All of it too normal, too safe, like layers of wallpaper over rot. She slipped upstairs, locked her door, and finally pulled the photo scrap from her pocket.

Up close, the paper was worse: Lydia's smile blurred from water damage, her parents' arms fixed around her like statues. The crease across her mouth cut the picture in half. Brynlee traced it with her nail until the edge bent.

A band of ceiling shadow cut across her face on the wall, bisecting her mouth exactly where the photo did.

She dropped the photo, chest heaving. The paper landed face-down on the carpet. When she picked it up again, her ribs flared sudden-hot. A bruise was already blooming there, dark under her shirt, though nothing had touched her.

The Spirits didn't need to speak this time. The message carved itself straight into her skin:

You saw. Now you owe.

Brynlee pressed her palm to the bruise until it hurt worse. "I'm going after her," she said, the vow small and steady. "Tomorrow." The silence shifted, satisfied.

The Search

Saturday stretched thin and colorless. Snow fell in halfhearted flurries that never stuck, dissolving on the pavement before they could call themselves winter. Brynlee sat hunched at her desk with the photo scrap pressed flat under a geometry textbook, as if hiding it under the weight could make it safer. The crease through Lydia's mouth still cut her smile in half.

She opened her laptop. The screen glow burned her eyes too awake. She typed *Old Town Winter Market* into the search bar. Autocomplete coughed up results—Instagram tags, event flyers, a handful of blurry photos posted by people—bragging about cocoa in plastic cups. Tomorrow. Dusk. The market. The words stamped themselves behind her eyes whether she looked at the flyer or not.

Her pulse quickened. Tomorrow was Sunday.

She clicked through photos. Rows of string lights sagged over stalls, steam fogging from paper cups, handmade scarves twisted into display racks. Normal. So normal it felt like a lie. And in one image—background, left edge—she swore she saw a cardboard box tucked beside a dumpster. Not central, not staged. Just there, ignored by the people who had filtered themselves in front of it.

Her fingers clenched the trackpad. Zoom only made the pixels worse. She leaned close until her reflection ghosted in the glass, face stretched. For a split second the reflection didn't move with her. Its lips shaped a word she didn't hear, but she knew the meaning anyway: *Go.*

She snapped the laptop shut, chest hammering. The noise in her ears was louder than the heater, louder than her parents downstairs arguing over groceries. The bruise on her ribs pulsed like a heartbeat, not her own.

Her phone buzzed. Harper: *You alive?* Then another: *Haven't heard from you since yesterday. Ping me when you land. I'm not letting go.*

Brynlee typed *I can't talk* and erased it. Typed *tomorrow* and erased that too. Finally sent nothing. The dots of Harper typing back came and went, then vanished.

She pressed her palms to her face, breathing through her fingers. When she pulled them away, the photo scrap had slid half out from under her book, as if it wanted to be seen. The crease through Lydia's mouth looked deeper in this light, splitting all the way to the edge of the page.

Brynlee slipped the photo into her pocket and stood. She didn't decide. The decision was already made the moment the Spirits dragged her into their world. *Tomorrow at dusk, she would go to the market.*

The room felt thinner as soon as she thought it.

From the corner of her mirror, her reflection smiled without her.

The Market

Dusk made Old Town look like a postcard someone had handled too much—edges softened, colors thumb-smudged. String lights sagged between lampposts, each bulb a small lie about warmth. Generators purred under vendor tables. Steam rose from paper cups and burned sugar clung to the air. Families moved in slow swells, kids dragging mittened hands along rails until static snapped them yelping back to their parents' coats.

Brynlee walked the middle of the street where the salt had half-solved the ice. She kept her hood up and her head down and still felt visible, like her name had been pinned to her shoulders. The photo scrap in her pocket had warmed to the shape of her hand. She could feel the crease through the denim, a fault line she had brought with her.

The first cardboard box sat where the alley opened behind a kettle-corn stand, tucked against a dumpster, its flaps gaping, stiff with old damp. Nothing about it announced itself. It waited the way a mouth waits. When she looked at it, the rest of the market receded, sounds thinning to tin. A child ran past with a string of lights tangled around his wrist and the bulbs went dead as he crossed the alley's mouth, winking back on when he returned to his parents' orbit.

She stepped closer, the cold inside the alley a different temperature from the street—older, used. The box breathed. Not up and down; in and out, a small draw like something trying not to be heard. She bent and the smell rose—wet cardboard, soap that never rinsed clean, the metallic ghost of old bleaches. When she braced a hand on the rim, the fiber rasped her palm and a welt erupted along the inside of her forearm, a thin raised line that burned like the memory of heat. She jerked back, breath hitching.

A sound unspooled beside her ear: words without voice, the texture of no one saying anything. *No hands to hold. No voices to call your name.* Loneliness didn't need to show itself to be believed; it wrote on her skin instead. She tugged her sleeve down over the mark and made herself look. The box held nothing but an indentation, the shape of someone's hips and shoulders pressed into the damp enough times to teach the cardboard the lesson of a body.

A violinist sawed through *Silent Night* two booths away, out of season now, the wrong song with the right ache. Brynlee pulled back into the stream of shoppers. She told herself to breathe. *She told herself she could leave and come back with someone who would believe her. She told herself she would not run.*

Past a line of scarves twisted like ropes, two men stood under the awning of a coffee stand, steam haloing their caps, talking in the posture of people not talking. Ball caps. Puffer jackets. Hands in pockets that didn't need them. One laughed once without moving his face. The other took a slow scan of the crowd that would have been nothing if she hadn't already seen him do it somewhere else.

Mall man number two. The one who'd blocked the corridor with his body like a door that had never opened.

He didn't see her yet. She changed her angle, using a group with a double stroller as a shield. She pulled out her phone and turned on the camera, lifting it as if to take a photo of the lights. The screen didn't show the stand or the men or the sag of bulbs. The feed flickered into a stage no one had set rows of empty folding chairs fanned under a white-hot bar of light, all facing a microphone that had no cord. The chairs creaked as if a crowd had just leaned forward at once. The word *ENOUGH* was chalked on the stage floor in a hand that had run out of strength. She blinked and the market snapped back, her phone's lens dutiful, the two men still under the awning and now both looking at her.

Recognition clicked in his eyes the way a camera does. He didn't frown. He didn't smile. He touched the brim of his cap in a gesture too polite to be anything but a choice.

She turned casually, the way people do when they are not prey. Pain moved with her, a slow bloom down her hip where bruise had already learned the terrain, as if to remind her which side she had chosen. She cut behind a booth selling carved spoons, past a table of beeswax candles shaped like churches, into the crowd where breath fogged and disappeared.

"Miss?" The voice was behind her, kind enough to be used. She straightened and did not stop. "Miss?" Closer now. "You dropped something."

She hadn't. She didn't look back. On her left a van idled at the curb, white paint grayed by salt, back doors scabbed with old tape. Not illegal here; vendors, delivery, the thousand excuses cities give vans. The exhaust made a low animal noise against the snowbank. Her heartbeat in time with it and then ahead of it, racing to prove it could. She crossed the street with a family whose youngest had lost a mitten and was wailing about it like the world had ended. The man behind her adjusted his speed to theirs, not hers. Not hunting; learning the rhythm of the herd.

She veered toward a stall where a woman in a knit hat sold cheap Polaroids to couples who wanted proof they had stood under these exact string lights. A clothesline of damp photos moved in the small wind. One image near the end had bled badly, faces run to watercolor and then winter water. A younger girl between two parents, smiles forced flat by flash. The photo had bled badly, flash flattening their faces until the smiles looked stapled on. Not Lydia's photo: a thousand families fit that pose. The sight still punched her the way a memory that isn't yours can.

The man from the coffee stand materialized at the corner of the booth. He held out his palm. A folded napkin lay there, stainless with intent. "You dropped this," he said gently, as if the napkin were a wallet or a name. Up close, his eyes were the color of the blur string lights make when you stare long enough. "Hate for you to lose something important."

"I didn't," she said, looking at the napkin, not at him.

"You were at the mall," he said, like the weather, like the time. "Funny thing, running into each other in a city this size."

"Lots of people go to the mall." Her voice held steady in the air like a coin she'd just flipped. It could land either way.

He leaned in a fraction, not enough to scare the couples, enough to make the air between their bodies his. "Not lots of people yell names they shouldn't know."

In the reflection on a thermos beside her hand, her face smiled back a beat too wide, too certain, like the glass had improved her. Her jaw clenched. "My mistake," she said.

"Sure," he said. He didn't move, didn't blink wrong, didn't show his teeth. "Mistakes happen. Be careful on your way home."

"Not alone," she said before she could stop herself.

"Smart." He turned his head slightly, and somewhere down the row a second white van, different salt scars, pulled away from a hydrant like it had never been there. "You keep being smart."

He stepped out of her way. The violinist had moved to something faster, cheerful and cruel. Brynlee took three steps and didn't run until she had turned the corner and the corner after that, until the market noise had thinned to generator hum and the smell of diesel. A welt flared across her upper arm, bright sting spreading under her coat like someone had lit a match on her skin. Loneliness didn't like that she hadn't called anyone; she could feel it writing that judgment into the welt's heat. Pain joined it lower, at her thigh, a bruise blooming without touch. The alley ahead narrowed, a throat. The window beside it threw her back at her like a stranger and then nothing at all for a blink, just the alley going on without her.

She pressed herself into the angle where brick met brick and counted backwards from twenty with her eyes closed. When she opened them, a group of teenagers swarmed past, too loud, smelling like gum and borrowed spray, the safest camouflage the world had ever invented. She stepped into their noise and let it cover her. For a second she envied their volume, the way safety made people careless enough to laugh too loud.

At the end of the block the first man had returned to the coffee stand, back to the posture of two friends not talking. He did not look at her. That was worse.

She walked to the far corner, forced herself to stop by a vendor selling pears and cheese, she bought a pear she didn't want, the kind of normal act that left a receipt. Proof she'd been here. Proof she wasn't only someone the boxes remembered. She put it in her pocket beside the photo scrap as if weight on one side of her body could balance the other. Her breath smoked the air. The welts throbbed. Somewhere behind the vendors, a van door thudded twice, far apart, like a heartbeat that had learned patience.

The Spirits had not saved her. They had not warned her away. They had done what they always did: peeled back the layer everyone else agreed to believe and watched what she did with the rawness underneath.

On the walk home she kept to the center of the sidewalk and checked every glass she passed. In one, she didn't exist. In the next, she did, too bright and clean to be trusted. When she crossed the last street before her block, headlights washed her in a square of light. The car passed. The square faded. Her body kept moving because stopping would make meaning out of standing still.

At her door, she fumbled the key twice and didn't look back down the street until she'd thrown the deadbolt. The house breathed its normal breath—heater, TV, her parents talking like they didn't know they sounded like comfort. She slid her coat off and hissed when the fabric scraped the welt on her arm. Under the bathroom light, the raised line flared angry, fresh. Below it, purple was already shouldering its way up through her thigh, the bruise shaped like fingers that hadn't needed to touch her to leave themselves behind.

She pressed her palm to both until her hand ached. Then she took the photo scrap out of her pocket, smoothed it against the mirror, and held it there at the edge where the glass wanted to turn away.

"They saw me," she said to the girl with the crease through her mouth and to the girl in the mirror who didn't always look back. "And I saw them. I'm not going to stop."

The mirror offered nothing. The house held its breath. Outside, somewhere far enough to pretend it was coincidence, a van engine turned over and idled until it didn't.

Splitting Glass

Dinner tasted like cardboard. Her mom's stew usually warmed the whole house, smelled like garlic and thyme before the lid even came off. Tonight, it was just heat sliding down, no taste, no comfort. Salt and nothing. The welt on her arm stung where her sleeve brushed it, the bruise on her thigh pressed every time she shifted in her chair.

"You're quiet," her dad said, breaking bread in half. "School?"

"Fine," Brynlee said.

Her mom tilted her head. "Fine like you don't want to talk about it, or fine like you're actually fine?"

"Fine like—fine."

They both looked at her, not suspicious exactly, but reading her like she was homework they couldn't help with. She shoved another bite in before they could ask again.

Her phone buzzed on her lap. Harper. *Pick up. Please.* Then again: *I'm not letting this go. If you don't talk to me, I'll come over.*

Brynlee typed *don't* and erased it. Typed *I can't* and erased that too. Finally shoved the phone back in her pocket and stabbed at a carrot that had gone soft.

The mirror above the sideboard fractured, not her reflection but the dining room behind it, chairs and sideboard splitting along a seam she couldn't unsee. She blinked, and the mirror was whole again, but her stomach had already dropped.

"I've got homework," she said, pushing her chair back.

Her mom frowned. "Bryn, you've barely—"

"I'm fine." She carried her plate to the sink before either of them could stop her.

Upstairs, she locked her door and leaned against it until her knees buckled. She yanked her sleeve up. Multiple scratches that looked like *ALO* but didn't finish. She hissed and pulled the fabric back down.

Her phone buzzed again. Harper: *I miss you. Don't shut me out.*

Brynlee's throat clenched. She almost called. Almost. The bruise on her thigh pulsed sharp, a warning from Pain this time. She set the phone face-down on her desk. *I can't*, she whispered to no one.

———

Monday at Ashwood, the halls were all gray coats and salt-wet floors. Brynlee kept her head low, one hand tugging her sleeve down tight over the welt. Harper passed her by her locker, curls frizzed from the damp. Their eyes met a second too long. Harper's hand twitched like she might catch Brynlee's sleeve, then fell back to her side when Brynlee turned away.

And there—halfway down the hall—Vivienne stood by Mara and Jacob, books balanced against her hip. She wasn't laughing. She wasn't talking. She just watched. Around her the hallway jostled with coats and lockers slamming, but Vivienne didn't shift, didn't blink. The stillness made her the only fixed point in a hall built out of motion. Her gaze caught on Brynlee's sleeve and lingered, heavier than words.

Brynlee dropped her eyes first.

The bell rang, lockers slammed, voices surged. Everyone moved. But Brynlee's ribs still burned with the echo of the welt's message, and Vivienne's look followed her into class like a shadow she couldn't peel off.

The Widening Gap

By midweek the bruise on Brynlee's thigh had gone sick yellow at the edges, but the scratches on her arm still flared red, hot enough she kept tugging her sleeve down like she could erase it—by hiding it. Every tug reminded her of the word she figured it had almost spelled. *Alone.* She wore it like a brand no one else could see.

Harper tried anyway. Between classes she popped up at Brynlee's side, copper curls escaping her braid, bracelets clattering as if sound could force a reply.

"Movie night tonight?" she tried, grin wide, desperate. "My place, terrible rom-com, popcorn with too much salt? We can heckle every kiss."

Brynlee shifted her books higher. "I've got work."

"Homework?"

"Yeah."

"You can do it at mine. You've done it a hundred times."

"I can't, Harp." The words came sharper than she meant. "Not tonight."

Harper's smile slipped, not all the way gone but cracked at the corners. "Okay. Not tonight. Tomorrow, then."

Brynlee walked faster. Harper kept pace two steps, then let her go. The echo of her bracelets followed like a question.

———

At lunch, Brynlee carried her tray to the far side of the cafeteria. Harper was already waving her over, but Brynlee pretended she didn't see. Her feet pulled her toward Mara and Jacob instead, though she didn't let herself sit with them. She hovered a table away, back to theirs, the sound of their voices threading into hers anyway.

Vivienne sat across from them, coat folded precise, posture perfect even on a cafeteria bench. She cut her apple into clean wedges, sliding one to Mara without a word. Jacob said something low, and Mara's laugh—small, genuine—lit the air for a second. Vivienne's mouth curved at the edge, not quite a smile, but enough.

Brynlee ate her roll dry, throat tight. She felt Harper's eyes from across the room, searching, waiting for her to turn around. She didn't.

———

After school, the halls thinned. Harper caught her by the stairwell. "Why are you doing this?" she demanded, voice breaking on the edges.

"Doing what?" Brynlee's voice was flat.

"Shutting me out. Pretending I don't exist. I've been your anchor since—since forever, and now you look at me like I'm the one you need saving from."

Her chest cinched, ribs refusing to open. For one breath she almost told her everything—the Spirits, the bruises, the market, Lydia. Almost. The cuts on her arm burned like fire. She flinched.

"I'm not pretending," she said instead. "I just... can't."

Harper's face crumpled, not into tears, but into something worse: hurt twisted into disbelief. "Then tell me when I stopped being enough."

Brynlee pushed past her. The hallway blurred.

———

Vivienne stood outside by the curb, waiting for her ride. Snow feathered down, catching in her hair like it belonged there. Vivienne lifted a hand, tucked one strand precisely behind her ear, and never looked away. Not asking. Not accusing. Just *seeing*.

It felt like being read in a language she didn't know she'd written.

The car pulled up. Vivienne slid inside without a word, gaze still fixed until the door closed. Brynlee stood in the falling snow long after the taillights disappeared.

Breaking Point

That night the house hummed steady—dishwasher cycling, her parents' muted laughter bleeding from the TV downstairs. Ordinary noise. Safe noise. Brynlee sat cross-legged on her bed with her laptop open, a geometry problem set glowing on the screen, untouched. The welt on her arm itched like fire, the bruise on her thigh pulsed like a second heart. She pulled her sleeve up, half expecting to see letters burned deep.

Nothing.

Just skin. A faint flush where she knew the welt should be, but nothing that would explain the pain biting her every time she flexed.

She scraped her nails over the spot until her eyes watered. Still nothing.

She yanked her phone out and flipped to camera. Held it up to her arm, to her thigh. The screen showed her skin smooth, blank, unbothered. She angled it different ways, tapped the light brighter. Nothing.

Her breath quickened. She pressed harder on the bruise until the air ripped from her throat. The pain was real. Her body screamed. But the proof wasn't there.

This was part of the cruelty — not only to hurt her, but to make sure no one could prove it.

Her door cracked—her mom leaning in with a laundry basket, cheeks flushed from the dryer's heat. "Hey, honey. Everything okay?"

Brynlee yanked her sleeve down so fast it pinched skin. "Fine."

Her mom's eyes flicked to the sleeve, lingered; her thumb paused on the laundry basket handle, as if to reach. The pause broke and she only said, "Don't stay up too late," and was gone.

Brynlee stared at the wood, skin crawling.

If no one else could see, no one else could believe.

—

At school the next day, Vivienne passed her in the hall. For the briefest second her gaze snagged on Brynlee's wrist where the welt throbbed under fabric. Brynlee froze. Her pulse screamed: *She knows. She sees it.*

Vivienne's brow creased faintly, almost a frown, then smoothed. She didn't speak. She just looked away, precise and deliberate, as if whatever she'd noticed hadn't been worth keeping.

Brynlee's stomach turned to ice. *She saw. And she didn't.*

She tugged her sleeve down harder, nails biting through the fabric, the phantom mark still burning. She imagined Vivienne thinking she'd seen a scar, a rash, some weakness Brynlee would have to explain away if it ever came up. An excuse. A lie.

Every step down the hall felt heavier. She wanted to scream: *It's there, it's real, it hurts.* Instead, she walked straighter, chin high, the lie that had always protected her hardening again.

—

That night, when she tried to sleep, the Spirits came back. Not in the room—worse. In the mirror.

Her reflection twisted at the edges, mouth bent out of sync with words she hadn't spoken. The mirror fogged from the inside, the breath cool and wrong. Letters scrawled themselves in the film — backward at first, then righting, spelling two words that made Brynlee's lungs empty: *YOU ARE OURS.*

Her wrist flared white-hot. Her thigh throbbed purple. Pain and Loneliness braided together until she choked on the silence in her own room. She pressed her face into her pillow, sobbing without sound, because even if someone came—her parents, Harper, anyone—they would never see.

Only she could.

The Last Anchor

By Thursday, the silence between them had turned into its own language—one Brynlee was learning to speak too well. Harper still sat near her in homeroom, still filled the gaps with jokes about teachers and cafeteria food, but Brynlee heard every word as a plea: *don't let this end like this.*

She kept her head down anyway.

After school, Harper caught her by the bike racks, fingers clamping Brynlee's wrist before she could walk past. The grip was familiar, the way Harper had always tugged her back into orbit.

"Stop." Harper's voice shook. "You don't get to ghost me forever."

Brynlee tried to pull free. "I'm not—"

"You are." Harper yanked her closer, her curls frizzing out from the damp, bracelets clattering like chains. "We've been best friends forever. "You don't just throw me away. For Vivienne? For Mara and Jacob?"

Brynlee's chest clenched. "It's not like that."

"Then tell me what it is!" Harper's grip tightened on her wrist. "Tell me why you look at me like I'm poison when all I've ever done is stand by you."

The welt under Brynlee's sleeve erupted like fire. Her knees buckled. She bit down on a scream and swallowed it with blood at the back of her throat. Harper's eyes widened at her flinch.

"What is it?" Harper demanded. "What's wrong?"

Brynlee shook her head hard. "Nothing."

"Don't lie to me. I felt you—"

The burn scorched deeper, carving upward until her arm shook. Letters gouged into her flesh, unseen but undeniable: NO HANDS TO HOLD. The verdict pressed in like walls closing.

She ripped her arm back, so hard Harper stumbled. "Don't touch me!" The words tore out sharper than she meant, too loud, echoing off the brick wall behind the racks.

Harper froze. The color in her face drained. "Wow."

"I didn't—" Brynlee's voice collapsed. "I can't—"

"No." Harper's laugh cracked, brittle. "Don't backpedal. You made it clear. You don't want me. Got it."

Her bracelets clashed as she shoved her hands into her hoodie pockets. "You know what, B? I hope Vivienne laughs at all the right times. Because I'm done. I hope Jacob and Mara fill every single silence. Because you just burned the one person who would've stayed, no matter what."

She turned and walked fast, curls bouncing, shoulders stiff. She didn't look back.

The welt throbbed, still searing. The bruise on Brynlee's thigh flared in sympathy. Pain and Loneliness had never braided this close before. She doubled over, breath strangled, forcing herself not to cry where anyone could see.

When she finally straightened, Harper was gone. Her bracelets' echo still clattered in Brynlee's head long after the lot went silent. The only sound was the hiss of the snowmelt drain, swallowing everything she hadn't said.

The First Crack in Vivienne

Monday blurred into the kind of gray that stuck to skin. Salt
chewed the curbs, buses wheezed like old men, and the halls of
Ashwood hummed with too many voices that weren't hers.
Brynlee kept her head down, headphones in without music,
sleeves tugged over wrists that still throbbed with phantom heat.

Harper hadn't texted all weekend. The silence cut sharper
than words. Every time Brynlee glanced toward their usual
spots—in the cafeteria, by the lockers, outside homeroom—
Harper was there, laughing at jokes she never used to find funny,
her voice bright enough to sting. And every time, Harper's eyes
skipped over her like she'd already been erased.

The bruise on Brynlee's thigh pulsed in time with each
glance. The welt under her sleeve flared if she thought too long
about chasing Harper down. The Spirits didn't need to whisper
anymore. Their punishment was built into her skin.

At lunch she sat alone, chewing a roll that tasted like dust.
Across the room, Mara and Jacob shared a tray, Mara breaking
crackers in half, Jacob nudging his half back like he hadn't needed
it anyway. Vivienne sat with them, posture so precise it made the
plastic bench look like it belonged in her world instead of theirs.

Her coat draped perfect. Her apple slices gleamed white where the skin had been peeled away.

Brynlee meant to look away before anyone noticed. But Vivienne's eyes lifted, cool and sharp, like a blade catching light. Not empty—never empty—but weighing. It was the kind of gaze that sifted. And it landed on Brynlee's sleeve. Not on her face, not on her tray. Her sleeve.

Brynlee's pulse stuttered. She tugged the fabric lower, but Vivienne didn't glance away fast, like most people would out of politeness. She watched long enough to make it deliberate. Then, without a word, she slid her last slice of apple across the table to Mara and lifted her water like nothing had happened.

Brynlee dropped her gaze, heat crawling her neck.

———

Later, the hall thinned after last bell. Brynlee dragged her books against her hip, eyes on the floor. Vivienne stood by her locker, spinning the dial like she had nowhere better to be. Her hair caught the light wrong—too glossy, too sharp. Brynlee slowed before she could stop herself.

"Your wrist," Vivienne said.

"What?!" Brynlee answered, heart fluttering. *Oh no she can see it!*

"You snagged it on something," Vivienne said, eyes flicking to Brynlee's wrist where the fabric had pulled. A faint thread dangled loose, nothing more. But Brynlee's stomach dropped all the same—because under that sleeve, the welt still burned, invisible to anyone else. For a second she was sure Vivienne had seen straight through to it.

The words landed flat, matter-of-fact. Not an accusation. Not kindness either.

Brynlee froze. Her arm burned under the fabric, welt invisible but roaring. "What?"

Vivienne tilted her head, eyes unreadable. "You're tugging at it like you don't want anyone to notice. Makes people notice more."

Brynlee's throat locked. She wanted to snap back, to deny, to lie. The words tangled. "It's nothing."

Vivienne shut her locker with a clean metallic click. "Sure." She slung her bag over her shoulder, the weight balanced perfectly. "Nothing always hurts that much."

And then she walked away, steps even, coat swinging.

Brynlee stood there too long, sleeve clutched tight, heart hammering against a mark no one else could see. Vivienne hadn't pressed. She hadn't pried. She had just said what she saw—and left it hanging, waiting to see if Brynlee would admit to the crack.

The silence in the hall filled with the echo of her footsteps, and Brynlee realized she wanted them back.

Unheard

Sunday night she decided to stop flinching and start moving. She spread a notebook open on her desk and wrote in block letters at the top of a page: **LYDIA: WHAT I KNOW.** Under it she stacked facts that wouldn't argue: *Mall. Service corridor. Two men. White vans (salt-scarred). Photo scrap (crease through mouth).* On the next page: **WHERE TO GO.** *Mall back corridors. Old Town vendors (coffee stand, kettle-corn, Polaroids). Ask about vans. Sketch exits.* She traced each word hard enough to dent the paper below it. When she closed the notebook, the indent still said **GO** in ghost letters.

Monday, Loneliness cut the sound out of the world.

It started in history when the teacher asked about food rations on the home front. Brynlee raised her hand because the answer lived on the edge of her tongue and because agency was a muscle and she was going to make it work. "Black markets," she said—

Nothing came out.

Her mouth formed the syllables. The air left her lungs. Silence dropped around her like a glass dome lowering, sealing her off from air. She saw her classmates' faces—Harper's pencil paused mid-doodle, Jacob's head half-turned, Mara already looking down to hide notice. The teacher frowned. "Speak up, Brynlee."

"I—" she tried again, forcing the word from the back of her throat.

Silence. The clock ticked. She could hear that, but her own voice didn't exist.

The teacher's gaze slid past her. "Anyone else?"

Hands went up. A boy two rows back said exactly what she'd meant to say, and the teacher nodded, chalk scratching approval. Sound rushed back in a blink: chair legs, paper, a cough, the scrape of chalk. Brynlee's heart hammered against ribs that now burned with heat that left no mark.

Second period she tested it. In the hall she said *hello* to a girl from algebra, louder than she meant. The girl glanced at her lips moving and then over her shoulder at someone who had actually made noise. In the bathroom she whispered *Can you hear me?* at the tiles. The heater clicked. The faucet dripped. The words fell at her feet. She texted herself a note—***I SAW LYDIA. DON'T LET THEM ERASE THIS.*** The message flickered, then vanished while she watched, letters smudging away as if the phone remembered something cleaner.

At lunch she chose a table and sat facing the room. She raised one hand at Harper across the cafeteria—simple, neutral. Harper's eyes flicked to her, then to Vivienne, then back to her tray. Brynlee stood anyway and crossed the floor because if her voice didn't carry, her feet still could.

"Harper," she said when she reached her. *Nothing.* "I need—" *Nothing.* She dug in her pocket, tore a page from the corner of a receipt, wrote **PLEASE LISTEN** and set it beside the fries. Harper stared at the words, then at Brynlee's face, confusion and anger wrestling. "You won't talk to me," Harper said, *louder than necessary.* "Now you want me to read your mind?" The girls at her table laughed, a little cruel. Brynlee's mouth moved again—*I'm trying*—and the sentence fell apart in her throat. She picked up the note, folded it once, twice, slid it into her sleeve like she was tucking gauze over a wound. She turned away before the heat behind her eyes could rise.

By last bell, the quiet had drained her bones. Pain didn't bruise this time; it pressed fatigue into her body until climbing the stairs felt like walking through wet sand. After school she detoured to the counselors' office because if the Spirits erased sound, paper might still count. At the sign-in window she slid the photo scrap across the counter and wrote on a sticky note: **I saw her at the mall. Two men. White van.** The receptionist smiled apologetically and rotated the scrap with two fingers like it was a lost locker combination. "If you have a concern, sweetie, you can fill out a safety form. We'll make sure it gets to the right place."

Brynlee filled out the form, printed letters steady, the story tight. By the time she reached the bottom of the page, the first half had paled to faint gray. She pressed harder. The graphite went darker and then ghosted again, as if the paper itself refused to hold her story. When she handed it back, the receptionist checked the top corner for the box where you wrote your name, saw nothing written there, and stapled the blank form to a stack of other blanks.

Fine. If the world refused her voice, she'd build a louder one.

In the library she printed a schematic of the mall from a decade-old planning commission PDF and marked the service corridors in red pen—trash lanes, dock doors, camera blind spots. She copied bus routes from her neighborhood to Old Town and wrote **SUNDAYS, DUSK** as if scheduling the harm could make it manageable. She flipped her notebook to a clean page and wrote a line she didn't want to forget **I am not waiting for permission.**

On the way out she passed Vivienne in the foyer. The air was full of wet wool and boys stomping salt from their shoes. Vivienne stepped aside without looking down, the movement neat, and then stopped short like she'd heard something other people hadn't. Her gaze slid to the notebook against Brynlee's chest, to the corner of the mall schematic sticking out—a row of small squares like a spine. Her eyes lifted. "What are you doing?"

For once, Brynlee didn't try to say it. She tore a strip from the edge of the map, wrote **Looking**, and held it out. Vivienne read the single word, fold-tightened it between two fingers, and tucked it into the inner pocket of her coat like a receipt she needed to keep. "Be careful," she said. Not warning, not comfort. Just fact.

At home that night, the house sounded normal and wrong. She sat on the floor and laid everything out in a grid: the photo scrap, the bus routes, the map with corridors inked red, a page of vendor names she'd copied from the market flyer, a list of questions that didn't have answers yet. **What time did the vans arrive? How many doors? Who saw them?** In the top corner she taped a Post-it to the wall above the baseboard: **You saw her. Don't let them erase it.**

The heater kicked on. The Post-it curled. She pressed it flat with her thumb until it held.

Her phone lit with an unknown number. She answered because she was done hiding. Static filled the line. Then a voice, calm and too friendly: "We received a tip from your school. Hard to process a blank form. If you'd like to come in and make a statement—"

"I—" She spoke into the phone and watched the sound die midair. No words traveled, just her breath fogging the screen. "Lydia," she tried, mouth forming the shape. Silence ate it. The voice on the other end kept talking as if she were there and already not.

She hung up. She wrote **_POLICE_** on a new page, underlined it, and then wrote **_NOT YET_** underneath because walking in without sound would get her dismissed, or worse—noticed by the wrong people first. She flipped to the map again and drew a small circle where the service corridor met the dock. **Tomorrow.** She pressed the pen so hard the nib bent.

She stood back and looked at the grid on the floor. It wasn't much. It was more than nothing.

"_I'm coming_," she said to the empty room, to the girl in the crease, to the space in the mirror where her reflection sometimes refused her. The words didn't carry into the air. That was fine. She could hear them. She taped the sentence to the wall in ink instead.

Erasure

Tuesday morning, Brynlee stared into the bathroom mirror and saw nothing. Not a blur, not a lag. Nothing. Steam blurred the glass, but even when it cleared, the space where she should've been stayed empty.

Her hands pressed the counter, knuckles white. She touched her cheek, lifted her chin, dragged her fingers down her throat. No image. Only the white tile behind her.

Her breath hitched. "Stop," she whispered, and even that carried no echo in the glass. The Spirits weren't bruising her this time. They were *carving her out.*

She shoved back, yanked her sleeve down to hide the welt only she could feel, and stormed downstairs before her knees gave.

———

At Ashwood, whispers swelled near the entrance. Another missing kid's face plastered across the news monitors in the lobby. *Samantha Ng, age fifteen. Last seen leaving a bus stop two towns over.* Brynlee's stomach dropped. She had never seen Samantha, but the girl's hoodie in the grainy footage matched the same brand one of the Williams kids wore every day.

Mara and Jacob stood stiff near the bulletin board, Mara gripping her backpack strap until her knuckles went white. Brynlee lingered close enough to hear Jacob's voice, low and steady: "We're not them. Don't think it."

Mara's eyes flicked to Brynlee—haunted, searching. Brynlee looked away first.

———

Third period, Vivienne caught her by the lockers. The hall buzzed with voices, but Vivienne's cut through, level and precise. "You look pale."

"I'm fine."

"You're lying badly."

Brynlee's laugh cracked. "You don't even know me."

Vivienne shut her locker with a deliberate click. "I know when someone's about to come apart. You're close." Her gaze flicked once more to Brynlee's wrist, then to her eyes. "Just be careful how much of yourself you let disappear."

The word disappear hit harder than any bruise.

———

After school she cut through the side lot, notebooks heavy in her bag. A van idled near the curb—white, salt-streaked, engine humming too low. Its headlights clicked on as she passed.

Her pulse spiked. Her throat locked; the sound of the engine tunneled through her chest. She forced her steps even. The driver's window lowered just enough for a voice to slip out. Calm, too calm. "Careful walking alone."

She didn't look. Didn't answer. She walked faster until the sidewalk bent, and when she turned back, the van was gone.

Her reflection in a shop window stared back a second too late—mouth still moving, eyes empty.

She pressed her palms to the glass, breath fogging. "*I won't* disappear," she whispered. And though no one else heard, the words stayed this time, scrawled in condensation: **I won't.**

Crossing Lines

Snow had calcified into ice ridges, every step after last bell a small decision to fall or keep moving. Students scattered into cars and buses, voices carrying high in the brittle air. Brynlee hung back by the doors, pretending to fuss with her phone while her eyes tracked Mara and Jacob weaving through the crowd.

They didn't take the bus. They never did. Instead, they walked. Not aimless—measured, as if they knew every crack in the pavement before they reached it.

Brynlee slipped into their wake.

She told herself it wasn't stalking. It was... *protection. Observation.* The Spirits had shown her their faces first, *not by accident.* If anyone had a thread that could lead to Lydia—or to whatever truth waited under all this—it was them. And she wasn't about to let the Spirits dictate who she could and couldn't follow.

The first punishment came half a block in.

The air thickened, swallowing sound before it could return. Her boots crunched the ice, but the echo never returned. Mara's laugh, soft and brief at something Jacob murmured, flattened before it reached Brynlee's ears. Silence swelled between her and them like an invisible wall. Loneliness. She gritted her teeth and pressed on, shoving her hands deeper into her coat pockets.

They turned down a narrower street, past houses with sagging gutters and Christmas lights still strung even though January had already worn into late weeks. Brynlee's pulse quickened. Her reflection in the darkened windows warped— elongated, eyes too wide, mouth blurred—as though Rejection wanted to remind her what it would mean if she pushed too close.

Mara glanced over her shoulder once, sharp as a corner. Brynlee froze, pretending to retie her boot. Mara's gaze lingered a beat too long before she turned back.

"You hear that?" Mara's voice carried, low but distinct.

Jacob shrugged. "Just someone behind us."

Brynlee's chest locked. She tightened the lace until it cut her glove, then stood and followed anyway.

At the corner, the siblings ducked into a small market with peeling red paint and a flickering OPEN sign. Brynlee slipped inside two breaths after them, keeping to the shadow near the freezer aisle. Fluorescent light buzzed overhead, washing everything in a tired glow. Mara and Jacob stood near the back, counting change between them before setting a carton of milk on the counter.

The man at the register didn't smile or look up—as if the light itself had already gone out for him. He just rang it up, handed them their change, and turned back to his radio.

Normal. Painfully normal. And yet Brynlee's ribs ached with a warning anyway.

She shifted, the floor tile groaning under her weight. Mara's head lifted instantly, eyes cutting toward the aisle. This time Brynlee couldn't pretend. Their gazes locked.

Mara's brow furrowed, suspicion written sharp across her face. Jacob turned too, more tired than alarmed, but his voice carried steady: "You following us?"

Brynlee's mouth opened. Nothing came. Loneliness hadn't given her sound back yet.

Her pulse roared instead, loud enough she thought they must hear it.

Mara's eyes narrowed, but she didn't say anything else. She just nudged Jacob toward the door. The bell over the frame jingled as they stepped out into the cold again.

Brynlee followed two beats later, the distance stretched tight between them.

Outside, the streetlamps hummed. A white van rolled slow past the corner, headlights sweeping. Brynlee flinched. When she looked back, Mara and Jacob were already halfway down the block, moving quick now, their shadows thinning into the night.

Her wrist burned under her sleeve, hot enough to blur her vision. The Spirits whispered through the dark glass of the storefronts, their verdict braided together: *You cannot keep them. You cannot save them.*

Brynlee shoved her fists deep into her coat pockets and walked faster, because moving was the only argument she had left.

The Seed

By morning, the grid on her floor had begun to climb the wall, like proof refusing to stay contained: bus routes taped in a ladder, the mall schematic with red corridors and dock doors, vendor names from the market in a narrow column—coffee stand, kettle-corn, Polaroids—plus a new sheet labeled **PLATES** with three empty lines waiting to be filled. Brynlee capped her pen and felt the ache not as bruise but as weight; Pain had learned a new trick, packing sand into her bones so every motion cost more than it should. She left the house anyway, the photo scrap in her pocket, the vow from last night still drying in ink on the yellow Post-it above her baseboard: **I'm coming.**

The lobby monitors screamed the same face over and over—Samantha Ng. Fifteen. Vanished. The ticker at the bottom warned about ice, about group safety, like any of that mattered when you could disappear anyway. Brynlee's stomach flipped hard enough she thought she might drop her books. Another girl gone. Different name, same hollow pit.

Attendance in first period skipped her name. The teacher's finger traced the list, frowned at the screen, and moved on as if Brynlee's desk were only the idea of a desk. She said "Here," too quickly, and the word landed dull; the boy behind her answered for her as a joke, got the laugh she needed, and the roll call rolled on. Rejection didn't need mirrors; it had spreadsheets.

Between bells the hall shoved and flowed. Loneliness took the hallway and turned it into a river that parted around her without meaning to; shoulders angled away, eyes slid past, space opened that shouldn't have. She cut through it like a ghost with a map. At lunch she didn't sit with Harper and didn't sit with Mara and Jacob either; she took a table that faced both directions and ate fast, watching patterns the way she'd started watching everything—where kids who didn't belong tried to belong, where security glanced, where the sight lines were clean. Vivienne sat across from the Williams kids again, precise as a placed object, sharing small things without ceremony: a napkin, a wedge of apple, the kind of gestures that made space without taking any.

After last bell, the weather shoved its cold fingers under everyone's collars. Brynlee fell into step a half lane from Vivienne outside, not beside, not behind—parallel enough for a shadow to think they were walking together. For half a block neither said anything. Then Vivienne spoke without turning her head. "You're walking like you expect something to step out of the shadows." *Maybe I do.*

Brynlee's throat tightened. "What's that supposed to mean?"

Vivienne's gaze cut to the dark shop windows they passed, where reflections smeared and re-formed. "Don't let them corner you. That's when they press hardest."

She stopped dead. *Them.* No one said it like that unless they meant more than boys in hoodies and vans with dull paint. "Who?"

Vivienne adjusted her coat like she hadn't said anything odd. "People," she said, too quickly to be casual. A breath later, softer, almost an afterthought that sounded rehearsed: "Some doors you don't open alone." Then she kept walking, shoes finding dry patches on the sidewalk like she'd mapped them in her head hours ago.

Her feet wouldn't move. The cold bit straight through her socks, ankles burning, but Vivienne's words clung heavier than the air. *Don't let them corner you.* Like she knew. Like she'd been pressed in the same way. Brynlee's heart stuttered. No—people didn't just say things like that. Not unless—

She went to the library instead of home. Printed a second copy of the mall schematic and slid it into a manila folder labeled **GEOMETRY** in blunt black marker. Taped a fresh Post-it to the inside of her locker: **SUNDAY—DUSK—MARKET.** Wrote an alarm into her phone with no words at all, just three emojis that meant exactly what she needed them to mean and nothing a filter could read. On the back of her bus schedule, she wrote **PLATES** again and drew three blank boxes, because the next time she saw a van she was going to come away with something the Spirits couldn't smudge.

On the walk out, the school's front doors flashed her back at herself in the glass. For one heartbeat she wasn't there—the hallway rolled on without her, bright and indifferent. Then her face snapped into place, a fraction too clean. "I won't disappear," she said under her breath, and her breath fogged the pane in the shape of the words. The fog held. When she lifted her hand, the print she left behind looked like someone else's.

The van that idled at the corner when she stepped into the lot didn't roll forward. It didn't need to. She memorized what she could at a glance—the plate bracket bent at one corner, the smear where the inspection sticker had been scraped, the thread of black tape on the rear window's edge—and walked on, counting letters on a plate two cars back instead, because attention had to look like it landed somewhere else when your life depended on it.

One of the notes had fallen, the yellow corner poking out from under the baseboard like something trying to crawl away. Her chest squeezed. She dropped to the floor, scraping it out with her nails. The ink had paled, almost gone, but the words still bled faintly: *You saw her.* Her throat tightened. "I still do," she whispered, and slapped it back on the wall with fresh tape. Hard: **Don't let them corner you.** She didn't know whether she was quoting Vivienne or the girl she wished she'd been six months ago. It didn't matter. The line held the wall like a nail.

Her phone lit with a number she didn't recognize and a voicemail banner she didn't listen to. Instead, she laid the plate page beside her bus routes and drew a small rectangle where the lot met the service lane. **Friday—trial run,** she wrote and underlined it. The ache in her bones settled like someone setting a heavy box down instead of dropping it. Outside, ice clicked on the gutters; inside, paper whispered under her hands. Somewhere between the two, the sentence Vivienne had left her kept turning itself over: *some doors you don't open alone.*

Maybe she wouldn't. Maybe she would hand someone else the key before she went through.

She capped her pen and didn't look at the mirror. The mirror didn't always look back.

Blind Spots

Friday, last bell. Geometry folder zipped tight, map folded inside like a secret burning through fabric. I keep the cap jammed low, hair tucked, hood up even though it makes me look like I'm hiding—because I am. Bus to the mall, the same sick-sweet pretzel smell bleeding through the doors before they open. I don't go inside. Not the bright part. I skirt the outer wall, past the compactor, to the back lane where the pavement turns to oil and gravel and the snow piles are gray at the edges. Cameras blink red in lazy arcs. I count them. One on the dock. One above the service door. One pointed the wrong way, thank God.

Pain doesn't come as purple this time. It packs my bones with sand. Every step down the cinderblock corridor feels like wading. *Fine. Be heavy. I'll carry it.* The air back here has a different temperature—grease and cold metal and the wet-sock breath of the compactor. A forklift beeps somewhere behind the wall like a heart monitor for a building.

I tuck into the shadow of a stack of broken pallets and wait. Trucks groan. Vans come and go. Most are nothing—plumbers, a florist, a mom-and-pop bakery with a cupcake magnet stuck crooked on the door. I make myself log them anyway because doing something is the only way to stop my hands from shaking.

Time thins; my phone says 4:12, then 4:19, then the same minute, twice like the signal is lagging. The cold works under my coat and licks the welt under my sleeve until I want to scratch my arm raw.

White van. Salt scars like fingerprints. Backing in slow. I step half out of the shadow and pretend to be a bored kid on her phone. I lift the camera and the screen shows—nothing. Plate area blown out to white, like the pixels forgot how to hold a number. "You've got to be kidding me," I breathe. Fine. Plan B. I squint, catch the curve of a K, the sharp leg of an X. I say them in my head hard enough to make a dent: *Seven. K. X.* The rest slides when I reach for it, like soap. I dig a pen out of my pocket with numb fingers and write on the heel of my hand. Ink skates on cold skin.. The N looks like an H. I press harder until it hurts. *7KX–* A man's cough snaps my head up.

Not the men from the mall. Dock worker—vest, badge on a lanyard, the bored kind of authority. "Loading zone," he says, not unfriendly. He doesn't meet my eyes. Like I'm a reflection someone hasn't quite lined up. "You can't be back here, sweetheart."

"I'm—my ride's late," I say, and Loneliness eats the first half of the sentence. He hears the end—*late*—and shrugs, already turning away. Rejection doesn't have to erase you completely; it can do it by inches until no one ever looks all the way at you.

Another van noses in, a different white, the paint more matte, a square of old adhesive on the rear window like a ghost sticker. I memorize the sticker shape, the dent near the left taillight, the way the driver's side mirror vibrates at idle. The plate is clean on this one, sun catching the emboss. I lift my phone again out of habit; the camera flares, then stutters to a smear. I want to hurl it. I don't. I write fast—*3, 1, 2? 7?* The numbers slide right to the edge of my brain and try to jump. I pin them with my mouth, whispering like I'm praying. *Three-one-two-seven. Three-one-two-seven. Three-one—* A door slams and my heart tries to bolt.

Footsteps. A shadow clips the pallet stack and keeps going. Just a kid in a store polo on a smoke break, earbuds in. He passes close enough that my sleeve snags on a splinter; the thread catches and tugs, biting. *You snagged it on something,* Vivienne's voice says in my head, too calm, like she's here. I yank free and pocket the loose thread, like it's a talisman.

The first van reverses, brake lights glowing red enough to stain the snowbank. The driver's wrist flashes in the side mirror: leather band, snapped at one hole too tight. I add **WRIST: LEATHER** to the margin because if the Spirits are going to smudge numbers, they can choke on details. The van noses out toward the lane, pauses at the bend like it's considering me, then slides away. The second idles, doors shut, just breathing. I drift farther along the wall, counting cameras again, looking like I'm not looking.

A security cart whines into the lane. The guard from the mall isn't in it. New guy. Same expression: practiced patience, risk calculation turned into a face. "You need to be out front," he calls, and the way he says *you* makes it clear he doesn't mean the vans.

"Okay," I say, because I can't afford to get thrown. He waits until I move. I move slow enough to see the plate when the second van finally pulls, the numbers catching the light one perfect second. *7KX312*. My brain floods with relief so hard my knees wobble. I look down and the ink on my palm has already blurred into a gray thumbprint. I write it again, harder, like carving: **7KX312** so deep the nib scratches my skin. The ink bit the groove; her pulse stuttered under it. I say it under my breath the whole way around the building, through the crowd of teenagers with sodas, past a mom wrangling a toddler out of a coin-op car. *Seven kay ex three one two. Seven kay ex three one two.*

On the bus home I fog the window on purpose and trace the plate into the condensation. The letters look like they belong to someone else's alphabet-like language. A boy in the next seat watches and smirks and looks away when I meet his eyes. The heater rattles at my feet. When the bus turns, the fog stutters and the numbers smear. I write them again. The smear follows. I switch hands and print on my wrist instead, ink bleeding through the heat of my skin. If the mirror won't hold me, my body will.

At my stop, the snow squeaks under my boots, the kind of cold that makes everything sound closer than it is. My phone buzzes—unknown number, voicemail I don't listen to. My street looks normal: trash bins, porch lights on timers, a dad dragging a sled back to the garage. When I reach my door, I check my palm. The ink has crawled, but the shape of it is still there. **7KX312.** I whisper it to the lock as I key in, like saying it to the house will make it part of the wiring.

Upstairs, I peel off my coat and lay everything out like evidence—geometry folder, map, my hand as if it's a page. I print the plate onto the **PLATES** sheet in block letters and circle it twice. The circle looks like a bruise. I stare until the numbers don't look like numbers anymore, just marks. I blink hard and they settle back into meaning.

The heater kicks on. The note above the baseboard curls at the corner and holds. My phone buzzes again: *Unknown caller. No voicemail.* I set it face down. The silence in my room isn't empty tonight; it's waiting. A moment later, a car rolls past outside, slow. Not a van. Normal. I don't go to the window anyway.

Some doors you don't open alone, Vivienne said. Friday was a trial run. Sunday isn't going to be. I cap the pen, press the plate with my thumb until the numbers warm under the paper like a pulse, and say it one more time in my head so the Spirits can hear me: *I got one. You can take everything else, but not this.*

Splinters

Sunday dusk dragged low across the rooftops—a gray so heavy it made everything look half-built, half-erased. Brynlee's bus lurched through Old Town in jerks, brakes squealing, windows rattling with every pothole. She sat rigid, palms damp, notebook jammed under her thigh like pressure alone could keep it safe. **7KX312.** She mouthed the plate over and over until her lips went numb. If she forgot it—even once—it would be gone.

The Spirits didn't bruise her this time. They pressed at the edges instead. Every reflection in the bus glass carried a fraction of delay, she moved her hand once just to watch it arrive late. her mouth moving half a beat late. Rejection stretching her in wrong directions. She dragged her hood higher and stared at the dark ahead, daring it to blink first.

The bus hissed to a stop two blocks from the market. Brynlee got off alone. Salt crunched under her boots. The storefronts along the square were tired from the holidays— garlands sagging, SALE posters slouching, frost feathering the edges of the glass. The same stall lights from her nightmare blinked awake: coffee steam curling into air that smelled like sugar and cold metal.

She hugged her coat tighter and slipped between vendors. Faces blurred. Voices came sharp, then muffled, then sharp again, as if Loneliness was testing how much she could take. She forced herself forward anyway, spine rigid, every step a mutiny against the weight in her ribs.

By the kettle-corn stand, a girl bumped into her—Mara. Thin coat, red scarf fraying at the ends. Jacob trailed close behind, expression flat but his eyes flicking everywhere at once, like they'd already mapped all the exits.

Brynlee froze, heart rattling against her throat. This close, she could feel it: the overlap. Nightmare and reality pressed together, identical lines drawn on different paper.

Mara's gaze snagged hers, recognition flashing—quick, wary. "You."

Brynlee swallowed hard. The word jammed in her chest, but she pushed it through anyway. "I know what you prayed for."

Jacob's shoulders went stiff. Mara's lips parted, breath showing white in the air. For a second, Brynlee thought she'd blown it—that they'd turn away, vanish back into the crowd.

Then Mara's voice, low and sharp: "Careful what you say out loud."

The market lights flickered once, hard enough to throw shadows long and wrong across the snow. Brynlee's skin prickled. She knew exactly who had been listening.

Tightrope

The crowd pressed in at the market, bodies brushing shoulders, bags clinking, voices layered so thick Brynlee had to fight to keep her focus. Mara and Jacob didn't vanish, though—they shifted sideways, the three of them caught in a strange orbit no one else could see.

"Don't follow," Jacob said, but his eyes never touched hers. He fixed them instead on the space behind her, like he was watching for something to lunge.

"I'm not—" Brynlee started, but the words came out raw, too sharp. She forced them lower. "I'm not following. I just... I see you."

Mara's stare was like glass—clear, cutting, reflecting too much back. "Then keep quiet. Seeing isn't safe."

The air thickened. Loneliness pressed against her eardrums until the shouts of vendors flattened into cotton. For a heartbeat, she heard only the scrape of her own breath. She bit down hard, refusing to flinch, refusing to let them see her fold.

"I know the van," she said instead, quick, before silence could eat it. "I know the plate. Seven K X three one two."

That got them. Jacob's head snapped her way. Mara's hand tightened on the strap of her bag until her knuckles whitened.

"You shouldn't know that," Mara said, voice low, almost a hiss.

The weight of the Spirits closed in—her sleeve burned hot, her reflection in the kettle-corn cart's glass showed her with no mouth at all—but Brynlee didn't stop. "I do. And if I can see it, so can you. We're not crazy."

Mara's throat worked. Jacob shifted closer, protective, suspicious. "You don't get it," he said. "Names. Numbers. They don't stay. They smear."

"I wrote it down," Brynlee shot back, heart pounding. "It's still there."

For a second, something cracked across Mara's face—not belief, not yet, but recognition, like the shape of a memory she'd tried to bury. She looked at Jacob. He shook his head.

"Careful," Mara whispered, eyes cutting past Brynlee, over her shoulder. "If you hold on too tight, they'll press harder."

The crowd surged, breaking the fragile knot between them. Mara and Jacob slipped into it, swallowed by coats and chatter and breath. Brynlee's pulse hammered. The kettle-corn lights burned her afterimage into the dark: two siblings, thin coats, eyes too old, walking away.

The Spirits whispered through the crowd's hum, voices braided into the clatter: *You cannot keep them. You cannot save them.*

She dug her nails into her palm, teeth bared against the sting. *Watch me,* she thought. *Watch me try.*

Echoes Between Stalls

The market was too bright, too alive—every light a needle, every laugh a fracture. Laughter burst sharp near the kettle-corn stand, music from a tinny speaker threaded through the crowd, air stinking of fried dough and smoke. Brynlee shoved her hands into her coat pockets and kept her eyes on the bobbing red scarf ahead—Mara. Jacob at her shoulder. If she could just keep them in sight—

The crowd bent wrong.

One blink, Mara's hair, Jacob's worn jacket. The next—gone. Only strangers, shifting coats, bags clutched close. Brynlee's chest seized. She lurched forward, weaving hard through shoulders, but every time she thought she saw them, the space collapsed into someone else. Her heartbeat thundered against the noise.

She stumbled near a booth draped in glass ornaments, their surfaces warped by string lights. Her reflection flashed back at her in a dozen globes—except none of them were hers. Faces blurred, mouths moving a fraction too late. One by one, the heads turned—slow, mechanical, as if pulled by strings she couldn't see, synchronized, glass creaking like bones under strain.

Rejection.

Her throat closed. She spun, desperate to find a real face, but the crowd bent again—people brushing past without touching, voices falling flat as if cotton stuffed her ears. Loneliness seeped in, curling under her ribs, swallowing the music whole. The air pressed thin.

"Stop," she gasped, but the word dissolved before it reached anyone. No one looked at her. No one even flinched. She could've been shouting fire and still been invisible.

Her pulse roared in her skull. She pressed her nails hard into her palms until it hurt enough to anchor her. *They can't erase me. Not here. Not now.*

In the ornament glass, one reflection lingered—her own this time, but hollow-eyed, lips pressed shut even as hers parted. It mouthed something she didn't say: *Give up.*

"*No.*" She bit it out, raw.

And just like that, the crowd snapped back. The music surged. A woman brushed her shoulder, muttered "sorry" without looking. The booths spilled light again, and the smell of sugar clawed her throat.

Mara and Jacob reappeared near the far exit, coins exchanged for a paper bag, as if they had never been gone.

Brynlee's lungs dragged in air too sharp, too fast. Her palms stung where she'd carved crescents into her skin. She wanted to scream, to run, to grab them and beg them to admit they'd seen it too. Instead, she dragged her hood higher, swallowed the panic, and walked the other way.

If they could erase her in a crowd, what would they do to anyone she tried to save?

Anchors and Echoes

The house smelled like cinnamon again—her mother's idea of comfort baked into every wall, too thick to breathe through. A candle flickered on the counter, cookies cooling on a wire rack. Her dad was at the stove, spatula in hand, making too much noise while making something as simple as scrambled eggs.

"Bryn!" Her mom's face lit up like she'd been waiting hours for this exact moment. "You're just in time. We thought—well, I thought—you might want cookies with dinner."

Her dad looked over his shoulder and grinned, wide, practiced, too bright. "Roadkill pancakes didn't do it for you? Fine. Tonight, it's breakfast-for-dinner. How's that for a deal?"

Brynlee dropped her bag by the door. Her bones still carried the market—crowd tilting wrong, glass mouths whispering *Give up*. The smell of butter and cinnamon wrapped too tight around her throat.

She wanted to say *stop*. Stop with the cookies, stop with the noise, stop trying so hard to stitch her into a family she didn't know how to fit anymore.

Instead, she dragged out a chair and sat, palms flat on the table so they wouldn't shake.

Her mother slid a plate in front of her, eggs steaming. "So. Tell us everything about your day."

The words landed like bricks. Brynlee's mouth opened, empty. *Tell us everything.* If she did—about Mara and Jacob, about the glass heads turning away, about the market van—her parents would break right in front of her. And if she didn't, she was already breaking alone.

Her dad leaned his elbows on the counter, he light from the stove warped behind his head, halo-bright, wrong, studying her face like it was a puzzle. The same look from Christmas morning—the one that made her skin crawl because it was too close, too desperate. Like he was reading a language he used to know by heart but had forgotten.

"Bryn," he said gently. "Are you okay?"

She stabbed her fork into the eggs. The metal squealed. "I'm fine."

Her mother smiled too quickly, relief painted on, as if *fine* was enough to anchor the whole house. "Good. That's good."

The silence that followed wasn't normal silence. It pressed. Heavy, brittle. The sound of them trying too hard not to say the wrong thing.

Brynlee shoved eggs into her mouth, chewed, swallowed. Her throat burned anyway.

Upstairs, in her room, she pressed her notes flat against the desk. **7KX312** circled in black. *Proof she was still here. Proof the Spirits hadn't scrubbed her out completely.*

She whispered it once, just to make it real. *"Seven Kay Ex Three One Two."*

The mirror whispered it back—same words, same tone—but its lips never moved.

Fractured Tether

Harper caught her before she could run.

"Don't even think about it." Harper's bracelets clinked as she blocked the hallway, copper hair frizzing out of its braid, and eyes locked sharp. "You've been ghosting me for a week. What is going on?"

Brynlee hugged her books tighter. Her pulse still hadn't smoothed from the market. The smell of kettle corn clung to her sleeve like a bruise. "Nothing's going on."

Harper snorted. "Yeah, and I'm the Queen of France. Don't lie to me. Not you. Not after—" She bit the sentence off, jaw tight.

Brynlee forced her mouth into something close to a smile. "You're being dramatic."

"*I'm* being dramatic?" Harper leaned closer, voice dropping. "You look like you haven't slept in days, you jump at shadows, and you keep staring at… I don't even know what. Corners? Windows? Like there's something there I can't see."

The words landed hard. Because Harper was right. Because Harper couldn't know.

Brynlee's nails dug half-moons into the cover of her notebook. "You don't get it." She hated how small her voice sounded—like she was twelve again, begging the dark to stay quiet.

"Then make me get it." Harper's voice cracked on the edge of something soft. "You're my best friend, Bryn. Since birth, remember? Whatever this is—you don't get to shut me out."

For a second, Brynlee almost told her. About Mara's prayer, about the van, about the way glass mouths whispered *Give up*. The confession sat right there raw, and clawing.

But the Spirits pressed in—their presence prickling the air, a phantom weight on her wrist. A warning. *If you let her in, she bleeds too.*

Brynlee swallowed hard, throat a raw scrape. "I can't."

Harper flinched like she'd been slapped. "Can't or won't?"

The bell shrieked overhead, bodies flooding the hall, breaking the moment into pieces. Brynlee turned sideways, slipped through the gap before Harper could grab her sleeve.

"Brynlee!" Harper's voice cut over the noise. "Don't you dare walk away from me!"

She didn't turn back. Couldn't. The crowd carried her forward, the tether stretched to breaking, and this time she didn't fight it.

When she finally reached her locker, her hands shook too hard to turn the combination. Her reflection wavered in the sliver of metal above the lock—eyes too hollow, lips pressed shut. Not hers.

The tether snapped—clean, final, and loud enough to make the silence ring.

The Rules

The house had that kind of hush that only sounds louder when you listen—heater ticking, the neighbor's dog offering one bark to the dark, the TV downstairs turning people into murmurs. Brynlee shut her door and pressed her back to it until the latch caught. Her wall grid waited on the desk like a dare: bus routes, dock map, **7KX312** circled so hard the paper almost tore.

"Why me?" It ripped out before she could swallow it. "If it matters that much—do it yourselves."

The air thinned, the kind of thing that made her ears pop. The ceiling light hummed, then steadied. Nothing stepped out of the corner. Of course, nothing. They never showed. They only bent things.

She pushed off the door and paced, palms raw from the way she kept pressing them to tables, to counters, to anything solid. "You want Lydia? You want the Williams kids safe? Then go get them. Stop—" Her breath snagged. "Stop stealing my voice. Stop erasing me. If it's so important, *do it.*"

Silence flattened, thick as felt. The note above her baseboard—*I'm coming*—curled at one corner and lifted like it wanted to leave. She slapped it flat, fingers shaking. The mirror on her dresser lagged, her mouth moving a beat late, then catching up. Rage crawled up her throat. "Look at me," she said to the glass. "If you can do that, you can—"

Her phone buzzed in her pocket. Unknown number. She didn't pick up. The buzz cut, then the voicemail banner bloomed across the screen without a missed-call line.

No one had called. The message was just there.

Her skin went cold anyway. She hit play and held the phone a little away, like distance could blunt it.

Static first, the cheap-plastic hiss of an empty room. Then her voice. Not now-her, but a slurred, underwater version, overlapped with something that wasn't a voice at all so much as pressure arranged into sound.

Her stomach dropped. She knew that voice. She just didn't know when she'd said it.

"There are rules."

Not a warning. A fact.

She stared at the waveform crawling across the screen, small mountains marching. "What rules? Whose rules?" Her voice came out too loud in the small room. She felt stupid the second she asked—like yelling at a locked door.

The message kept playing, more static, tape-chew edges. In the smear under the words, she thought she heard other scraps— breath, a hum that might have been a faraway generator, the click of a clock losing a second. Then nothing. The clip ended itself. The screen jumped back to her home page like it was relieved.

She played it again. The same six seconds. The same sentence in her own mouth, braided with theirs. The same refusal to mean more.

"There are rules." She said it back at the room, at the mirror that didn't quite hold, at the Post-its that wanted to peel. "What does that even—"

Her lamp dimmed and brightened, a heartbeat out of time. The heater kicked on and exhaled cold for three breaths before remembering heat. The house had hands, suddenly, and all of them were on her. Not bruising—pressing. Herding.

"It's not enough," she said. "I'm not your puppet." She grabbed a Sharpie and wrote across the top of the **PLATES** page: **NOT YOUR HANDS. NOT YOUR VOICE.** The smell of ink punched the air. Her head throbbed like a storm rolling in behind her eyes. She wrote anyway. *I choose what I do.* She underlined it until the line bled through the paper into the desk.

Her phone vibrated again. Same banner. Same message time stamp. No new call. She didn't press play. If they wanted to say more, they could break their own rules to do it.

She dragged the chair to the dresser and climbed up until she could see herself clean and head-on. For a second the glass held nothing—just her room continuing without her. Then she snapped into place, pale, eyes too bright. "You don't get to own me," she told the girl in the mirror. "You don't get to own them, either."

The mirror didn't answer. The corner of her Post-it stayed down.

Downstairs, her dad laughed at something on TV and coughed in the same breath, like even laughter hurt a little now. Her mother called up the stairs, too cheerful, "Bryn? Cocoa?" The word sounded like a lifeline tossed from shore.

"I'm good!" she shouted back and hated the way it came out—too fast, too high, a lie trying to sound like normal.

She climbed off the chair, palms blackened with ink where she'd braced them against the desk. She wiped them on her jeans and set her phone face-down beside **7KX312**. "You have rules," she said to the room, to the dead voicemail, to the pressure that made the light hum. "So do I."

Her rules fit into the space left by theirs: **Find Lydia. Keep Mara and Jacob breathing. Don't let Harper bleed. Don't disappear.** She didn't write that part down. She didn't have to. It was already carved into how her body held itself.

She hit play one more time as if there might be a different ending. There wasn't. *There are rules.* Fine. Keep them. She would keep hers.

The lamp stopped flickering. The heater settled. The house exhaled.

She didn't.

She sat with the grid until the numbers steadied in her head, until the words on the wall looked like iron instead of paper, until she could imagine walking into Sunday without folding. When she finally turned off the light, the mirror caught a slice of her and lagged, then matched. The room went dark. The phone stayed face-down.

On the other side of the door, her parents kept talking like the world wasn't bending. She listened to the shape of their voices and let the sound bruise her in a way the Spirits couldn't control.

Tomorrow, she'd move. Not because they said so. Because saying no had finally meant something.

The Gathering

The flyer came two weeks ago—glossy gold script pretending grief could be elegant: "*Ashwood Community Fundraiser: Building Hope for Missing Youth.*" Brynlee's mom stuck it to the fridge with the dog-shaped magnet and circled the date in red like it was sacred. Now, Saturday night, they were here—Ashwood High's gym strung with twinkle lights, folding tables dressed up in rented linen, the faint smell of polish and floor wax clinging under the perfume and cologne.

"Isn't this beautiful?" her mom whispered, clutching Brynlee's hand too tight as they walked through the entry. Her dad nodded like hope was something you could rent by the hour.

Brynlee's throat was already tight. She wanted to peel her hand away, shove it in her pocket, hide the marks the Spirits left. She wanted to go home.

The gym buzzed with the kind of energy that wasn't joy— just money and grief colliding in the same space. A silent auction table displayed gift baskets and sports memorabilia. Teachers in suits mingled with police officers in dress blues. At the center, a podium waited for speeches no one wanted to hear.

Her parents tugged her along, stopping to smile, to nod, to answer questions about "supporting the cause." Brynlee barely heard them. Her gaze snagged on the far corner.

The Turners.

Lydia's parents stood stiff near the refreshment table, untouched glasses of punch in their hands. Mrs. Turner's face looked like paper left in the rain—creased, worn thin, impossible to smooth. Mr. Turner had lost weight; his suit hung on him like it belonged to someone else. They didn't smile. They didn't speak. They just existed, like shadows pinned in place by the lights.

Brynlee's stomach dropped. She'd seen them on the news before, sure. But in person—grief had weight. It bent them smaller.

Then movement—Mrs. LeClair.

Vivienne's mother shimmered across the gym in a tailored dress, diamonds at her wrist catching the light. Mr. LeClair trailed behind, phone in hand, eyes already scanning the next conversation. They looked like they'd stepped out of a magazine. Out of place and yet perfectly at home.

Mrs. LeClair stopped in front of Mrs. Turner. Smiled, soft, like memory. Reached to touch her arm.

Mrs. Turner flinched. Pulled back. Her voice carried just enough: "I can't—please. *Not you.*"

The words carved the room. Silence spread in a ripple, then smothered itself in awkward chatter as people turned away. Mrs. LeClair's smile cracked, frozen for a beat before she let her hand drop. She nodded once, small, and retreated into the crowd.

Brynlee's chest ached. She saw it now—years of barbecues, vacations, birthday parties that had tied those families together. Gone in a single abduction. The LeClairs had risen higher, brighter. The Turners had collapsed. And Lydia's absence lived in both outcomes.

Her mom squeezed her hand again. "See, Bryn? This is why we show up. This is what matters."

Brynlee's nails dug into her palm. She kept her eyes on the Turners, on the way Mrs. Turner's shoulders shook once before she smoothed her dress and stood straighter.

The Spirits didn't whisper this time. They didn't need to. The room had learned to haunt itself.

Shadows on the Road

The ride home should have been quiet. It wasn't. Her mom hummed low in the passenger seat, one hand fiddling with the program folded in her lap. Her dad kept both hands on the wheel, jaw set, like the silence on the road demanded respect.

Brynlee sat in the back, forehead tipped against the cold glass. The reflection of twinkle lights still burned behind her eyelids—the Turners' hollow faces, Mrs. LeClair's hand dropping, the whole gym bent around a grief no one could name out loud.

The streetlamps stuttered by in orange blurs. Then she saw it.

White. Parked crooked against the curb half a block ahead, back tires kissing snowbank. Van body salt-scarred, back door handle darker than the paint around it.

Her lungs forgot what to do.

She sat up fast enough that her seat belt bit her shoulder. "Dad—slow down."

"What? Why?" He checked the mirror, puzzled.

She couldn't say *that's it, that's the one, I know it's the one.* Her throat clamped on the words, pressure pooled behind her eyes, the kind that meant the Spirits were listening. "Just—please."

Her mom twisted around. "Honey, are you—?"

The van's brake lights flared. The engine coughed to life, exhaust spilling white into the night. It rolled away from the curb as they passed, turning down a side street too narrow for the SUV to follow without it being obvious.

Her pulse hammered against her ribs. She craned around in her seat until the curve of the road swallowed the van whole.

Her dad frowned in the rearview. "Bryn, what was that about?"

"Nothing," she lied. Her voice sounded scraped raw.

Her mom didn't press. She only reached back, fingers brushing Brynlee's knee. Too gentle. Too much.

The rest of the drive blurred. By the time they pulled into the driveway, her notebook was already burning a hole in her bag.

Upstairs, she flipped it open, hand shaking as she scrawled: **Van—salt scars, back handle dark, left rear tire bald?** She pressed harder, ink pooling, but the words already seemed to blur. She rewrote them twice, three times, until the page looked like a mess of scratches.

The mirror caught her face in the corner. Her lips moved out of sync. The reflection whispered the words she hadn't dared in front of her parents: *They're still moving her.*

Her stomach knotted. Lydia wasn't gone. Not yet. The men were out there, circling. And if Brynlee couldn't hold on to the details, if the Spirits kept erasing them, then Lydia's face would vanish like a reflection turned away.

She slammed the notebook shut and pressed both palms flat, like holding a heartbeat she refused to let stop.

Crossing Orbits

The cafeteria had never been this loud. Or maybe Harper had just been loud enough to drown it before. Brynlee hadn't realized how much her best friend's bracelets, her chatter—her orbit of noise—had shielded her from the static. Now the room pressed in—laughter too sharp, trays slamming, shoes squeaking on tile— and Brynlee sat alone at a table near the back, her tray untouched.

She'd made a point of not sitting with the Williams twins today. Not with Harper either. Just... nowhere. The air still hummed like glass after the fundraiser. After the van. Her notebook burned in her bag, words she wasn't sure would still be there when she opened it again.

A shadow fell across the table.

Brynlee glanced up. Vivienne LeClair set her tray down with careful quiet, not asking, not explaining, just sliding into the seat across from her. The cafeteria chatter blurred around them, two islands in the noise.

Brynlee's throat tightened. "Shouldn't you be with—" she gestured toward the table where Mara and Jacob sat, backs bent toward each other in private conversation.

"I usually am," Vivienne said. Her voice was steady, low, like she didn't care who overheard but also didn't expect anyone would. She unwrapped her sandwich without looking at it. "Today I thought I'd sit here."

Brynlee poked at her potatoes, pretending she didn't care—until Vivienne's gaze slid across her wrist, and Brynlee's whole body went stiff.

"What?" she snapped.

Vivienne's expression didn't change. "You flinch like they're still touching you."

The plastic fork slipped from Brynlee's fingers. Her chest went tight. "What are you talking about?"

Vivienne peeled the crust from her bread, methodical. "You know." *The words lodged like static between them, waiting for someone to name it.*

Brynlee's stomach turned cold. "No. I don't."

Vivienne finally looked up, and for a second it felt like *glass cracking between them.* Her eyes were steady, sharp, too old for sixteen. "They don't care about saving you. Or saving anyone. They care what you'll do when you're bent far enough. *That's how they work.*"

The words dropped like stones into Brynlee's chest. She opened her mouth, but nothing came out.

Vivienne smoothed the napkin beside her tray, as if she hadn't just shattered the air between them. She didn't elaborate. Didn't soften. She just went back to her sandwich, her silence practiced and sharp as a blade.

Brynlee couldn't eat. Couldn't move. The cafeteria blurred—the noise, the colors, the smell of grease. All she could see was Vivienne across the table, her guard pulled tight, her words coiled like a warning she hadn't wanted to give.

Her fork trembled, catching the light — a mirror of every rule she'd tried to hold.

The Weight of Words

Vivienne's words didn't leave. They lingered — smoke that knew where to settle, curling in the back of Brynlee's throat long after she left the cafeteria.

They don't care about saving you. They care what you'll do when you're bent far enough. That's how they work.

Bent far enough.

Brynlee sat cross-legged on her bed that night, notebook open across her lap, pen clenched too tight. She wrote the line once. Then twice. By the third time her hand shook so badly, the words tangled into each other, black ink smearing across the page. She flipped to a clean sheet and tried again. The same.

Finally, she dug the Sharpie from her desk drawer and slashed the sentence in thick strokes across the margin: **BENT FAR ENOUGH.** Then she pressed harder, scratching it out until the paper tore.

Her lamp buzzed overhead. The shadows in the corner stayed still, but the stillness felt like listening.

"Is that what you want?" she muttered at the dark. Her voice sounded too loud in the small room. "To see how much I'll snap? How much I'll take before I break?"

The mirror didn't ripple. No voice bled back. Just her reflection staring, jaw tight, knuckles white on the pen.

She slammed the notebook shut, as if paper could muffle what it had already learned to repeat, like hiding it might change anything.

Downstairs, her parents were laughing—loud, messy, trying too hard over some game show. Her mother's voice rose, warm and fragile: *"I knew you'd guess that one—see? You're good at this!"* Her father chuckled, deep and tired, like he wanted to prove he was fine.

Brynlee crept halfway down the stairs, listening. For a second she wanted to step into the room, sit between them, let herself belong. But Vivienne's voice slid in sharper than her parents' laughter. *They don't care about saving you.*

She turned and climbed back up before either of them saw her.

In her room she pulled the blanket over her head, like she used to when she was younger, cocooning herself in heat and fabric. She whispered into the dark: "I'm not going to break." Her chest rose, shallow, defiant. "I won't."

But even saying it, her stomach knotted. Because if Vivienne had felt them once too, if she'd recognized their touch—then maybe she knew something Brynlee didn't. Maybe *snapping* wasn't the end. Maybe it was the point.

Sleep pressed at the edges of her eyes, heavy, reluctant. She fought it until her body betrayed her. The dark didn't rush — it waited.

Bent Reflections

The dream arrived without warning — no fall, no fissure, only the quiet wrong of familiarity. No fall, no fissure, no sudden drop through the floor. Brynlee simply opened her eyes and the room was wrong.

Her walls were there, her desk, her dresser—but multiplied. The mirror above the dresser had spread, spilling across the walls until every surface gleamed with her face. Hundreds of Brynlees stared back, rows stretching into a horizon.

She moved her hand. Some followed. Some didn't.

One smiled when she didn't. Another pressed fingers to her throat. A third just stood there, staring at the floor, like she'd already given up.

Her chest locked. "Stop." The word fractured, too many voices echoing it back.

The mirrors groaned like glass bending under pressure. The faces tilted one after another, turning away from her. Not in unison. In waves. First the Brynlee near her, then the next, then the next, until a tide of her own faces shifted their gaze aside, refusing to see her.

She ran to the nearest pane and slammed her palm against it. "Look at me!"

The reflection blinked, delayed, lips pressed tight. Then it whispered, without sound: *You don't matter.*

"No," Brynlee rasped. Her breath fogged the glass. "That's not true. I matter. I—"

The next mirror cut her off. *Easiest to break.*

Her stomach hollowed.

She backed up, stumbling, but there was no corner—only more mirrors, more versions of herself refusing her. Some with bruises, some with empty sleeves, some with nothing at all behind the eyes. A hall of discarded Brynlees, bent into shapes she couldn't name.

"You're lying," she said, voice shredding.

The glass nearest her rippled. A hand shot out—not hers—and clawed her wrist, nails biting cold into her flesh. She yanked back, but the grip was iron.

"You bend," the reflection hissed, smile widening. "That's all they ever make you for."

The mirrors cracked in unison, spiderwebs racing through every surface. The sound was bone snapping, wood tearing, a hundred voices turning their backs.

"No!" She fought the grip, nails tearing her own skin in the scramble to pull free. "I'm not like that. I won't—"

The hand released. She fell back onto the floor, breath ragged. Every mirror showed her sprawled, small, weak. And then—one by one—they vanished, black screens swallowing her face until the room was dark.

When her eyes snapped open, she was in her own bed, sweat chilling her skin.

She staggered to the dresser, heart still hammering. The mirror caught her, but only after a beat too long.

Her reflection lifted its chin slower than she did. Its lips parted, but no sound came.

She pressed her hand flat to the glass. It was warm, like something breathing beneath.

"Not me," she whispered. "You're not me."

But the reflection didn't answer.

Static Between Rooms

Brynlee woke with her throat raw, and her sheets twisted, like she'd been fighting something all night. The mirror looked harmless in daylight — sunlight softening the glass, pretending it was only glass. Still, she couldn't make herself glance too long. The memory of those multiplied faces—their turned heads, their mouths whispering *easiest to break*—clung like static.

Downstairs, the smell of bacon and coffee drifted up. Her mom's voice carried from the kitchen, bright, too bright: "Bryn, breakfast!"

Normal. Too normal.

She dragged herself out of bed, pulled on jeans and a hoodie, and forced herself down the stairs. Her parents were already seated at the table. Bacon popped in a pan, orange juice sweating on the counter. They looked up in unison when she entered, as if they'd been waiting.

"There's my girl," her dad said, smiling too wide. His gaze flickered across her face like he was trying to decode it. Again. That silent plea to know what she wasn't saying.

Her mom set a plate down in front of her. "Eat. You're pale."

Brynlee sat, fork felt heavy in her hand. She wanted to tell them everything—the mirrors, Vivienne's warning, the van. But the words stuck like barbed wire in her throat. They wouldn't understand. Worse, they'd try to, and the Spirits would make them pay for it.

She chewed, swallowed, and nodded like she was fine.

Her dad cleared his throat. "We've been talking about maybe doing a family night this weekend. Bowling, maybe? *His voice wavered on maybe, like even the word was too hopeful.* Or a movie. It'd be good, don't you think?"

Her mom touched his arm, hopeful. "Something normal. Together."

The fork clattered against her plate. "I can't." The words slipped out too fast, too sharp.

Both parents froze.

Brynlee shoved her chair back, the legs scraping the tile. "I've got… school stuff. Group project." A lie, ugly and obvious.

Her dad's jaw worked, like he wanted to say something but didn't know what. Her mom's eyes softened, searching. "Brynlee—"

"I said I can't."

The kitchen felt like a room bending in on itself, walls pressing in. She grabbed her bag and escaped before either of them could follow.

On the porch, the air bit her lungs clean. She leaned against the railing, head tipped back, fighting the sting in her eyes. Inside, their voices rose in muffled fragments—*what do we do, how do we reach her, she's slipping away*—but she couldn't let herself listen.

Her phone buzzed in her pocket. No caller ID.

Her stomach lurched.

She pulled it out, thumb hovering. One new voicemail. No missed call.

Her pulse throbbed in her ears as she hit play.

Static. Then a whisper, jagged, her voice braided with theirs: *They see you. They see too much. Don't let them in.*

The message ended.

Her parents' laughter broke through the window, forced and hollow, like they were trying to stitch the world back together. Brynlee stared at the phone, fingers trembling.

If the Spirits were watching her house, if they could leave their voices on her phone while her parents were two rooms away—then no one in her orbit was safe.

Not Mara.

Not Jacob.

Not Vivienne.

Not Harper.

And maybe, not even her parents.

Between the Stacks

The Ashwood Public Library smelled like lemon cleaner and loss—a place too clean to remember what it used to hold. Fluorescents buzzed overhead, steady, unblinking. Brynlee traced her finger along the spines of books as she moved down an aisle, not reading titles—just needing something solid under her hand.

She told her parents it was for a history project. That wasn't a lie, not exactly. But she hadn't opened her notebook since lunch. Not since Vivienne's words kept replaying: *They only care what you'll do when you're bent far enough.*

The stacks muffled everything. No clatter, no chatter. Just silence, thick enough to carry her own heartbeat back at her.

"Quiet makes it worse, doesn't it?"

Brynlee startled, her hand jerking against the books. A cover slipped and dropped to the floor.

Vivienne leaned against the end of the shelf, hair falling loose around her face, her blazer too sharp for a girl her age. She didn't smile. She didn't soften. She just waited, eyes steady.

Brynlee bent to grab the fallen book, buying herself a second. "You following me now?"

Vivienne's shoulders lifted in the smallest shrug. "I come here."

"To read?"

"To breathe." She pushed off the shelf and stepped closer. *"Noise keeps them back. Here? They press harder.* You know that."

Brynlee's throat tightened. She clutched the book to her chest, knuckles whitening. "Stop talking like you know what I know."

Vivienne tilted her head, studying her as if she were a puzzle she'd already solved once. "You flinch at quiet more than noise. You keep your sleeves pulled down even when it's hot. You scan a room like you're waiting for something to peel out of the corner."

Her voice stayed calm, even clinical, but Brynlee's stomach dropped.

"You've felt it," Brynlee whispered. It wasn't a question.

Vivienne's mouth curved, not a smile, more like the trace of something bitter. *"Felt it. Lived it.* That's why I said—" she lowered her voice, almost a hiss— "they don't save you. They shape you. Until you're useful."

Brynlee's breath snagged. The silence in the stacks thickened, pressing against her ribs. "Why me, then? Why not you?"

For the first time, Vivienne's gaze slipped—not away, but inward, somewhere Brynlee couldn't follow. Her jaw tightened. "Maybe—they tried."

Her fingers toyed with the edge of a sleeve, pulling it lower over her wrist. Too fast. Too deliberate. And Brynlee's pulse spiked because she *knew* that gesture. *Hiding. Covering.*

Vivienne turned before Brynlee could say more. "Don't stay here long." She walked down the aisle, the sound of her steps too soft against the carpet.

Brynlee pressed her back against the shelf, book clutched so tight her hands ached.

The lights buzzed. The silence leaned closer, like breath on her neck.

She fled before the silence could decide she was alone.

The Friend Who Stayed

The knock came just after dinner, cutting through the kind of quiet that pretends to be peace. Brynlee's mom wiped her hands on a dish towel, humming, then her voice lit like a struck match: "Harper! Oh, honey—come in!"

Brynlee froze at the top of the stairs.

Harper's laugh floated up, thin around the edges, followed by her dad's rumble: *"Well look who it is. Haven't seen you in forever."*

Her mom called, "Brynlee, come down. Look who's here!"

Brynlee's stomach twisted. Her body moved anyway.

Harper stood in the doorway, hair frizzed from the damp, bracelets jangling as she shifted her weight. She looked the same, except she didn't. Shadows clung under her eyes, and her smile wavered like she was holding it up by strings.

"Surprise," Harper said.

Her dad clapped a hand on Harper's shoulder, steering her toward the living room. "I'll grab some Cokes. You two catch up."

Brynlee's mom added softly, just for her, "It's good she came. You girls need each other."

So that was that. No escape.

They sat side by side on the couch, two sweating cans between them on the coffee table. The TV flickered muted light, some game show no one was watching. Brynlee folded her arms tight.

"You gonna say hi, or should I?" Harper asked.

Brynlee forced a smile. "Hi."

"Wow. Heartfelt." Harper popped the tab on her Coke, the fizz too loud in the quiet. "Your mom's been texting mine. Thinks we're in a fight. That if I come over, we'll braid each other's hair and fix everything." She took a sip, bracelets rattling. "So... here I am. Playing *my* part."

Brynlee lifted her can, just enough to look like she was drinking. The carbonation stung her lip, flat already.

"You let me disappear," Harper said, and the way her voice cracked sounded like she was realizing it in real time. "You didn't even chase me. Do you know how bad it got? I've been faking sick, skipping school, because I couldn't stand to sit there and watch you walk past me like I was no one."

Brynlee's chest pinched. She kept her face neutral, her smile stretched thin for the walls, for her parents listening in the kitchen. "I'm here now, aren't I?"

"That's not the same and you know it." Harper leaned in, eyes sharp and wet all at once. "Every memory I have is with you. Every single one. You're my person, Bryn. Always have been. But if you're gonna keep doing this—" Her voice cracked. "Then maybe I don't have a person anymore."

Brynlee swallowed hard. The air buzzed between them, louder than the TV. She wanted to say she was protecting Harper. That she was bleeding so Harper wouldn't have to. But the words jammed like glass in her throat.

Instead, she whispered, *"It's better this way."*

Harper stared at her, breath shaking out slow. Then she nodded once, sharp, as if carving the moment into stone.

She stood, grabbed her bag, and didn't slam the door when she left. The quiet was worse.

From the kitchen, her mom called lightly, "Everything okay, girls?"

Brynlee closed her eyes. "Fine," she said, voice steady. *"Everything's fine."*

The Coke kept fizzing, soft at first, then slow, then gone —
the only thing left still trying to fill the silence.

Shared Silence

The gym echoed after hours, a hollow heart still beating with the day's noise. Bleachers folded against the wall cast long ribs of shadow. Brynlee slipped inside because the hallways felt too crowded, too loud, even when they weren't.

She froze halfway across the floor.

Mara and Jacob sat on the lowest bleacher, backpacks at their feet, talking low between themselves. Their voices didn't carry, but their presence did—solid, quiet, like they belonged—to this hush.

Brynlee considered turning back. Then Jacob glanced up and caught her in the doorway. No judgment. No invitation. Just acknowledgment.

Her feet moved anyway.

She sat a few feet down, not too close, not too far. The wood was cold through her jeans. None of them spoke at first. Mara picked at the strap of her backpack. Jacob leaned forward, elbows on his knees, gaze fixed on the court lines painted bright against the dull floor.

The silence didn't feel empty this time. It had weight, but the kind that steadied, not crushed.

"You don't usually sit here," Mara said at last, not looking at her.

"Don't usually have a reason," Brynlee muttered.

That earned her the ghost of a smile from Jacob, quick and crooked before it slipped away.

The side door squeaked open. A woman entered, her coat thin against the late-winter chill, her hands red and raw from work. She carried a tote bag heavy with something that clinked.

"Sorry I'm late," she said, voice warm but tired.

Mara stood instantly, relief flashing across her face. Jacob gathered both backpacks without being asked.

The woman's gaze landed on Brynlee. Her eyebrows lifted, surprised but not unkind. "And you are?"

"Brynlee." Her voice came out too fast, too small. "From school."

"Ah." The woman smiled, a real one despite the exhaustion. "I'm Mrs. Williams. You're welcome here."

Something in Brynlee's chest twinged. *Welcome.* She hadn't realized how long it had been since anyone said that without strings attached.

Mara touched her mother's arm gently. "Can we give her a ride home?"

Mrs. Williams hesitated only a moment, then nodded. *"Of course."*

They walked out together, their steps soft against the polished floor. In the parking lot, Brynlee slid into the back seat of a car that smelled faintly of takeout and laundry soap. Mara sat beside her. Jacob climbed in front.

The heater sputtered to life, filling the car with a low hum. Brynlee stared out at the dark, streetlights smeared across the window glass.

For once, the silence didn't press her down. It held her up.

Outside, something flickered against the gym windows, but she didn't look back.

Erased

A couple days had passed since Mrs. Williams's warmth, still pressed against her ribs like a phantom heartbeat. No wonder Mara and Jacob loved her so fiercely. Gentle even in exhaustion, smiling softly when the world had scraped her raw. If money didn't grind them down, Mara would be sketching in a studio somewhere, Jacob building engines instead of scrounging coins for lunch. They deserved better.

That thought sat heavy now as she leaned on the park bench beside them, backpacks piled at their feet, the air sharp with thawing snow. Almost safe. Almost belonging.

Mara rested her chin on her knees, braid slipping loose, while Jacob flicked pebbles toward the curb with the same precision he carried in every movement. They argued about nothing—the vending machine eating his dollar again, the way math class felt like torture. Brynlee laughed, startled by the sound spilling out of her own throat.

And then—blink.

The air tilted wrong. Sound drained, muffled like her head shoved under water. The basketballs on the court, the voices, even the bite of wind—gone. Only her pulse slammed against her skull.

"Mara?" Too sharp. "Jacob?"

No answer.

Her chest cinched tight. She waved a hand between them, frantic. "Hey—I'm right here."

Jacob flicked another pebble. Mara stretched her arms overhead, slow and careless.

"Guess she had to go," Mara murmured, glancing at the empty spot beside her.

"Yeah." Jacob shrugged. "*Didn't say bye.*"

Ice dropped in her stomach. She grabbed for Mara's sleeve, desperate, and her hand slid through like smoke.

"No." The word tore out raw. "Don't—please, don't leave me."

They stood, shouldering their backpacks.

"Want to stop for fries?" Jacob asked.

"Yeah."

And they walked away, voices warm, easy, without her.

Brynlee staggered after them, throat splitting as she screamed. "I'm here! Please! Look at me!"

The path warped, stretching like elastic between them. The distance stretched like a rubber band that would never snap — only pull. By the chain-link fence, a blur leaned against the metal. Woman-shaped. Edges refusing to stay solid. The Spirit of Rejection.

She screamed until her voice shredded. The figure didn't move. Didn't speak. Didn't even *see* her. The gaze—if there was one—slid past, dismissive, like she'd never existed.

Her knees hit wet grit, cold soaking through her jeans. "*See me,*" she begged, voice breaking. "Please—just see me."

The Spirit tilted her head, almost curious, almost bored. *Then gone.*

When Brynlee lifted her head again, the court was empty, *even her footprints had blurred.*

First Fracture

The last bell had rung an hour ago, but Brynlee still walked the hall like one wrong step might erase her again. Fluorescent lights buzzed overhead, pale and cold, throwing her shadow too long across the lockers.

She stopped at her own, fumbling with the lock. Her hands still shook, memory of the park burning under her skin. Mara's shrug. Jacob's casual voice. *Guess she had to go.*

The clang of another locker cracked the silence. Brynlee flinched.

Vivienne stood three doors down, blazer too sharp for the washed-out light, her hair pulled into something careless that looked deliberate anyway. She didn't glance over right away, but Brynlee felt her eyes eventually—steady, assessing.

"You look like you've been erased," Vivienne said at last, her tone flat, almost clinical.

Brynlee's stomach dropped. "What did you say?"

Vivienne shut her locker with a soft click. She tugged her sleeve down, too quick, too practiced. The motion drew Brynlee's eyes—and she caught it. A welt, just above the wrist—thin, angry.

Her breath caught. "They touched you."

Vivienne didn't deny it. Didn't look away. "*Touched. Bent. Same thing.*"

The hallway seemed to shrink around them, lockers leaning in.

"Why—why didn't you tell me?" Brynlee whispered.

Vivienne's gaze cut cold, but her voice carried something already dead. Something hollow. "Because it doesn't matter. I let them. Easier that way."

Brynlee's chest tightened until it hurt. "You let them?"

Vivienne stepped closer, lowering her voice until it cut like glass. "You think they chose you because you're strong? No. They chose you because you were *easiest to break.*"

The words landed like a bruise.

Before Brynlee could answer, Vivienne was already walking away, her steps echoing down the empty corridor until she turned the corner and was gone.

Brynlee stood alone, sleeve pulled tight over her own wrist, and for one awful second, she understood why Vivienne had done it.

Unseen at Home

The kitchen smelled like garlic bread and tomato sauce—the recipe her mom used to anchor them when the air got too thin. Plates already set, glasses sweating with ice. Her dad cracked jokes about the basketball game on TV, voice too loud, like he thought words alone could hold back the silence.

Brynlee stabbed at noodles she couldn't taste.

Her mom's smile flickered. "So—school?"

"Fine," Brynlee said.

"That's it? Just fine?" Her mom leaned in, searching her face. "No tests? No friends to gossip about?"

The word *friends* hit like a bruise. Harper. Mara. Jacob. Vivienne. Each name burned for different reasons. Brynlee forced a shrug. "It's whatever."

Her dad cleared his throat, tried again. "There's a winter formal coming up, right? You going?"

She shook her head. "Not my thing."

He gave her that look again—like he was trying to read a language he used to know but had forgotten the words for.

The fork felt heavy in her hand. For one second, she wanted to blurt everything: the bruises, the dreams, the Spirits, the way she'd disappeared on that bench like she'd never been alive at all.

Her mom would hold her. Her dad would storm into action. *That's what parents did. That's what adults were for.*

Seventeen-year-old girls weren't supposed to carry this. When things got bad—*and they were bad*—you told your parents. You went to the police. That thought sat sharp and simple in her chest, the first clean edge she'd felt in weeks.

But when she opened her mouth, nothing came out. A pressure lodged there, thick as glass.

Her mom reached for her hand. "Bryn? You okay?"

She nodded, quick, forcing a small smile. "Just tired."

They bought it. They wanted to buy it.

But when she excused herself to her room, closing the door softly behind her, the truth pressed so hard it nearly cracked her ribs: she couldn't keep this in much longer. If it got worse, if they pushed her even one inch further, she'd tell. Parents. Police. Someone.

The question wasn't if. *It was whether she'd still be herself when it did.*

Glass Over Ice

The library hummed—fluorescents, heater, the soft machinery of pretending everything was fine, warm against the sting of March air leaking through old windows. Brynlee had come here to hide—no Williams twins, no Harper, just shelves and silence.

But Vivienne was already there.

She sat at a back table, posture sharp even in her slouch, a textbook open but untouched. Her hair fell like a curtain against one cheek, neat except where it frayed. She didn't look up when Brynlee slid into the chair across from her, though Brynlee knew she'd been seen. Vivienne saw everything.

"You're watching me," Brynlee said, sharper than she meant to.

Vivienne turned a page she hadn't read. "You wear it like a sign."

The words scraped something raw in Brynlee. *Obvious*—like the shaking hands, the pale skin, the way she flinched at shadows. She wanted to laugh it off, to play untouchable, but instead the question slipped out before she could stop it.

"You've seen them too, haven't you?"

That made Vivienne's eyes lift. Slow. Cool. They locked on Brynlee's face long enough to make her throat burn. Then, without a word, she tugged at her sleeve. Just enough.

The welt glared across her wrist, thin and red, raised like it had been carved there yesterday.

Brynlee's breath hitched.

Vivienne let the sleeve fall back into place. "Satisfied?"

"Why didn't you tell me?" Brynlee whispered. Her pulse thundered in her ears. *I'm not crazy. I'm not the only one.*

Vivienne leaned back, voice calm, too calm. "Because it won't help. Knowing doesn't stop them. Fighting doesn't either."

"Then what?"

Her eyes were unreadable, glass over ice. "You break. Or you bend. That's the choice."

Brynlee shook her head, heart hammering. "No. *There has to be—*"

Vivienne cut her off, tone still flat but edged now, dangerous. "You think they chose you because you're strong? They chose you because you were easy. *The easiest one to bend.*"

The words landed like a slap.

Before Brynlee could fire back, Vivienne stood, collected her untouched books, and walked away without a sound.

Brynlee sat alone, the welt burned into her vision, echoing like a brand, it throbbed behind her eyelids even when she closed them.

Splintered Hands

The classroom hummed with the sound of laptops—keys tapping, chargers buzzing in the wall sockets, the faint whir of the projector fan overhead. Brynlee stared at her screen, cursor blinking against an unfinished graph. Numbers swam. Lines blurred. She told herself to focus. Just finish the assignment. Pretend everything was normal.

But Jacob's hands kept cutting in. The cracks across his knuckles, the raw red lines that never seemed to heal. Like the world punished him just for holding on.

She flexed her own fingers under the desk.

Pain shot up her arm. Sharp. Blinding.

Her pencil slipped from between her fingers and hit the floor with a hollow clatter. Her breath stalled. She looked down.

Her skin had split—thin cracks spreading across her knuckles, blood seeping slow from each joint.

Her stomach dropped. She hadn't earned this. Hadn't touched anything. Still, the wounds gaped, wet and real.

The room tilted.

Someone's voice carried from the front—teacher, distant, muffled under the roar of her pulse.

Brynlee yanked her sleeve down, clenching her fist tight against her thigh to hide the blood. "*Fine*," she whispered, though no one had asked.

Every click of the keyboards after that sounded like bone grinding. Every throb in her hand matched Jacob's too perfectly.

When the bell rang, she shoved her laptop into her bag and bolted before anyone could look too closely.

In the bathroom stall, she peeled her sleeve back. The splits ran deeper now, skin wet and angry.

A whisper slid over her ear, inside her ribs.

"Pain doesn't fade. It only spreads."

Her vision blurred. She pressed her hands together hard, nails digging into her palms, choking back the scream climbing her throat.

The worst part wasn't the blood.

It was knowing the hurt wasn't hers—and that it never would stop finding her.

Borrowed Hurt

Her parents had been hinting for weeks. *Bring a friend home. Let us meet someone. Let us know you're not drifting away.* Brynlee always deflected, claimed she was busy, but tonight the words slipped out before she could choke them back.

"Can Mara and Jacob come over?"

Her mom's eyes lit like she'd been waiting months to hear it. "Of course! I'll make dinner."

Her dad clapped his hands together. "Finally. Names with faces."

Regret curdled in Brynlee's stomach, but it was too late. An hour later, the Williams twins sat stiff at her kitchen table while her mom dished out pasta and garlic bread.

"Eat, eat," her mom said, smiling too wide.

Mara's polite thank-you was quiet, Jacob's quieter. Their shoulders stayed tight, as if they weren't sure if they were guests or intruders. Brynlee watched the way Jacob's fork hovered, how Mara's fingers smoothed the edge of her napkin.

Her mom filled every silence with questions—classes, hobbies, siblings. Brynlee wanted to sink through the floor. The twins answered carefully, never too much. When her dad cracked a joke, Mara forced a laugh. Jacob gave half a smile, quick and vanishing.

The food steamed, perfect and ordinary. Everything looked safe—too safe, like a photo staged for proof.

But Brynlee's chest ached. All she could see was the way Mrs. Williams had smiled through exhaustion, the way coins had clinked too light on a cafeteria tray. And here—her parents piling seconds on their plates, asking about dessert—felt obscene.

Her fork scraped her plate, nails biting into her palm under the table. The Spirits didn't have to say it aloud. She could feel the truth pressing hard: this wasn't generosity. It was a mirror. A reminder of what Mara and Jacob didn't have.

Later, when the twins stood to leave, Brynlee's mom was already bustling at the counter. "Here," she said, sliding a plastic container across, still warm, still steaming. "There's plenty. Take some for later."

Mara blinked, caught between thanks and refusal. Jacob murmured, "We don't—"

"Please," her dad cut in, gentle but firm. "Humor us. We'll just eat too much if it stays here."

Mara tucked the container against her chest like it was fragile. Jacob nodded once, sharp, almost embarrassed. They both said thank you, soft, voices tight.

Her mom smiled, proud. Her dad looked satisfied.

Brynlee only saw the way their fingers clutched the container too close, like if they let go it might vanish.

Her mom turned to her beaming, "See that wasn't so bad."

Brynlee nodded, lips tight. She went upstairs before her parents could see how raw her hands still shook.

In her room, the reflection in her darkened laptop screen stared back. Not her face—just the faint shape of bruises blooming across knuckles that hadn't touched anything.

The punishment wasn't over. Inviting them in hadn't balanced anything.

It only made the house quieter, the air thick with the kind of weight that couldn't be shared.

Unspoken Confession

The news murmured in the dark, all static and names, while Brynlee sat on her bed, pretending to scroll through homework she wasn't touching. The anchor's voice carried names—missing kids, fresh faces on the screen—Lydia's among them. Each photo lingered a beat too long, the silence between words louder than the words themselves.

Her hand trembled around her phone. She pressed it to her chest, as if she could keep the images out by pinning them there.

This isn't mine to carry. I'm seventeen. When girls my age are in trouble, they go to their parents. They go to the police.

Her throat locked around it, but the thought burned anyway. She could picture herself walking into the station, blurting it all, begging them to look closer. She could picture her dad's face— confused, then furious, then ready to fix everything, the way fathers were supposed to when the world still made sense.

The air shifted. Her lamp flickered.

Her phone buzzed in her hand.

The screen lit—not with a message, not with a call, but with a recording. Her own voice, played back, warped and wet at the edges.

"I'll go to the police. I don't care what you say."

Her stomach flipped. She hadn't said it out loud. Not yet.

The playback twisted, slowed until the words bled into each other:

"You'll take us to them."

The screen went black.

Her pulse thrashed in her throat. She dropped the phone like it burned, breath tearing in and out.

The Spirits had heard her. They'd always hear her.

And if she told—if she even tried—who else would they hollow out to keep her quiet?

Cold Witness

Mom needed milk and bread and something 'easy' for dinner—the kind of errand people run when they still believe the world works. Fluorescents buzzed over the grocery aisles, too bright, too clean. Carts squeaked. The floor smelled like lemon and cold air. Mom handed over the list and a smile that tried too hard. "Grab the milk? I'll meet you at the register."

Cold rolled out of the freezer cases in little breaths. Frost webbed the corners of the glass. Brynlee tugged the door and a sheet of air knifed up her sleeve.

Her reflection didn't come with it.

Not her face. Not her coat. The glass held a room that wasn't this aisle—concrete gray, a bare bulb swinging slow, a door with paint chewed off around the lock. A shape in the corner, knees pulled tight, wrists bound with dull tape, edges frayed.

Lydia.

Not a photo. Not the box. Alive. Shaking. Hair matted to one cheek, breath fogging the air in stutters. She pressed a torn photograph flat against her chest as if it could muffle the sound of her ribs.

Heat flooded Brynlee's throat. Her palm hit the freezer door and left a smear. "Lydia." It came out as breath, not sound.

Boots crossed the floor in the reflection—two sets, heavy, careless. The door rattled; a bolt scraped. A voice she recognized without ever having heard it clean: low, bored, a thread of meanness that didn't need to be loud. "Get up."

Lydia flinched. Didn't move.

The woman-shaped blur slid into the fringe of the glass, too close to be in a grocery store, too far to be inside that room. Edges refused to hold. The gaze—if there was one—passed through Brynlee like a draft. Rejection didn't knock. She just... existed, the way an empty chair exists in a room where no one sits.

"You asked what happens when no one sees," the glass seemed to say, though the Spirit never opened a mouth. Cold pressed harder. "Look."

One of the men slammed his hand against the wall by Lydia's head. The sound arrived late, flattened by distance and glass, but it hit Brynlee's bones anyway. Lydia flinched so hard the bulb swung wider, shadows dragging the room into angles that hurt to look at. The other man crouched, spoke too close to her face. The words didn't reach—just a tone that said don't waste my time.

Brynlee's body tried to move—cart aside, fist through glass, anything—but the door bit at her palm. Cold soaked through, a warning in the shape of pain. Her breath fogged the glass, frantic, her own reflection drowning under the smear.

"Stop," she rasped toward the blur. "Show me where."

The freezers hummed. The blur didn't blink.

Lydia's mouth formed a word without voice. *Help.* Lips cracked, barely there. She tried to stand and folded. The crouching man's fingers tightened on her arm. Not hard enough to bruise in the moment, hard enough that the future would remember.

Pain ate into Brynlee's forearms, a heat that wasn't heat. She looked down—unmarked skin, nothing there—and still the hurt crawled under it, as if her body had been told how to ache and obeyed. Invisible. Like the welts before. Like the erasures. A private brand.

"*Tell me where*," she begged the blur again. "Please."

The bulb in the glass flared. The door in the reflection slammed. Darkness shook the frame. For one heartbeat the picture stuttered—three cuts spliced out of order: Lydia's eyes, too bright; tape pulling hair; a bucket in a corner that should never have to exist. Then the glass went honest again—just shelves of milk, her face, wide and white and wrong.

"Bryn?" Mom's voice from the end of the aisle, easy, oblivious. "You find it?"

Brynlee's fingers slipped off the handle. The door thudded shut, and the cold breathed against her legs. Words snagged like barbed wire under her tongue. If she opened her mouth, the whole store would hear the scream.

"Yeah," she said, voice steady enough to pass. She tugged a gallon free with hands that didn't feel like hands. The plastic sweated under her grip, little beads tracking down to her wrist, where nothing showed and everything burned.

Mom met her at the registers with a box of pasta and a smile that tried to land. "You okay?"

"Fine." The lie held because it always did when someone needed it to.

On the way to the car, the sky sagged toward evening, low and dirty, streetlights ghosting on in a row. Brynlee's phone was a weight in her pocket. The police lived there. Names, numbers, a front desk that would put her on hold for a minute and then say come in, tell us everything. Parents lived there too—two rooms back in her house, waiting to be told what they could fix.

Seventeen-year-old girls call for help. That's what they do when the world is wrong.

She slid into the passenger seat and buckled in. Mom started the car. Heat sighed from the vents, thawing the cold lodged in her sleeves.

Brynlee closed her eyes, and Lydia's face lived there behind the lids—blown light, cracked lips, terror held in so it wouldn't spill. *Help.*

"I'm coming," Brynlee whispered, not sure if it was a promise to Lydia or a sentence for herself.

How to Tell Without Telling

The back stairwell always smelled like wet concrete and old gum. Echoes hung there longer than voices had any right to. Brynlee found Vivienne between landings, one hand on the rail, blazer too neat for the scuffed steps, eyes fixed on the wired glass window showing nothing but brick.

"Tell me how to find her." No hello. No preamble. The words scraped on the way out. "I saw her. Not a picture. A room. They showed me."

Vivienne didn't flinch. A muscle ticked once at her jaw. "Where?"

"In a freezer door." Saying it sounded crazy. It didn't matter. "Concrete. A bare bulb. A bolt. She mouthed *help*." Heat climbed her throat. "If I go to the police—"

Vivienne cut in, voice even, razor-thin. "Say it wrong and you'll hand them more than Lydia."

Brynlee closed her fist on the rail until metal cut white crescents into her palm.

"Them who? The men? The Spirits?"

"The ones who listen—people who'll take what you hand them and hand it to whoever's closest." Vivienne's gaze slid from the window to Brynlee's face and held. "The ones who punish proximity. You name people, you point light, and the light burns what it touches first. The nearest."

"Nearest like Mara and Jacob." It wasn't a question. It hurt like a pulled tooth anyway.

"Nearest like anyone you stand too close to." Vivienne's tone didn't lift, didn't soften. "You think I don't know what happens when you tell? I tried." She looked back at the wired glass, and for a heartbeat the emergency light washed her skin a sickly green. Her sleeve shifted with the move; a shadow of yellow bruises bloomed above her elbow, gone as soon as she tugged the fabric higher. "They don't stop. They adjust. I named a street once—next week someone near it vanished."

"You let them," Brynlee said before she could swallow it. The words came out like a shove. "You said that. You let them bend you."

"It was easier." Flat. A truth already embalmed. "Easier than watching them take it out on everyone else."

"That's not a choice."

"It was the only one I had." Vivienne took the last step down to Brynlee's level, close enough that perfume, winter air, and something antiseptic threaded together. "You're thinking about the police. Good. Think. Plan. But don't walk in with names. Don't go alone. Don't call from home." A beat. "Don't say *police* in your house."

"They can't hear the word."

"They hear the want." Vivienne's eyes didn't blink. "They heard mine."

The stairwell hummed with the building's breath. Somewhere above, a door banged; laughter spilled, then died. Brynlee swallowed the iron taste in her mouth. Lydia's face lived behind her eyelids like an afterimage: cracked lips, blown-out light, the word that hadn't made sound.

"If I don't go, she dies." Saying it made the air thinner.

"If you go careless, she dies, and you don't get to pick who they take with her." Vivienne's hand lifted as if to touch Brynlee's sleeve, stopped an inch short. "There are rules. They won't save anyone. They'll only make it impossible for you not to try."

The sentence lodged like a splinter. "Then help me try."

Something in Vivienne's expression flickered—there and gone, like a light deciding whether to catch. "I'll tell you what not to do." She stepped back, the space between them snapping cold. "Don't give them a crowd. Don't make a scene. Don't bring a friend to be brave. If you choose a door, you go through it alone."

Alone. The word hit the bruise Rejection had left and pressed.

"Why are you telling me this?" It came out smaller than she meant. "If you think I'm easy to bend, why help at all?"

Vivienne's mouth curved without warmth. "Because you're still moving." Her gaze slid past Brynlee, up the well of the stairs where gray light pooled. "I stopped."

Footsteps drummed on the landing above. Vivienne was already climbing, voice drifting back without a backward look. "You want them to listen at the station? Walk in with *facts, not fear.* Time, place, faces. No names they can use to hurt anyone but you."

Brynlee stood with her hand welded to the rail until the echoes burned out. Facts, not fear. Her head spun with what she had and what she didn't: the market's glow, the van's blank panel, the freezer glass that wasn't a freezer anymore, the bolt, the bulb. A room can be anywhere. A bolt can be anywhere. But that door, those paint scars around the lock—

I can find that. If it exists once, it exists somewhere else. Hardware repeats. Habits repeat. People repeat.

She forced her fingers to unclench, air sawing in and out. Don't say police at home. Don't drag anyone to be brave. Don't give them a crowd. The rules tasted like rust, but they were something to hold.

Lydia's mouth moved in her head again: *help.*

"Facts," Brynlee whispered to the wired glass. "I'll bring you facts."

Echoes That Lie

The thaw had turned the park path to a ribbon of grit and mud. Brynlee walked with Mara and Jacob toward the bus stop, late light skimming bare branches, the air smelling like damp earth and last snow. Jacob told a story about a science lab gone wrong—vinegar volcano breaking bad—Mara snorted, elbowed him. Brynlee let their noise carry her. Breathing felt easier beside them, like the world loosened a notch.

A scream split the path.

Mara's voice. Not possible. Not here. Not this close—

The sound hooked under Brynlee's ribs and yanked. She spun so fast her ankle slid in a patch of melt. "Mara?"

Mara blinked at her from two steps away. "What?"

Another scream—behind the trees this time, the exact shape of Mara's voice in fear. Leaves rattled where no wind moved. Brynlee ran before her body asked permission.

She left the path, mud clutching her shoes. "Mara!" Branches slapped her sleeves, wet bark skinned her palm. Breath tore high and hot. The scream came again, edges serrated, *help*, then nothing—just the cough of a far-off car and a dog somewhere losing its mind at a squirrel.

"Bryn!" Jacob's voice from the path, normal, annoyed, a little winded from catching up. "Where are you going?"

She crashed through a last clump of brush into nothing: a scar of old leaves, a crushed beer can, the dent of someone's shoe from yesterday. No Mara. No one.

Her phone was already in her hand. She fumbled the camera open and hit record because *facts, not fear,* because Vivienne had said bring proof, because if her brain was breaking she needed a way to nail it to something real. The screen jittered—trees, blur, her own breath too loud; the audio caught only the chuff of air and Jacob's bored Where are you going.

She lowered the phone. The quiet came back wrong—too even. Her pulse wouldn't climb down.

"Hey." Mara, from the path, amused and confused in equal parts. "We don't have time for you to go feral in the woods."

Brynlee stumbled out, swallowing bile. Both twins stood where she'd left them, backpacks slung like always, faces clear, unhurt. Jacob lifted an eyebrow. "You good?"

She made her mouth work. "Thought I heard—" The word *you* lodged like a fishbone. "—something."

"Probably that dog," Mara said, pointing across the field. A golden retriever bounced after a stick, tail high, the owner waving like the world had never known a bad thing.

Brynlee nodded because anything else would loose the scream rising in her throat. They started walking again. Her hands wouldn't stop shaking. She slid the phone into her pocket and pushed her fingers hard against the fabric to make them behave.

At the bus stop shelter, water had pooled in a shallow dip in the concrete. The puddle held the three of them in a dull oval—Jacob taller than the reflection granted, Mara's braid cutting a dark line down her back, Brynlee's face pale and thinned by light. She stared because she couldn't not.

Her reflection's mouth moved one word too slow.

Her own mouth didn't. Air sawed in. She blinked, and the puddle went honest again—three kids, nothing else, a ripple where a drop fell from the shelter roof.

A woman-shaped blur leaned—no, *didn't* lean—against the side panel of the shelter where ads for phones and fries lived behind fogged plexiglass. The space around it bent without touching. The gaze, if there was one, slid off Brynlee like water off wax.

"Bus in five," Jacob said, checking the app without looking up. "If it shows."

Mara frowned at Brynlee's sleeves. "You're shaking."

"*Cold*," Brynlee said. Too fast. She jammed her hands deeper into her pockets.

The dog barked again. Nothing else screamed.

The bus arrived with a sigh of brakes and a wash of diesel that made her eyes water. They climbed on, took their usual row. Mara talked about an art contest she might enter and then laughed it off because who had time. Jacob stared out the window like he could bend traffic with will alone.

Brynlee watched the glass. Her reflection lagged a heartbeat behind and then caught up, only a smear in the corner she could pretend was dirt. She pulled out her phone under the seat edge and replayed the thirty seconds from the trees. Leaves. Breath. Jacob's *Where are you going* sounding bored. No scream. No proof.

Facts, not fear.

Her chest throbbed, edges catching on every breath. If Rejection could feed her false losses, she could make Brynlee sprint to shadows—while the real danger lived in a different room with a bolt and a bulb. Make her chase ghosts until everyone decided she was one.

At the next stop, an old man climbed on slow. Mara scooted to make space; Jacob reached to steady his elbow without making a show of it. Kindness hurt worse than fear—it reminded her what could be lost.

Brynlee closed her eyes. Behind them, Lydia's mouth formed that word the freezer glass had stolen—*help*. She pictured a door with paint chewed away around the lock. Not a scream. Not a trick. A thing that existed, specific enough to find.

You can bend a scare. You can't bend a hinge.

When she opened her eyes again, her reflection stared back from the bus window, in sync this time. No message. No mouth moving on its own. Just her, pale and stubborn and shaking, counting bolts in her head like a prayer.

Cracks in the Table

Dinner smelled of pinto beans and ham, potatoes crisping in the pan, cornbread cooling on the stove. Her mom only made that spread on nights she wanted the house to feel steady, like comfort could be cooked back into the walls. Brynlee sat at the table with her hands around a glass of water she hadn't touched.

Her dad slid into the chair across from her, grin ready, voice too casual. "So, how's school treating you? Any teachers I need to threaten?"

She tried to match the smile, but her lips barely moved. "It's fine."

"*Fine,*" he echoed, rolling his eyes toward her mom. "Always fine. Never spectacular."

Her mom carried the beans to the table, ladled them into bowls. "You've lost weight." Not a question.

Brynlee's throat went dry. She shook her head. "Just tired."

Her mom set the ladle down, leaned in, brushed hair back from her temple—the way she hadn't since Brynlee was little. "Your hands are shaking."

Brynlee shoved them under the table, pressing her palms against her thighs until it hurt. "It's cold."

"It's March," her dad said, trying to joke, but his eyes didn't laugh.

Something inside her cracked under their stares. Words clawed at her throat—*Lydia, the Spirits, the van, I'm not safe, none of us are safe.* She almost let them spill, almost begged her mom to hold her the way she used to when bad dreams still lived in closets, not her head.

But Vivienne's voice lived in her head now: *Don't say police at home. Don't say names. Don't bring them too close.*

Her chest cinched, ribs refusing to widen, breath scraping shallow. She pushed back from the table, chair legs scraping the tile. "I've got homework."

Her mom's hand caught her wrist for half a second—warm, solid, human. Brynlee flinched before she could stop it. The touch fell away.

"*I'm fine,*" she said again, forcing the words out flat, empty.

She went upstairs before their faces could show her what she already knew: they didn't believe her.

In her room, she shut the door and slid to the floor, pressing her forehead to her knees. Downstairs, her parents murmured to each other—low, worried, not meant for her ears.

For the first time she could remember, it sounded like they didn't know what to do. Neither did she anymore.

The Van in White

Late-afternoon light fell in pale bars across the nearly empty library. Brynlee sat with a stack of books she wasn't reading, notes spread open like evidence she didn't believe in. Her pen tapped, tapped, tapped until she pressed it flat and made herself stop.

Facts, not fear. She'd told herself that every day since Vivienne's warning. But what good were facts if the walls kept bending, if nothing held still long enough to catch?

Her eyes drifted to the glass wall at the far end, where the town sprawled below. Parking lot, street, two blocks of brick buildings with faded awnings. Ordinary. Solid.

Until it wasn't.

Two men leaned against a white van by the curb—ordinary, forgettable. Until her ribs forgot how to move. But her chest caved as if her ribs had been kicked. She knew the slope of his shoulders, the careless sprawl of boots braced on the curb. The other tipped his head back, laughing at something too quiet to reach her.

She didn't know their names. She didn't need to. They belonged to the bolt and the bulb. To Lydia.

Her pen slid from her hand.

One of them turned his head, and for one impossible second she swore his gaze locked straight through the glass, pinning her. The kind of look that said, *I see you even if you think you're hidden.*

Her pulse slammed so hard it hurt. She jerked back from the table, nearly knocking her chair. Her notes fluttered to the carpet.

When she looked again, the men were climbing into the van. Doors slammed. The engine turned over. The van pulled away, swallowed by traffic like it had never been there.

She stumbled to the glass, palms hitting cold. She told herself to memorize—*license plate, dents, any marker*—but her eyes blurred with panic, and all she caught was the panel's blank white side as it slid into distance.

Behind her, a cough echoed between the stacks. The sound cracked the silence clean in half. Brynlee turned, throat tight.

At the far end, a blur leaned against the endcap of biographies. Woman-shaped, edges slipping in and out like the glass couldn't hold her.

"*You asked for proof,*" the not-voice pressed through her. Rejection didn't look, didn't move. She just existed, empty as an unused chair.

Brynlee's mouth opened. "Why show me this?" It broke in the middle. "Why now?"

The blur wavered, the air bending as if it had shrugged. No answer.

Her stomach heaved like she might be sick. She snatched her books and shoved them into her bag, fingers fumbling, vision tunneling.

If they were here—on her streets—then Lydia wasn't a nightmare. She was near. Near enough to touch. Near enough to lose again.

The Reflection's Warning

The drive took an hour. Her dad played old songs too loud, drumming the wheel like a kid showing off. Her mom laughed the way she always did—head tipped back, eyes crinkled. Brynlee leaned against the window and pretended to sleep. The blur of highway lights made it easy.

The spring festival sprawled across three blocks—smoke from food trucks, strings of lights, music wheezing from speakers too cheap for the bass. Children ran with balloon animals already sagging at the ears. The air smelled like cinnamon and grease.

Her mom hooked her arm through Brynlee's. "See? Not everything has to be heavy."

Her dad pressed a funnel cake into her hands, powdered sugar already clinging to his jacket. "You loved these when you were ten."

The sweetness hit her throat like chalk. She managed a bite, forced a smile. "*Still do.*"

They walked under lanterns strung across the street. Her parents stopped at a booth selling handmade soaps, debating lavender versus peppermint. Brynlee drifted, letting the crowd fold her in. For one brief, fragile second, she almost believed in ordinary—noise, light, the crush of strangers.

Then the crowd bent.

Music warped. Voices stretched to static. Light stuttered out in a ripple.

In the gap between booths, Mara stood—hair tangled, eyes wide, mouth open in a silent scream. Brynlee's chest tore open. It was her worst nightmare wearing her best friend's face. She shoved forward, nearly dropping the funnel cake, hands outstretched—and blinked into empty space.

Only a woman in a red jacket frowning at soap prices.

She staggered back, sugar dust sticking to her palms. Her parents were waving her over, smiles easy, unaware.

"Bryn?" her mom called. "There's live music starting!"

Her dad added, "Don't pretend you're too old for it."

She tried to laugh, but it scraped. "I'll be right there."

They didn't hear the shake in her voice. They turned toward the stage, arms linked.

The bulbs overhead flared back to life. The music smoothed, bright again. Laughter spiked like nothing had cracked at all.

In the window of the raffle booth, her reflection lagged. When it caught up, the mouth moved without her: *You can't hold them.*

She dropped the funnel cake in the nearest trash can, sugar trailing down her sleeve.

You can't hold them, but you can lose them.

By the time fireworks bloomed above the dark horizon, her parents had their arms around each other, faces lit in bursts of color. Her mom leaned close and murmured something Brynlee didn't catch. He laughed, kissed her temple.

"They're happy," Brynlee whispered to no one.

Her chest ached with how badly she wanted to stay inside it, safe. But the hollow pressed harder—until even the fireworks sounded like glass breaking.

Three Screws

The drive home left grit in her teeth—sugar, diesel, fireworks still popping behind her eyes. House lights made soft squares on the lawn. Her parents moved around each other in the kitchen, rinsing cups, brushing shoulders. Normal filled the air—solid, heavy, impossible to move around.

Desk. Lamp. Notebook. *Facts, not fear.*

Brynlee clicked the lamp on and sat. The bulb hummed. The second hand stuttered once, like the clock was thinking about stopping. She set her phone face up beside the notebook. 10:42.

She printed a title because titles felt like control: **WHAT I KNOW.**

—White van. Panel sides. No windows.

—Two men. One slouches, one squares his shoulders.

—Bolt on door. Paint chewed around lock.

—Bare bulb. Swinging. Concrete floor.

—Lydia alive. Mouth formed *help.*

—Market alley. Freezer door. Not a freezer.

Her pen dragged to a stop mid-stroke. The hum of the lamp thickened, a mosquito trapped inside glass. The second hand twitched. Twitched again. She looked at her phone—10:43—looked back—10:41. Blinked. 10:44.

"Stop," she whispered to the room. The word hit the air and went nowhere.

She pressed back in. **WHERE TO LOOK.** Warehouse rows. Storage units. Any place with a bolt inside the room. Any place where a door's paint would wear in half-circles from the same hand missing the handle and hitting the lock, over and over.

Her pen felt heavier. The line she drew furrowed too deep; the paper furred under the nib. The letters widened like a child's block print. **HELP.**

No. She didn't write that. She lifted the pen; the word kept repeating. The word kept repeating—HELP in the margins, HELP inside loops of letters—until every inch of white space whispered it.

Her breath climbed fast and thin. She set the pen down, palms flat, and watched the clock to anchor the second hand—a full minute, two—no, not a full minute, because when her eyes burned and she blinked them clear, the phone said 11:09 and she didn't know where the time between had gone.

Ink stained her fingers. The pad of her thumb had a fingerprint pressed in blue, whorls she didn't remember making. Her notebook lay open to a page she hadn't turned. The *WHAT I KNOW* list was gone under a field of small drawings: the same door over and over, rectangle stacked on rectangle, each with the hinges sketched on the **left.** Three screws. Three screws. Three screws. Arrows. Notes crammed into the margins in a pinched version of her own handwriting.

- hinges left
- bolt right
- paint worn in a crescent
- drain in corner—iron ring
- sound—low hum
- smell—bleach + damp

She touched the page. The words weren't wet. A smear still came away on her fingertip, like whatever wrote them hadn't finished drying.

The room pressed close. Air didn't move. Her clock said 11:10. Her phone said 11:27. Her lamp buzzed like it had been buzzing forever.

"Lydia?" It came out before she decided to say it. Not a summoning, a question for an empty room.

Nothing answered. The only reply was the old house settling and her own blood in her ears.

She flipped to the next page. A map she hadn't drawn spidered across it—a mess of lines and boxes with no labels. In one corner, a square ringed in dark like someone had pressed too hard. Arrows converged there. No street names. No compass. Just pressure, like the paper knew where without knowing how to tell her.

Her phone lit on its own. 12:03. A notification blinked and then wasn't there, a ghost of a banner she couldn't catch. She unlocked out of reflex. Blank home screen. She checked the recording app. The last file sat at the top labeled with the time she'd lost: **23:52–00:01.** She hadn't hit record.

Play.

Silence rode a hiss for a long breath. Then the faint hum she'd written, the sound of a bulb working too hard, the scrape of something hitting concrete in slow strokes. At the end, a breath—hers? —and a word so quiet she felt it more than heard it.

help.

She snatched the phone to her chest. Stop open stop play no—her thumb fumbled, and the file ended in its own hiss.

Laughter rose thin from downstairs—her dad saying something about the fireworks traffic, her mom answering with that soft *mm* she saved for him. Safe sounds. The ordinary kind. Tears stung because she couldn't drop this into their laps like a tray and ask them to carry it.

Vivienne's warnings braided with the ink on her fingers. Don't say police at home. Don't hand them names. *Facts, not fear.*

She forced her pen into her grip again. She wrote what the recording gave her. **low hum. scrape. breath at end**. She drew the door one more time, careful, controlling the lines, marking the three screws, left hinge, right bolt, the crescent of paint worn back to wood.

Her clock said 12:11 now. Her phone said 12:23. The second hand landed hard on a mark and stopped. The hum in the lamp rose, rose, pressed—

Everything snapped back. The hum fell to a normal whir. The second hand lurched on like nothing had argued with it. The house sounded like a house.

She sat with her hand cramped around the pen, breath coming in small, measured pulls. The notebook lay open, messy and certain all at once. *You can bend a scare. You can't bend a hinge.* The thought clicked into place like a notch.

She turned the page and wrote the words she needed to see with her own eyes to make them true: **I will find the door.**

The bulb flickered. Held.

She capped the pen and left the notebook open, the pages breathing on their own.

Borrowed Mouths

The cafeteria clattered with trays and chatter, the air thick with reheated pizza. Brynlee sat with Mara and Jacob, their laughter knocking against her like it might catch if she let it. She stabbed at the slice on her plate, grease slicking her fork, and told herself this was normal. This was proof she still belonged here.

"Bryn?" Mara's braid slipped over her shoulder as she leaned in. "You okay? You look…" She searched for a word, settled on, "Not okay."

Brynlee opened her mouth. Air moved. Lips shaped. Nothing. Panic scraped her ribs raw. She tried again, harder, forcing sound up from her chest.

Mara frowned. "What?"

Jacob cocked his head. "She's fine. Just tired. Right?" His tone carried that casual cover, giving her a way out.

She thought she said yes, but what reached her ears wasn't hers at all. A flat voice, hollow, breaking on the edges: *help.*

Her fork clattered against the tray. "No," she whispered—or tried to—but the word came back, warped and wrong, empty of tone: *help.*

Her hands shook so hard she gripped her thighs to still them. No one else reacted. Mara just broke her roll into tiny pieces, Jacob talked about a test he didn't study for. The noise of the cafeteria swelled, laughter cracking across the room, trays thudding down. To everyone else, she was just another girl with too much on her plate.

Inside her head, the word kept echoing. Not her voice. Not Lydia's. Something stolen between them. *help. help. help.*

She shoved back her chair. "Bathroom," she managed, but it came out a split second after her lips stopped moving, like someone else had chosen the delay.

In the mirror over the sinks, her reflection stood pale and wide-eyed. The reflection's mouth lagged half a breath behind— mouthing help, Lydia's shape, Lydia's silence—before it caught up.

Her throat cinched tight. She gripped the porcelain until it creaked.

The *bathroom* door swung open behind her, girls laughing, oblivious. Brynlee plastered on a smile that felt like it might crack her teeth. She slipped past, heart pounding, her throat raw though she hadn't made a sound.

Back in the hall, lockers slammed. The noise should've grounded her. Instead, it rang like a countdown.

If they could hollow her words, how long before they used her mouth to betray them all?

Voice Test

The lamp buzzed faintly, steady but ready to burn out. Brynlee sat cross-legged on the floor, phone in her lap.

She opened the voice memo app—new recording, red light pulsing.

"Say something normal," she whispered, breath scraping her throat. She forced the words out slow. "My name is Brynlee Hall. I am seventeen years old."

Stop. Play.

Her voice played back steady, tired, hers.

She swallowed. Tried again. "I live on Sycamore Street. I go to Ashwood High. I—"

Playback: *help*. Flat. Not hers.

Her stomach dropped. She squeezed the phone until the plastic creaked.

Again. "Today is Wednesday. It snowed a little. My parents are downstairs watching TV."

Playback: "Today is Wednesday. It snowed a little. *help*."

She slapped stop, chest heaving.

She shut her eyes. Tried once more, louder. "I'm fine."

Playback: "I'm—*help*."

Her thumb trembled on delete. She couldn't. Proof lived there. She shoved the phone under her pillow instead, as if the weight could smother the sound.

Downstairs, the laugh track of a sitcom bled faint through the floorboards. Normal. Safe.

She pressed her fist to her mouth, bit down until she tasted copper—until she was sure any sound that slipped out wouldn't be hers.

The Assembly

Ashwood High herded students into the gym, sneakers squeaking, chatter ricocheting off rafters. Folding chairs scraped concrete. Teachers lined the walls, arms crossed, pretending to enforce order.

Brynlee sat wedged between Mara and Jacob, her knees pressed too tight together. The air smelled like floor wax and popcorn oil baked into the bleachers.

A uniformed officer stepped to the mic at center court. His voice carried the tone of practiced seriousness. *Awareness. Prevention. Community partnership.* Behind him, a slideshow flickered on the projector: names, faces, missing posters with phone numbers bold across the bottom.

Her stomach turned to stone when Lydia's photo flickered onto the screen—the same one from the news, crooked smile, sunlit hair. *Alive. Alive. Alive.*

"This is our community," the officer said. "These are our kids. We ask that you keep your eyes open. Report anything unusual. Don't dismiss what feels wrong."

Her pulse screamed in her ears. Report it. Say it. The van. The men. She had details no one else did. She could raise her hand, shout it across the gym, force the world to look.

The words swelled, too big for her throat. Someone had to say it.

Her hand twitched halfway up. Mara glanced at her, eyebrows knitting.

She opened her mouth.

Nothing came out.

Her throat locked—air scraping inside her like it had nowhere to belong. A sound scraped loose—flat, empty, not hers: *help*.

Mara's frown deepened. "What?" she whispered.

Jacob nudged her elbow, distracted. "Shh."

The officer's voice filled the space again, smooth, unbroken: "If you see something, say something. Don't wait. Don't assume someone else will."

Brynlee's nails carved half-moons into her palm. She wanted to scream *I did see something*—but her lips shaped words she didn't choose. The echo came out thin in her head: *We'll take it from here.*

Her vision swam. She clamped her mouth shut, hard, as if her teeth could barricade whatever else might slip free.

The slideshow moved on. More faces. More numbers. The gym hummed with the restless shuffle of kids waiting to be dismissed.

Her parents would have told her to speak. The officer told her to speak. Every bone in her body begged her to. And still— the Spirits had welded silence into her ribs.

When the dismissal bell rang, the room dissolved into chatter again. Mara and Jacob stood, but Brynlee stayed seated a beat too long, hands shaking in her lap.

If they could lock her throat in a room full of cops and teachers, then help wasn't coming—unless she broke them first.

Sideways Looks

The hallway buzzed louder than usual—assembly energy spilling into locker slams and sneakers squeaks. Posters curled on the walls—fundraisers, bake sales, soccer tryouts—bright paper ghosts after faces on a projector.

Brynlee kept her head down, books hugged too close.

"Hey." Mara's voice cut clean through the noise. She slid in beside Brynlee, braid swinging, eyes sharp. "Back there—you were gonna say something. Weren't you?"

Her chest locked. "No." Too fast.

Mara's brow arched. "Your hand was up. You opened your mouth."

"I was…stretching." It sounded weak the second it left her lips.

Jacob caught up, bumping Brynlee's shoulder with his. "She doesn't like assemblies, that's all. Too many people, too much drama."

Mara didn't answer right away. She just stared, quiet enough that Brynlee felt pinned.

The hallway thinned, kids peeling into classrooms. For a moment it was just the three of them.

Mara lowered her voice. "You were scared," Mara said. A beat. "Not bored. Not annoyed. Scared."

Brynlee forced a laugh, brittle. "Maybe I'm allowed to be human."

"Maybe," Mara said. Her gaze stayed steady, unblinking. "Or maybe you know more than you're saying."

The bell shrieked before Brynlee had to answer.

She ducked into her classroom, heart pounding, Mara's words echoing like a stone rattling down a well.

Vivienne slipped into the desk behind hers, moving like shadow. "She's watching you," she murmured, just loud enough for Brynlee's ear.

Brynlee froze.

Vivienne leaned closer, her perfume faint but sharp. "Careful what you give away. You think breaking their rules hurts?" her nails tapped the desk once, deliberate. "Wait until you see what they'd do to her."

Brynlee stared at the worksheet on her desk, letters blurring, throat tight.

Vivienne straightened, mask of indifference sliding back over her face. To anyone else, she looked like a girl already half-bored with class.

To Brynlee, the warning still hummed against her ribs.

Vivienne wasn't wrong. Mara wasn't either. Which left her nowhere to stand.

The Pushback

The night held its breath. Brynlee sat on her bed with the blinds cracked, watching the empty streetlight outside hum in its halo. Every shadow twitched wrong. She didn't care—tonight she had something worse to face. Her phone was in her hand, thumb hovering over the call button. Mara's name glowed on the screen.

If you tell her, she'll believe you. The thought beat in rhythm with her pulse. *She already suspects. You won't be alone anymore.*

Vivienne's warning whispered back, sharper: *Wait until you see what they'd do to her.*

Her throat tightened. Her thumb pressed anyway. The ring tone bloomed once—

The lamp blew out.

Her phone screen snapped black.

The air thickened, heavy with mildew, iron, frost. She knew this place before her eyes adjusted—knew it in her ribs, in her skin. Dreamscape. Not hers.

The room lengthened into corridors. Shadows peeled up and shaped themselves.

Pain stood first, skin too clear, bruises sliding under it like oil through water. His cracked nails dripped dark down his wrists.

Loneliness uncoiled beside him, all brittle limbs and hollow eyes, grin cut too wide.

Rejection was already there, blurred at the edge of her sight, steady as an empty chair.

"You think you can defy us?" Pain's voice dragged like gravel across bone. New bruises bloomed wherever she looked.

"You don't own me," Brynlee shot back, though her chest heaved like the air was knives.

Loneliness tilted his head, brittle fingers reaching. "Not yet. But almost."

Rejection didn't move. Her not-voice bent the air itself: "If you speak, she bleeds."

Mara's face flashed—braid, steady eyes, suspicion burning—and her stomach knotted.

Pain surged forward, hand clamping her arm. Agony jolted down to the bone, blooming purple beneath her skin before she even looked.

She screamed.

Her voice echoed wrong, folding back on itself, until the sound wasn't hers anymore. Until it bent into Lydia's.

"Help," the scream said.

Brynlee's throat tore. She yanked free, arm pulsing with fire. "You want me to save her, then let me try. But I'm not shutting up. Not for you. Not anymore."

The corridor around her fractured, spiderweb cracks racing across the dark, swallowing the Spirits piece by piece.

For one heartbeat, silence.

Then Rejection's blur leaned closer, edges wavering like static. "Every choice has a cost," Rejection murmured—not to her, but through her.

The floor ripped out.

Brynlee slammed back into her bed, lamp flickering on, phone buzzing with a dead screen. Her arm burned. She shoved her sleeve up—already darkening, bruise spread like ink in water.

She pressed her palm over it, shaking.

Next time she pushed back, something else would break—and it might not be her.

Frayed Edges

Lunch reeked of fryer oil and fruit gone just past ripe. The fork slipped, tines scraping plastic. Pain flared up her arm, fast and hot, blooming beneath her sleeve. She flinched before she could stop it.

Mara stilled, eyes locking on her. "Who did that?"

Blood drained fast, heat rushing in to replace it. *Don't show. Don't give it away.* "Did what?"

"You keep jerking like somebody hit you," Mara said, voice low, clipped.

Jacob leaned in. "We're not guessing, Bryn. We've seen this before."

No. Too close. Her pulse clawed at her throat.

Mara pressed harder. "At church—there was a girl. Her mom's boyfriend. Same look. Same pulling away. We didn't ask until it was too late." She swallowed. "It's the same signs."

Her tray blurred. Words thickened in her throat. *Not that. Not them.*

"It's not—" Her voice cracked, splintered. "No one's hurting me."

Mara leaned closer, gaze sharp as a knife. "Home, then? Is it your parents?"

Her chest cinched. Mom laughing in the kitchen. Dad watching her face like he could read something written there. The thought of their names in anyone else's mouth snapped panic through her ribs.

"No," she spat, too fast. Too defensive.

"School?" Jacob's voice softened. "Some jerk? Tell us."

"It's nobody," she said, plastering on a smile that didn't reach her eyes. "I'm just…off. That's all."

Mara's jaw tightened. She didn't buy it.

"I don't need you to pretend," Brynlee added, quieter, desperate to shut it down before the words *counselor* or *police* could crawl into the space between them.

"So, what do you need?" Mara asked.

Help. Please, help. The word rose hard in her throat, burning, impossible to release. She forced something else past it. "I need you to trust me."

Mara's stare cut through. "That goes both ways."

The bell screamed. Chairs screeched back. Jacob slung his bag over his shoulder, torn between them.

Mara didn't move. Her voice wasn't a question anymore. It was a verdict. 'If this gets worse, I'm telling someone."

Brynlee nodded like the promise didn't gut her. "Okay."

Not okay. Never okay.

The crowd shoved her toward the door. She clutched her books tight, sleeves down, pulse roaring. *I'm protecting you,* she told herself. The lie landed heavy as stone. *Even if it looks like I'm the one breaking.*

The Telling

Ashwood Police looked too small to hold something as big as an answer. Brick, glass, and a flag whipping in gray air. Brynlee stood on the curb too long, fingers dug into her sleeves until her nails left crescents in her skin.

Then she pushed inside before she could turn around.

The receptionist barely glanced up. "Can I help you?"

"I...need to give a tip. About a missing girl."

Clipboard. Pen. Brynlee scrawled her name before the shake reached her fingers. No school. No parents. Just what they asked.

A detective came for her within minutes. Blazer, hair in a no-nonsense knot, eyes that missed nothing. "Detective Kearns," she said, voice flat but not unkind. She led Brynlee into a small interview room that smelled like dust and burnt coffee. Two chairs. A table. Walls the color of cardboard.

Kearns set a recorder down but didn't switch it on. "You said you have information?"

Brynlee pulled her phone from her pocket and unlocked it with a thumb that shook. "I saw her," she said. "Lydia Grace Turner. At the mall. She looked at me. She mouthed 'help.' I managed to take this before they pulled her away."

She shoved the phone across the table.

The photo glowed under fluorescent light—Lydia blurred at the edge, two men flanking her. One short, square-shouldered, close-cut hair. The other slouched, boots turned out against the floor. Behind them: a white van, dent low on the rear panel. The plate was clear as print, letters and numbers sharp enough to carve.

Kearns leaned in. The air in the room shifted. "This is recent?"

"A few weeks ago. They saw me. They know I exist now. I don't think I'm safe."

Kearns's gaze flicked from the photo to Brynlee's face, measuring, weighing belief against procedure. "You're saying these two men abducted Lydia Grace Turner and that you witnessed it?"

"Yes."

"And you're seventeen?"

The word stuck. "Yes."

The folder snapped shut. "Then we need your parents here before I can go further. Legal requirement."

"No—please, no, I can't—"

"Brynlee." Kearns's tone cut off protest. Calm, steady, immovable. "This isn't optional. You did the right thing, but we proceed by the book."

The room tilted. She dug her nails into her palms. She'd come here to keep her parents clear—and now they were about to be dragged in anyway.

Her sleeve slipped. Skin smooth. No bruises. No welts. No punishment—only proof.

The rules were clearer now. Not *don't tell. Don't tell the wrong people.*

Minutes stretched. Then the door banged open. Mom first— hair wild, fear naked in her face. Dad right behind, jaw locked, his eyes searching hers the way they used to when she was a kid who couldn't explain what hurt.

"What's going on?" Mom demanded, voice too high.

Kearns didn't sugarcoat it. "Your daughter has given us photographic evidence in an ongoing case. She claims she personally witnessed Lydia Grace Turner at the mall, in the company of two men. We'll need to take her statement formally and secure this photo as evidence."

Her mom's hand clamped her shoulder. "Brynlee…you saw her?"

Her throat closed around it, but she forced the word out anyway. "Yes."

Dad's face broke. His mouth worked like he had ten things to say and none would come. Finally: "You were right," he whispered. No disbelief this time. Just fear.

The room blurred, heat behind her eyes. For months they'd looked at her like she was making it up, or worse—losing her grip. And now? Proof.

She clung to the edge of the table as relief and dread knotted inside her. She'd told. She'd been believed. And her parents were in it now. Relief flared—sharp, fleeting—before she saw her mom's shaking hands. The price wasn't her silence anymore. It was them.

Kept Safe

They drove home like a sharp turn might break her. Porch light already on. Her dad's keys shook against the deadbolt and then he checked the door twice after it closed, palm flat to the wood like he could feel danger on the other side. Her mom moved in circles that didn't land—phone on the counter, off, on again— before giving up. 'I'm ordering everything,' she said. Menus fanned like cards; no one thought about cooking.

The house smelled like lemon cleaner and whatever they'd sprayed last weekend to make the place feel new. Her shoes left wet crescents on the mat. The detective's card pressed a rectangle against the inside pocket of her bag, right where she'd zipped it— a small, hard certainty. Upstairs felt far away; the kitchen light made islands of all of them.

"Detective Kearns will call as soon as they pull cameras," her dad said, too brisk, finding the words like tools and laying them out. "We'll get the doorbell cam up this week. Motion lights. I'll talk to the neighbor about keeping an eye—"

"We're not leaving her alone," her mom cut in. "Not until— " She didn't finish the sentence. Her eyes kept going to Brynlee's face and then away, like the looking itself might bruise.

"I'm okay," Brynlee said. The truth in it startled her. The word came out clean, no lag, no hollow in the middle. Her throat didn't seize. The lamps didn't flicker. Pain didn't tighten her fingers when she set her bag down. Reward, then. Or permission. Either way, the quiet felt earned—and temporary. Either way, the air wasn't crowded the way it gets when the Spirits want her small.

They ate at the table from boxes that sweated through paper. Her mom kept pushing cartons toward her like full plates could plug a leak. Her dad asked if the school should be notified, if she needed time off, if she wanted him to drive her everywhere for a while. The questions stacked like barricades. She answered the ones she could. "Maybe." "For now." "Please." He searched her face the way he did that morning in December—like trying to read a language he'd once known but forgotten the grammar for.

"I wish you'd told us sooner," her mom said softly, not an accusation, just grief. "I would have—"

"I know." She pressed a knuckle to her mouth and let her hand fall before it looked like she was hiding. "I know."

Upstairs, the mirror over her dresser held steady. No lag. No second mouth moving underneath hers. She said her name under her breath, and it belonged to her, all syllables present. The bruise that should have been blooming from last night's defiance hadn't risen; skin lay ordinary over bone. The quiet felt earned. Or bargained for.

Downstairs, her dad opened and closed the back door again to test the lock; the click carried through the vents. Her mom's voice on the phone—low, careful—gave the detective the same details Brynlee had given, then said, "Thank you," like she was thanking a doctor who couldn't promise anything. The words floated up the stairwell and sat outside Brynlee's door, listening.

Text bubbles on her screen glowed from Mara and Jacob. *You okay? Call if you need me.* She typed *Home*, then erased the rest. The nearest burn first. The rule lived under her tongue now. You can tell the machine built for catching monsters; you don't feed the names of the people you love into its teeth.

Her mom knocked once and came in without waiting, blanket over one arm, that mug she only filled when someone was sick in the other. "Sleep in our room if you want. Or I'll sleep on your floor." She said it like she meant it, like her back could ransom a whole night's rest.

"I'll be okay here." The bed dipped when her mom sat, the blanket spreading over her knees. Fingers brushed Brynlee's hair back from her forehead, hesitant, then steadier when she didn't flinch. "We'll keep you safe," her mom said, and it wasn't a promise so much as a pledge she was making to herself out loud.

Kept safe. The words warmed and chilled at once. Safe from men with vans and dented panels and paint on their boots, maybe. Not from the thing that stood in the corner when the lights went out and rearranged the walls.

After the house went dark, the ordinary kind of dark, she lay on top of the covers and listened to her parents move in their room—the closet door, the soft thud of a drawer, her dad murmuring something about cameras and timers and calling the alarm company in the morning. The security of it pressed and didn't quite reach. She slid the detective's card from her bag and traced the numbers with her thumb until she could recite them without looking. On her desk, the notebook waited open to the sketch: left hinge, right bolt, crescent of paint worn thin. The lines held. The clock second hand ticked forward without stuttering.

Being kept safe wasn't the same as being safe. One was mercy. The other was a miracle. But for the first time in weeks, the house didn't feel like it was listening for her to make the wrong sound. She turned off the lamp and let the dark come all the way in. The last thing she told herself before sleep took her was as plain as a plate number: tell the right people, and doors open. Tell the wrong people, and the door opens under you.

The Shift

News traveled faster than doors locked, faster than warnings could catch up. Even when the detective said *quiet, careful, let us work*, the whispers ran anyway—through church basements, through Facebook threads, through mothers who carried the memory of missing kids like scar tissue. Eleven years gone, and now Lydia Grace Turner's name beat against every mouth again. Not dead. Seen. Alive.

The men heard. They always heard.

Brynlee didn't know it until the dream opened beneath her. The dark thickened around her bed, the walls of her room softening until they fell away. Cold rushed in, and she stood barefoot on concrete slick with a thin sheen of water. The air stank of mildew and unwashed skin. Her breath smoked out in front of her like she was already outside.

"Brynlee."

Not one voice. Three. Woven together until she couldn't tell which mouth spoke first.

Shapes unfolded from the shadows—bone-stretched skin, bony shoulders under a ragged coat, the blurred woman-shape whose gaze slid past her like she was already gone. The Spirits. Whole here. Flesh here.

The floor shivered under their steps.

They didn't drag her this time—she followed because the air itself forced her lungs to. Down a narrow corridor, into a room with a single light hanging bare.

Lydia was there—hands bound, face swollen from crying, hair clumped into tangles. Human again. Terribly, beautifully human. She rocked against the wall, her knees drawn in, whispering words Brynlee couldn't catch.

A scrape of metal. A door opening on the other side. Two men—shadows she knew anyway—stepped inside.

"She was meant to be gone already," one said, his voice a rasp from too many cigarettes.

"More valuable older," the other muttered. "Worth the wait."

Lydia flinched at both voices but didn't lift her head.

Her stomach hollowed. She slammed her fist against the vision, but it passed through air. "Stop—" Her voice hit the walls and came back smaller.

The Spirits shifted, their presence thickening.

"They will move her," the Spirit of Pain rasped, words dragged over splintered glass. "Gone before the week ends."

"You cannot let them." Loneliness's mouth twitched too wide, the echo of a smile with no joy in it.

Rejection stood still, her outline blurring every time Brynlee tried to focus. Her voice landed flat, as though it had already been written: "If they take her, she vanishes. Not into death. Into absence."

Brynlee shook her head, chest burning. "Then tell me where. Tell me when."

The Spirits didn't answer.

Instead, her phone lit in her hand—though she hadn't pulled it from her pocket, though she hadn't remembered carrying it here. A recording bled onto the screen, grainy but unmistakable: Lydia's voice, hoarse, whispering, *I can't hold on.*

Another voice overlapped—the men's. *Load her up tonight. She won't make it another run.*

Then the screen blinked black.

Brynlee's knees buckled. "You can't expect me to go to the cops with a dream."

The Spirits leaned closer, the three voices braided into one. "We expect you to act."

Lydia lifted her head then, and for a split second her eyes locked onto Brynlee's like she *knew* she was there. Bloodless lips shaped a single word: *Hurry.*

The room shattered around her, concrete dropping away, water rushing upward, and she slammed awake in her own bed with a scream raw in her throat.

Her phone lay on the nightstand. The recorder app open. No file.

Her reflection in the dark window mouthed it back—her voice, but not hers: *You cannot wait.*

The Lockdown

Morning came with rules.

Dad stood at the counter with a legal pad: *No walking alone. No rideshares. Call when you leave, call when you arrive. Doors locked. Location sharing circled twice*, the pen leaving grooves you could feel.

Mom poured coffee and kept reaching for her phone like it could fix something if she held it hard enough. "We'll drive you," she said. "Everywhere. School. Practice. Nowhere alone until this calms down."

"I don't have practice," slipped out, useless.

"Then home and school," Dad said, voice bright with the kind of cheer that means *not up for debate*. "We'll get the alarm company out. Cameras. Motion lights."

A fortress, built out of love and paper, and already cracking.

The house hummed with new sounds—beeps when a door opened, the chime of the app Dad installed, the lock thudding twice because he had to hear it. Every noise said *inside*.

"I can't miss school," she tried. The truth: the walls pressed if she stayed still too long. "Midterms."

"We'll clear it with the office," Mom said. "Detective Kearns said to keep routine where we can, but I'm not risking—" She stopped. The word hung there anyway: *you.*

"I'm fine," came out whole, clean. No stolen echo threading it. No stab of pain in her hands when she wrapped them around a glass. The quiet reward sat on her tongue like a coin that wouldn't spend.

Dad set the pen down and cupped the back of her neck like he used to when she had a fever. "We're keeping you safe," he said, and meant it with his whole body. "Okay?"

Okay. The smallest prison word.

By afternoon, a new keypad blinked by the back door. Dad tested the siren twice; the house shrieked and then apologized in little beeps. Mom stocked the pantry like storms lived in the forecast. The doorbell cam blinked its red light like an unblinking eye.

She breathed through the press of it, through the texts lighting up in her pocket—*Did you really see her? Is it true? You're a hero* with star emojis that made her stomach flip. She typed *don't* and deleted it. The rule lived under her tongue: tell the right people. Don't feed the wrong mouths.

"Early night," Dad said at eight, like you could tuck fear in with the dishes.

She tried. She lay on top of the covers and listened to alarms arm, locks thud, her parents' steps soften into the hallway and then into their room. Her pulse kept counting. The ceiling held still. The dark came in the right way.

And then it didn't.

The room thinned. The hallway stretched. The carpet under her feet went soft and then softer until it wasn't carpet at all, just a dark that held the shape of a floor. The house stood up around her like a model built too carefully—walls too straight, corners too clean, windows shining without light behind them.

Downstairs, the TV glowed blue on her parents' faces. They sat side by side, hands laced, eyes forward. News static whispered without words.

"I'm here," she said, stepping into the spill of light.

They didn't turn.

"Mom." Louder. "Dad."

The blue wash didn't blink. Their profiles stayed perfect and wrong, like pictures in frames.

Something breathed behind her—slow, wet, measured. Pain drifted past, bruises blooming beneath clear skin, cracked nails tapping each lock—one by one by one. With every tap, a lock duplicated, brass multiplying like mold. The door sagged under the weight.

Loneliness unfolded from the shadow near the stairs, coat hanging off sharp shoulders. He tilted his head at the couch, at the two figures fused by the television's blue, and smiled that not-smile. The sound from the TV changed—crowd noise, a hundred voices muffled like under water—close enough to make the bones in her ears ache, too far to hear a word.

Rejection stood at the window, an empty-chair presence, outline blurring whenever she tried to take her shape in. The glass reflected the room wrong: no couch, no parents, just a small figure sitting very still in a house that had swallowed itself.

"I don't want this," she said, throat raw. "Let me keep them. Let me keep this."

Pain's cracked knuckle brushed the mountain of locks again. The door bowed. The siren wailed thick and distant, like the house screamed from under a pillow.

Loneliness sank onto the other end of the couch, eyes fixed on the blue light that wouldn't show him a face. "Safe," he said, voice soaking into the air. "So safe."

The word landed like a lid.

Rejection didn't look at her. "Still is not safe," she said, each syllable flat, final. "Still is silence."

On the TV, the picture sharpened for a heartbeat. Not news. A hallway somewhere that didn't belong to this house. A girl moving between two men, head down. The image blurred again before her mouth could form *Lydia*. The remote on the table had no buttons.

"Let me go," she said. To them. To the locks. To the model of a life that held too tightly. "I'll move."

Pain's hand opened, palm up. A single lock fell from the pile and hit the floor with a small, awful sound. Metal on wood. A dent.

The TV froze on an empty doorway. No bodies. No faces. Just the frame—waiting.

Rejection spoke without turning. *If you let them hold you, she goes.*

The living room stretched longer, longer, the blue light farther away, her parents' faces losing even their edges. The alarm's beeps spaced out into a slow, drowsy hush. Safe as sleep. Safe as stone.

"I get it," tore out of her. "I get it. I won't stay."

The locks stopped multiplying. The siren cut. The TV went black.

She woke with her heart in her mouth and the taste of cold metal under her tongue. The house sat ordinary around her— alarm armed, hallway the right size, a glow under her parents' door. For a long time, she lay very still and listened to the not-screaming silence and the soft, human noise of her dad clearing his throat in his sleep.

Then she slid out of bed and dug in her backpack for the little things that meant moving: a folded hoodie, the cheap flashlight from the junk drawer, the detective's card. She tucked them into the pocket of her coat and set the coat by the chair where no one would notice it in the morning. Phone on the charger. Ringtone off. The second hand on the clock stepped on, steady as pulse.

Kept safe wasn't safety. The house could hold her. It couldn't hold back what waited if she didn't move.

When sleep took her again, it was shallow and bright. In the last skim of it, a lock clicked once, and not from the door. From something inside that had decided.

Tomorrow, school. After that, whatever breaks the stillness — or breaks her.

The Fallout

By first bell, her phone burned. Thumbs-ups from numbers she didn't remember saving. DMs with wide eyes and prayer hands. Screenshots of posts that said *SHE SAW HER* in block caps over a grainy crop of Lydia's face everyone swore they weren't sharing. In the hall, heads tipped together and then snapped up when she passed. Hero in one mouth. Liar in the next. Same breath. A freshman whispered *Turner* like it was a ghost story and flinched when Brynlee looked his way.

The office called her down second period. The secretary pretended it was ordinary, a pass slid across glass, but the waiting room had new gravity. Principal Krantz in his tie with the school crest. Detective Kearns in the corner, face unreadable. A counselor with soft eyes and a spiral notebook open to a blank page as if she could catch falling things with paper.

"We scheduled a conversation," Kearns said. The neutral voice from the station. "The family asked to meet you."

Family. The word hit low—alive, not dead. The rumor had outrun caution; of course it had. Eleven years turns strangers into kin.

They used the library conference room because it had a door and a long table and windows that looked like transparency. Mr.

Turner stood to shake her dad's hand; the grip was there, the warmth wasn't. He'd shaved but missed a nick; a square of toilet paper clung to his jaw like a flag of surrender. Mrs. Turner didn't stand. Her hands were knotted in her lap around a rosary whose beads had rubbed matte from use. When she looked up, it felt like standing too close to a fire.

"Thank you for coming," she said, and the thank you sounded like I'll die if you lie to me.

Kearns set her recorder down and didn't press it yet. "We'll keep this focused. What Brynlee can share is limited to what she personally observed."

Dad sat close enough that his knee touched hers. Mom's palm found the back of her shoulder, warm through the fabric. They felt like bookends; she felt like the folded pages between.

Mr. Turner tried to be the one who didn't break first. "Did she look…hurt?" His voice went sideways on the last word.

Alive, Brynlee wanted to say and knew that wasn't the question. "Scared," came instead. "Tired. She mouthed 'help.' She moved like she'd been pulled too hard too many times." The table edge bit her forearms. "But she walked. She looked right at me. She knew where she was. She knew me seeing her mattered." Each sentence laid down like a plank. Don't say the dream. Don't say the room. *Facts, not fear.*

Mrs. Turner's breath left in a sound with no shape. Her fingers crushed the rosary so tight the crucifix left an imprint in her skin. "Was anyone…was anyone kind to her?" Not hope—hunger.

No. The word wouldn't come out. Brynlee swallowed the truth and gave the only thing she had. "She had her eyes. That's all I could save."

Silence, thick enough to chew. Kearns cleared the room with procedure—thank you, next steps, we'll be in touch—and still nobody moved, like pushing the chairs back would scatter the good out of the air. Mr. Turner nodded too many times. Mrs. Turner stood as if gravity had been adjusted while they sat and she was learning the new math of it.

Movement at the far side of the glass caught and held—another family, a different kind of polished. The LeClairs. Her name said like a headline even when the adults used first names only. He carried his wealth like a pressed suit; she wore hers like a second skin. The foundation that wrote checks for missing youth bills stood in the doorway and made the teachers twitch.

Mrs. LeClair stepped inside without waiting for an invitation. "We're so grateful for anything that helps," she said to the room at large, voice tuned to gala volume and then softened too late. Her gaze landed on Mrs. Turner like a hand on a bruise. "We're here for whatever you need."

Mrs. Turner's face tightened—not anger, not exactly. A flinch made of ten years of holidays they didn't share. She set the rosary down like a line on a map. "I can't do the past today, Vivienne." The first name came out like a slice.

Mr. LeClair lifted his hands, palms placating. "We don't want to intrude. The event committee thought—"

"Not today," Mr. Turner said, gentle because it cost less that way. He smoothed the wasted square of toilet paper off his jaw with a thumb and didn't know what else to smooth.

Behind them—half-hidden by the doorframe—Vivienne watched, careful not to touch the threshold. Not the gala version. Hair back in a simple tie, uniform neat without trying, posture careful like one wrong move might spill something she couldn't get back. Her eyes snagged on Brynlee and held too long. There it was—the pull. Not curiosity. Recognition without naming.

Kearns erected a boundary with her body and her badge. "We'll coordinate through me," she said to the LeClairs without looking at them, and the sentence put a fence around the Turners big enough to breathe in.

The adults filtered out in polite little eddies—principal's handshakes, counselor's murmured *any time*, Dad's practical questions about patrol cars near the house tonight. Mrs. Turner took Brynlee's hands in both of hers before she went. The skin was thin and hot; the rosary had printed a tiny cross into the soft meat of her palm. "If you remember even a scrap," she said, voice down to its wire, "you call. You don't wait. You don't wonder if it's silly. You call."

"I will." The promise clicked into place like a key because it was one she could keep.

They left with Kearns between them like a current.

The library returned to shuffling and whispers. Kids in the stacks peered over spines, pretending not to. Her mom smoothed the front of her sweater; her dad squeezed her shoulder hard enough to ask if she needed out. She nodded and they moved as a unit into the hall where the noise was easier to hide inside.

A cluster by the water fountain pretended to be about Algebra but leaked words anyway—*plate number* and *library cam* and *hero*. Someone hissed *or she's making it up*, and the friend smacked his arm like shut up, idiot. Her name rode all of it like a raft.

Vivienne had trailed the grown-ups out and then not left, as if the threshold itself was a decision. She stood by the trophy case, eyes on the floor until they weren't. When Brynlee passed, the look they traded landed like a note slid under a door: later. Not here. Not with all these eyes.

By lunch, a parent page had posted a blurred screenshot of the mall photo with a caption that read *credible lead confirmed* and a paragraph begging people not to share it. Someone had already made it a story with a blinking heart and tagged Brynlee's handle wrong and still right enough. Her tray went cold while the screen scrolled itself. Every notification tasted like pennies. She put the phone facedown and kept breathing.

In last period, the intercom coughed and Principal Krantz said something about community and vigilance and *respecting the privacy of those involved*. Half the class looked at her. The other half pretended not to.

After the bell, she hit her locker and closed her eyes a second longer than blinking buys you. When she opened them, a reflection waited in the metal—a version of her with her mouth closed and her shoulders squared, an older steadiness that didn't feel like hers yet. The reflection nodded once. Or maybe that was just the way fluorescent lights stutter when they've been on too long.

Down the hall, a girl cried into her phone. Somewhere, a rumor changed hands and got a new ending. In the shadow at the end of the corridor, Vivienne stood like a question with legs and didn't ask it.

Brynlee shouldered her bag and went to meet the part of the day that still had to be lived, the detective's card a rectangle against her ribs, the Turners' thank you a bruise she chose to keep. The internet chewed names like candy and spat out saints. Tomorrow would bring more eyes. Tonight, would bring the kind of dark that carried orders. And between them—her, learning which doors to open without getting swallowed.

Hairline Cracks

The house felt thinner after the meeting. Not in size—Dad still stalked from room to room, double-checking locks like muscle memory. Mom still called her name from the kitchen for help with nothing. But the air had edges. Too many names hung in it now—Turner, LeClair, Lydia—splintering against the drywall, sharp as glass that wouldn't sweep up.

Upstairs, her phone lit every five minutes. Notifications she didn't open: classmates tagging her handle in disappearing stories, cousins she hadn't heard from in months asking *is it true??*, strangers with profile pictures of candles sending *prayers*. She flipped the screen face-down and still felt the light pulsing through the case.

She tried homework. Words blurred. She tried music. Lyrics bent wrong until they all sounded like *help*. By nine she'd given up and stared at the ceiling until the cracks shaped themselves into maps she couldn't read.

Her parents padded in to say goodnight like they used to when she was ten. Mom smoothed the blanket that didn't need smoothing. Dad pressed a kiss to her hairline. "You did good today," he said, voice rough from disuse, as if praise wasn't a language he'd had to practice until now. "You gave them hope."

Hope scraped. She swallowed the answer that wanted out: *Hope isn't enough. Hope doesn't stop vans.*

When their door closed, she turned her lamp off and lay in the quiet. For a few minutes it held. Then the floor thinned under her bed. The air sharpened until it whistled in her lungs.

A handprint appeared on her ceiling—too long-fingered, the outline bruised into plaster. The Spirit of Pain's voice seeped down, dragging over splintered glass:

Hope doesn't keep her.

Another voice rose from the floorboards—Loneliness, echoing like boots in an empty stairwell:

Hope doesn't find her.

And from the window, a blur that bent her reflection wrong—Rejection, flat and final:

Hope doesn't save her. Hope only shines.

The handprint deepened until flakes of plaster dusted her pillow. Brynlee squeezed her eyes shut and whispered, "I'm moving. I'm not staying still." The words came out cracked, but the house steadied anyway. The air softened. The handprint faded, leaving only a pale outline like chalk.

She breathed again.

Sleep came shallow, fragile, threaded with Lydia's eyes beyond the glass. Eyes that didn't need hope. Eyes that needed a door open.

The Question

By midweek the noise hadn't died down—it had multiplied. Every hallway at Ashwood carried it: whispers that paused, heads tipping together, phones angled like mirrors. Even the teachers seemed to glance too often, voices tight when they said her name during roll.

Brynlee kept her hood up between classes, earbuds in with no music playing, just so she could pretend she wasn't listening. The detective's card pressed against her notebook — sharp-edged through the paper. A reminder of which mouths she *could feed*. Not these. Not any of these.

At lunch she didn't sit at the Williams table. Didn't sit with Harper, who barely looked at her now. She claimed the corner table near the vending machine, tray untouched, staring at the soda labels until the colors bled together.

A shadow fell across her. "This seat taken?"

Vivienne. Polished without trying, her hair smoothed back, her uniform perfect as if it had ironed itself. But her eyes— uncertain, sharp in a way that cut inward instead of out.

Brynlee shook her head. Vivienne slid in across from her, setting her tray down without ceremony. For a few minutes they didn't speak. Noise carried over from the rest of the cafeteria—

metal clattering, laughter breaking too loud, the low tide of gossip always circling.

Finally, Vivienne leaned in just enough that Brynlee had to look up. "Is it true?"

The words landed heavier than a slam.

Brynlee blinked. "What?"

"That you saw her." Vivienne's fingers tightened around her fork, knuckles whitening. "Lydia." Her voice broke softer on the name, like it wasn't supposed to leave her mouth out here in the open. "Was it really her? Or is it just another rumor?"

Heat climbed Brynlee's throat. "It was her," she whispered. "I wouldn't—" She stopped, breath catching. "I wouldn't make that up."

Vivienne watched her, weighing each word like it might tip a scale she didn't trust anymore. "I didn't know if I could believe myself," she said finally. Her tone was low, almost drowned by the cafeteria hum. "There were nights I thought I saw her. Felt her. After she was gone. I thought I was…losing it." A laugh that collapsed halfway. "Turns out maybe I was just too afraid to trust myself."

The silence between them sharpened. Brynlee swallowed hard. "You weren't wrong."

Something flickered in Vivienne's face then—relief tangled with grief, a splinter of something that looked almost like trust but not yet. She sat back, pushing her untouched tray away. "Thank you," she murmured, but it didn't sound like thanks. It sounded like a vow she hadn't worked out the words for yet.

The bell rang. Chairs scraped. The cafeteria emptied into the current of students. Vivienne stood, smoothing her sleeve, mask back in place before anyone else could see the crack. "Later," she said, not a question.

Brynlee watched her walk out, shoulders stiff, head high. The air left behind felt heavier, like something unseen had exhaled. The spirits hadn't shown themselves, but she could feel them all the same—pressing, listening, waiting.

Because if Vivienne could almost believe, then maybe she was part of this too.

Unspoken

It started with Mara and Jacob.

The cafeteria had emptied but for a few stragglers trading chips and half-hearted jokes. Brynlee sat across from them at the Williams table, tray untouched, a knot tightening in her stomach with every second they didn't speak.

Mara's braid was frayed, fingers working the end like a nervous tic. Jacob sat rigid, arms folded, jaw locked around something he wasn't ready to say.

Finally, Mara's eyes lifted, red-rimmed from a night she hadn't slept. "Why didn't you tell us?"

The words cracked in the middle, softer than anger, sharper than a plea.

Brynlee's throat went dry. "Tell you what?"

"Don't," Jacob cut in. His voice had weight. "You saw her. At the mall. You've been carrying it since then." His gaze flicked to her sleeve, to the way she kept rubbing her wrist. "We pray with you. We sit with you. And you couldn't—" His voice caught. "You didn't trust us with that?"

The cafeteria buzzed somewhere far away. Brynlee opened her mouth, closed it again. How could she explain that telling the wrong people wasn't safe? That the Spirits' rules weren't made for sharing? That silence wasn't betrayal—it was survival?

Mara leaned forward, tears bright but not falling. "We're your friends. You let us eat beside you every day. We'd have believed you."

Would they? The doubt scraped. Even Harper hadn't.

The thought summoned her before Brynlee could brace. Harper's bracelets jingled against the table as she dropped into the seat beside her, sliding her tray down like it belonged there. Copper curls frizzed around her face, eyes wide and determined.

You should've told me first," Harper said, no preamble. "You always told me first. I thought that meant something.

Brynlee's chest cinched. "Harper—"

"No." Harper's voice climbed, then wavered. "Do you get what this did? You let everyone else believe before you let me. You let me—" She broke off, shaking her head. "You made me the one who didn't believe. You broke us, Bryn. Not because you saw her. Because you didn't trust me to carry it with you."

Silence pressed between them, thicker than shouting.

Harper's eyes shone, but she didn't wipe them. "Every memory I have is with you. Every stupid laugh, every night I thought I wasn't alone in this world—it's you. And you're telling me I'm not worth the truth?"

Her bracelets clattered against the table as she stood. "I thought we were unbreakable."

Brynlee reached for words—any words—but they stuck, jagged in her throat. Because Harper was right. She hadn't believed. And that fracture couldn't be sealed, not even if Brynlee begged.

Mara wiped her cheeks with the heel of her hand. Jacob looked away first, jaw tight.

The bell rang. Chairs scraped. The cafeteria emptied again.

Brynlee stayed still in the echo, Harper's words etched into her ribs. Even the silence had shape now—and it looked like her. *You made me the one who didn't believe.*

The Spirits didn't need to mark her this time. The wound was already there.

Shadows Move

Sleep didn't last.

Brynlee lay flat on her back, breath steady, as if pretending for an audience—but the dark pulled her under crooked. Not the soft dark. Not the kind that meant rest. This one had teeth.

She opened her eyes into a room that wasn't hers. Concrete walls, gray paint flaking in sheets. A single bulb swung from the ceiling, buzzing, light stuttering like a dying heart.

And Lydia.

She sat hunched on a low cot, knees drawn to her chest. Her hair hung dull around her face, strands clinging where sweat had dried. Wrists chafed red from rope that had been tied and retied too many times. She stared at the floor like she'd forgotten the ceiling existed.

Two men moved in the corner, voices bent low. Their faces blurred like smeared paint, but their words snapped sharp.

"Too long."

"Heat's on."

"Move her tonight."

One dragged a duffel bag across the floor; the zipper's rasp knifed through the air. The other checked the window bars, fingers testing each weld. "No mistakes. Next stop, she's gone."

Brynlee lurched forward. Her hands hit the floor, but no sound followed. Her breath scraped loud in her own chest, but the men didn't hear.

She tried Lydia's name. It tore her throat raw and left her mouth empty. Silence swallowed it whole.

The Spirits didn't appear, but their fingerprints pressed everywhere: the buzzing bulb, the ropes that tightened, the men's words like verdicts. *Gone.*

Lydia shifted then—slow, aching, her head lifting just enough. Her eyes caught the bulb's sputtering light. Not hope. Not even fear. Just the last filament of fight stretched thin.

Their gazes locked.

Brynlee's throat closed. Her pulse hammered: *She knows I'm here. She knows.*

One man slung the duffel bag over his shoulder. The other turned toward Lydia, hand reaching, shadow spilling across her small frame.

"No!" Brynlee lunged—but the floor cracked open like ice, black water rushing up to swallow her.

The air shuddered once, like lungs exhaling. The bulb flickered out.

She hit her bed hard enough to rattle the frame. Sheets twisted tight around her legs. Sweat slicked her skin, hair stuck to her face. Her chest heaved, lungs dragging air that didn't feel real enough.

The digital clock bled 3:12 a.m. Red, accusing.

Move her tonight.

The words clanged like chains in her skull. She sat up, palms over her mouth to keep the sound in. If the police only knew. If anyone only knew. But the message had already found her.

Her phone buzzed on the nightstand. Blank screen. No caller. No text. Just one line, already typed into the notes app she hadn't opened:

You have hours.

Surrender

The heater hummed. The clock blinked. The house slept—but not her.

Her body didn't.

It started in her wrist—white-hot, twisting, like someone grinding bone in their fist. She cried out, clutching it, but the pain spread, bruises blossoming invisible up her arm, crawling into her ribs. Each breath cut jagged, like glass.

"Stop," she whispered.

The house obeyed—too much.

The hum cut out. The pipes stopped ticking. Even her own pulse vanished. The silence pressed in, thick as concrete. She opened her mouth, tried to scream—her throat moved, but nothing came.

Her reflection stared from the window — except it didn't blink. The eyes slid away. The lips stayed shut. Behind the glass, photos curled black: Harper's bracelets, Mara's braid, Jacob's crooked half-smile. All erased, burned to ash.

"No," she croaked, but her voice was nothing here.

Her body doubled when her ribs cinched tighter, like iron bands squeezing. Pain arced down her spine, heavy, endless. Her legs turned to stone. Her jaw locked until her teeth ached.

The window reflection blinked. And suddenly she wasn't in her room anymore.

She saw Harper laughing—louder, brighter—at someone else's jokes.

Mara and Jacob bowed their heads over dinner, lips moving, prayer spilling—but her name wasn't there.

Her parents at the table, two plates, two chairs, no empty seat waiting. Her father's laugh sounded lighter without her. Her mother's face easier, not strained.

The school hallway passed in a blur—lockers slammed, kids shouted, and her seat in homeroom sat empty. No one noticed.

The news played, Lydia's picture lingering on screen. The anchor's voice carried one word: *unidentified*. Without Brynlee, there had been no mall, no photo, no hope. Just another girl lost.

Her chest convulsed. She clawed her arm, dug her nails deep, scratched her name into her skin—letters crooked, bleeding. The blood spelled it louder than sound ever could.

Proof she was still here.

But the marks vanished. Skin smoothed blank. Her name slid out of her ears, out of her mouth, out of memory.

"Say it," the silence urged. It wore Harper's voice. Then Mara's. Then her father's. Then her own. "Say what you already know."

She shook her head hard, tears hot, ugly. Her body shook so violently the mattress rattled. Her scream tore up her throat but broke before it hit the air.

"You belong to us."

The words echoed back in her own voice, slowed and distorted until it didn't sound human.

Her ribs screamed. Her body folded smaller. Her forehead pressed to her knees. Her nails dug deep into her palms until blood slicked the sheets.

"Fine." The word broke, useless, already too soft.

The silence leaned closer. Waiting.

Her chest heaved once. Twice.

"TAKE ME!" The scream ripped her throat raw."

"I'M YOURS!"

The world buckled. The photos turned blank. Her reflection turned away forever. Her parents' voices cut out. Lydia's image winked to black.

Everything snapped shut.

Silence hit absolute. Crushing. Final.

The room spun once—then black poured in and swallowed her whole.

Wake

She surfaced hard, like breaking through ice—breath catching, ribs refusing the air. Ceiling. Fan blade unmoving. Blind slats leaking gray morning. The heater's low hum stitched the room together in a way that felt almost obscene after the silence that had crushed her. She lay very still, pulse hammering against the inside of her mouth, waiting for the next blow. Nothing came. Her wrist throbbed with heat beneath the skin; her ribs ached in a tight, mean ring. Her throat burned raw. The room smelled like sweat and dust and the lemon cleaner her mom used on Saturdays. Ordinary. Wrong.

Memory poured back in a rush that made her curl. She'd said it. The words had torn out of her like something dead leaving. Take me. I'm yours. The world had gone black the way doors slam. For a nauseous beat she couldn't tell if she was still inside the black and this house was the trick.

She shoved the heel of her hand into her sternum until pain sharpened and held. She sat up. Sheets twisted tight around her calves. Fingernails had carved crescents into her palms; the half-moons stung when she uncurled her hands. She pulled her sleeve up. Skin bare. No welts. No new bruises where they should have been if the night belonged to the laws of gravity and bone. The ache lived anyway, a memory in the muscle. Her voice came out wrecked: 'No.' One syllable, splintered and hers.

It hit then—not relief, not exactly. Fury, clear as ice water. If they could make her believe she'd given up, if they needed her to think she was already theirs to keep her leaning their way, then they were not omnipotent. They needed her moving. They needed her hungry. They needed her to be the hand that turns the key. They'd shown her what the world looked like without her in it because fear is a leash. They'd jerked it hard. She felt the burn around her throat. She put a finger under it and pushed.

"You don't get me," she said to the quiet, voice ragged and steadying as it went. No echo came back in her own mouth the wrong way. No light flickered. The mirror didn't lag. The window threw back her face—the real one, swollen-eyed, hair stuck to her cheek, human. She held her own gaze until the part of her that expected the reflection to turn away gave up and shut its mouth.

The clock bled 5:42. Hours. The word from the screen in the middle of the night hummed in her bones like current. Lydia on a low cot under a buzzing bulb. The slosh of water on concrete. Flaking paint gray as newsprint. Bars across a window a man tested with his fingers like a habit. A duffel rasping open. Move her tonight. Once she was gone she was absence, they'd said, and absence has no doors.

Her parents shifted down the hall—a cough, a toilet tank glug, two bodies re-stitching morning. Her brain wanted to hand the weight over just to stop carrying it. The picture rose—her dad's jaw tight, his eyes trying to read a language he used to know; her mom making lists until the paper wore through. They could flood the house with cameras and promises, and it wouldn't matter. Kept safe wasn't safety. She needed open doors, not locks.

She swung her legs over the side of the bed and put her feet flat on the cold. The shock steadied her further than breathing exercises ever had.

She dragged her backpack onto the bed and laid everything out on top like she was building a body: phone; charger brick; the cheap flashlight from the junk drawer; hoodie balled small; detective's card, numbers by heart and still she wanted the weight of the cardstock; a black marker; a folded page from her notebook where she'd sketched the dent in the rear panel of the van and the crease near the plate, the left hinge scored, the crescent of worn paint; and a new page, clean.

She wrote without thinking: **Concrete wet. Flaking gray. Single bare bulb buzz. Bars—old welds. Chemical mildew. Two voices: one smoker rasp, one slouch low. Duffel. Hours.** Under that she drew a crude window and hashed it, then wrote **windows barred = ground-floor or basement with window well?** She added **where does concrete sweat?** and **near water line / drainage / old warehouse with sump** and **bus route to Depot, rail spur, river district** and, finally, **tell Kearns what's useful, not why.** The rule slid into place like a bolt. Tell the machine built for catching monsters. Do not feed names of people you love into its teeth. Do not tell the ghosts what you plan.

Her throat ached too much to risk a call now; she pictured the first word snagging and her mom on the other side of her door asking if she was okay and the plan collapsing under concern. She thumbed open messages and typed to Kearns: **Remembered details about the van damage & environment—think they're prep to move. Need to share fast. Please text back when you're up.** She stared at the sentence until it felt like a real thing in the world, then hit send. The bubble hovered. Delivered.

She pulled the marker cap with her teeth and wrote on the inside of her wrist, just at the pale place the welts liked: **I belong to me.** The letters bled into skin; the smell of solvent scraped her nose. She pressed her thumb across the words until the oils blurred it slightly, proof she wasn't glass. She wrote again, higher on her forearm, Lydia's name and under it **tonight.** Harsh. Plain.

The house creaked the way houses do in winter. She dressed quiet: worn jeans, dark T-shirt, hoodie, the shoes that didn't squeak on tile. She slid her coat to the end of the bed where her mom wouldn't notice it missing if she came in to do her morning hovering. Phone into back pocket, charger and flashlight into the inner pouch. The detective's card she tucked into the flat zip that pressed against her ribs when she wore the backpack; she wanted to feel it when she breathed.

She paused with her hand on the light. *Surrender,* the chapter they'd tried to write for her, sat heavy in her chest. She let herself feel it all the way—the shame of it, the way the words had torn her throat, the clean cold of the silence after. If they ever clawed at her again with *you already belong to us,* she would hold this feeling up like a mirror and watch them choke on it.

Her throat still burned with the echo: *I'm yours.* She pressed her hand over her chest, leaned into the sting, and answered it aloud, sharp as a blade across stone:

"You were wrong. I'm not yours."

The clock ticked loud in the silence.

Hours. That was all she had. Hours before Lydia was gone. Hours before the countdown the Spirits had started hit zero.

And this time, she wasn't surrendering.

The house hummed again, unaware the girl inside it wasn't sleeping anymore.

Thin Hours

Her phone buzzed before sunrise turned the snow from blue to gray. *Call in ten*, Kearns had written, and ten arrived like a verdict. She answered on the first vibration, voice sandpaper. He didn't waste time on comfort; his voice already belonged to the case. "Tell me what you've got."

She gave him only what a report could hold. Chemical mildew, concrete sweating, a single bulb that buzzed high—old ballast or cheap fixture—bars with soft welds, a duffel dragged across sealed floor, two voices: one torn up by cigarettes, one lazy-low like he slouched even when he stood. "They said *tonight*. It felt like last-minute, like heat on them." Plate and panel damage he already had. She didn't say how she knew, only that she did.

"River district fits the profile," he said. "Old warehouse lines, basement window wells, storm runoff. We've got a list. I want you to come in."

"My parents—" The word snagged, a skitter in her throat. "School. I'll meet you after last bell."

He didn't like it. She could hear him think in the pause. "Share your location with your parents and with me. You go nowhere alone."

"Okay," she lied, because *kept safe* wasn't safety, because *hours* had already fallen to less, because if she waited she'd be watching a news crawl with *unidentified* where a name should be. She ended the call with the numbers in her head and the plan she could live with under her tongue: give him what he can use; move where he can't yet.

Downstairs, her mom had eggs on the pan and worry in her mouth. Dad had the doorbell cam up on his phone like it could replace a hand on her shoulder. "We'll drive you," he said, like the rules were love. "Straight there, straight back."

"Please," her mom added, and the word was softer than the food she pushed toward Brynlee.

"Fine." She ate because it let them unclench. The marker ink on her wrist—**I belong to me**—hid inside her sleeve, warm against the pulse that kept insisting she was still here. Lydia's name written higher burned like a brand. She let Dad turn the locks twice, let Mom tug her scarf straight, let the front door close her between them and the cold. She held both of their eyes at the curb and told them she loved them, then slid out at the Ashwood drop-off with the lie of routine zipped around her like a coat.

She lasted one period. Krantz's voice came thin over the intercom about *respecting privacy; rumors harm families*, and half the class looked, and the other half didn't, and the clock moved like it was chewing molasses. At second bell she was a shadow in the back stairs, a hood up, a door that didn't catch all the way on a hinge the building had stopped caring for in 2004. Outside, the air bit like a clean knife. The bus shelter at the corner stank of salt and old cigarettes. She bought a day pass with hands that didn't shake and chose the route that cut south and then east, toward the spine of warehouses and the river's iron-smell breath.

On the bus she sat where she could see the driver and the doors, and her reflection warped in the scratched plexiglass petition. She kept her head down and her eyes up and read her notes again until they weren't notes but a map the city had given her for free: flaking gray paint, a buzzing bulb you can hear above a bad heater, bars that live closer to dirt because the windows sit low, concrete that sweats when the river air presses through it. Every turn redrew the vision over asphalt. By stop eight the snow wore a black crust along the curb and the buildings turned from retail to storage to something less honest. She got off where the street names lost their trees and started being numbers and men unloaded pallets in coats that weren't thick enough while a forklift beeped in a way that made anger in her jaw.

She walked like she belonged to that morning. The river pulled left. She followed storm grates and the smell of wet dust. Three blocks down, a building hunched into itself—old brick skinned with gray paint that peeled in thumbnail curls, a loading bay with a roll-up door, a row of window wells cut into the sidewalk, bars welded in before someone stopped caring about code.

She stood above the nearest well and let the smell hit: damp, old bleach, a fat mildew that lives in walls, the way concrete breathes when it's near water. The glass below wore a skin of condensation; a drop fattened and slid and left a clean snail trail through the film. Somewhere under her the faintest high whine trembled—a ballast starving or a coil burning down.

Her phone camera made a soft insect click as she took the shot and then another: bars, weld bloom, condensation on glass, a tire scuff at an angle that suggested a van had nosed up to the bay without loving the fit. She crouched fast, fingers to the scuff, salt pressed into rubber grit. Fresh. Not hours old. Less.

A door somewhere inside banged low. A voice said something she couldn't catch and then came closer, flatted by concrete into a smear. Cigarette rasp. The smell hit a second later—menthol and old clothes. She slid behind a dumpster that leaned out of the alley like a drunk and ground her back into cold metal until she felt like she could pass for shadow.

The roll-up groaned. The van's nose edged into view—white under a rash of road grime, the panel dent exactly where it should be, the crease near the plate that made her hand start to shake just thinking about how close she'd been to getting this wrong. The engine coughed and caught and settled into a low animal sound that vibrated the metal against her spine.

She texted Kearns one-handed, thumb rattling against glass: *Possible location—Pierce & 11th. Window wells barred, smell matches, ballast whine audible, fresh tire scuffs, white van at bay with left-panel dent.*

Three dots. I'm in the alley behind a dumpster. Not moving. She added *Now* because that's what the clock said and hit send.

Footsteps thudded two floors below. Another voice answered, lazier, younger, like sleep was a thing he wore even when he worked. A zipper rasped; fabric dragged. The duffel in her head. Through the well glass a shadow crossed and disappeared.

A gull screamed above the river, thin and too clean for this street. The engine idled, shuddering in her bones. She could feel the minutes falling away like coins down a grate. She could picture Lydia's knees pulled to her chest under a bad bulb. She could picture the black that comes after the last picture if you blink too long.

Her phone buzzed. Kearns: *Units en-route. Do. Not. Approach.* And a second: *Stay hidden. Keep eyes.* Her breath fogged her bare knuckles white. She tucked her hands into her sleeves to stop the stupid instinct to reach, to act now, to yank a cable or smash a headlight with the wrong adrenaline. *Tell the right people. Don't feed names to the dark.* Fine. But if the dark moved, she would move with it.

Voices flared again inside, closer now. "Hold her." Boots scuffed. Something knocked—wood on concrete, hollow.

The van's brake lights bloomed red against dirty white. The roll-up climbed another foot. A strap buckle clinked. She could almost count the seconds in that clink.

Hours had become *minutes.* She pressed her palm flat against the ink under her sleeve and repeated in her head what she'd said to the quiet at dawn. *You were wrong. I'm not yours.* The van's idle deepened. The door banged open all the way.

She leaned closer to the dumpster's edge until the metal bit her shoulder and held herself there at the exact point where falling forward would mean showing her face. A shadow crossed the bay—broad, then narrow, then something small between them, moving like breath under weight. Her phone buzzed in her pocket again; she didn't look. Every part of her had turned into a clock hand aimed at zero.

Zero Point

The van's engine rattled low, the sound swallowing the alley like an animal guarding its meal. Brynlee's breath clouded once, twice, and she forced herself still. If she twitched, if she shifted weight, metal would scrape concrete, and the men would know.

The roll-up clanged the rest of the way up. A man stepped out—broad-shouldered, jacket shiny at the elbows, smoke curling from his mouth. Behind him, another man, thinner, a hoodie hood cinched tight. Between them—movement. A girl's shape, stumbling, pulled forward by the elbow.

Brynlee's fingernails dug half-moons into her palms. Every nerve screamed to run, to shout Lydia's name, to claw them apart with her hands. But her sleeve pressed tight against her wrist, the marker words burning underneath: **I belong to me.** She couldn't move. Not yet.

They shoved the girl into the van. She tripped on the bumper, caught herself on her palms. The flash of raw skin— scraped, angry red—seared into Brynlee's vision. Lydia folded herself small the second she was inside, knees tucked to chest, as if she could make her body disappear.

Her phone buzzed in her pocket. She slid it out, thumb shaking: *They're moving her. Now. Van leaving. White. Plate matches.*

She hit send without looking at the screen, eyes fixed on the back of the van like she could anchor it with sheer hate.

"Shut it," the broad one muttered. The roll-up clattered down, half-caught on its track, juddered, then settled. Brake lights flared, then dimmed. Reverse beeped once, a short pulse.

The van rolled back into the street.

Brynlee's heart tore against her ribs. *This is it. She's gone. She's gone if you don't—*

She lunged out of the shadow before thought could catch her. The cold hit her throat, burning, as she snapped the photo—headlights, plate, the dented panel—then saw the flash bloom and knew she'd doomed herself.

The broad man's head jerked toward the light. His eyes caught hers. For one beat too long, he saw her.

Brynlee froze, the air sucked out of her lungs.

The van lurched forward. Tires screamed on salt. It tore down the street, fishtailing once before it straightened, the sound of the engine clawing out into distance.

The alley fell empty; Brynlee's pulse slammed back in, hot and frantic. She staggered against the dumpster, chest burning like it would split.

Her phone buzzed again: *Units less than three minutes. Stay put.*

Three minutes. But the van already had a head start.

Her reflection wavered in the dirty metal of the dumpster—eyes wild, face ghost-pale, lips moving without sound. For a split second she thought it wasn't her at all, that Rejection had found her even here. Then the image steadied. Just her.

She stared at herself. "Not without her."

The Pursuit

Sirens split the air before her pulse could steady. Red and blue stuttered against wet brick, smeared across the gray slush. Tires chewed salt. The river stank of iron and thaw, the wind carrying it up the alley like a warning.

She pressed back into the dumpster's shadow, breath knotted high, as the cruiser swung in hard. Doors slammed. Radios spat coordinates— "white van, dented left panel, headed south along Pierce."

She couldn't move. Couldn't blink. Lydia's scraped palms burned behind her eyelids, the way she folded herself small, knees tucked like she could make her body disappear. That image throbbed harder than the lights, harder than the sirens.

"Stay here," one officer barked without even looking her way, already sprinting back to the car. The cruiser lunged. Lights ricocheted across warehouse glass. The howl of pursuit tore after the van.

Brynlee staggered out from behind the dumpster, her legs stiff, the alley yawning empty where Lydia had just been. She couldn't breathe right. Each inhale clawed. The wet pavement reflected her face wrong, warped thin, as if the street wanted to erase her too. For a second she thought Rejection had caught her again—until the sirens snapped her back.

The van was out there, engine grinding south, minutes ahead. *Three minutes had turned to one. Now maybe less.*

Her phone buzzed. Kearns: *We have eyes. Don't move.*

Another ping a breath later: *You did good. Stay put.*

Stay put. The words cut sharper than the cold. *While Lydia's gone. While she's folded small in the dark.* Her nails dug into her sleeve, straight into the marker letters on her wrist. **I belong to me.**

The river air pushed damp into her lungs. She started walking anyway—out of the alley, toward Pierce, boots sinking in slush that sucked like the city wanted her ankles.

Traffic snarled at the intersection. People craned necks at the sirens flashing deeper into the grid. A woman clutched her kid's hand tighter, eyes flicking past Brynlee without seeing. She kept walking, every step a fight against the instinct to sprint, to scream Lydia's name into the thaw.

Up ahead, the wail fractured—one siren swerving left, another echoing right. Too many streets, too many places for the van to vanish. Brynlee's chest locked.

She reached the curb, breath tearing, and saw it—just for a blink—white van fishtailing through an intersection, dented panel flashing red-blue in the lights before it vanished behind warehouses.

Her throat closed around the scream she wanted. She gripped her phone so hard her knuckles whitened. The reflection in the dark screen showed her wide-eyed, unblinking, every part of her face shouting one truth:

She was the only one who'd seen Lydia alive. If the van disappeared tonight, so did Lydia.

Street-Level

Sirens forked, thinned—teeth on the wind.

Red and blue smeared across wet brick, then slid off and were gone. Slush chewed the gutters. The river breathed iron and thaw. Brynlee stepped out of the alley like the ground might punch back.

Traffic on Pierce stuttered, heads craning at the lights knifing south, then east, then nowhere. A bus hissed past and threw gray water at her shins; cold climbed through denim and took her calves hostage. She didn't flinch. The sound in her head was still the van—low, animal—paired with the one thing she couldn't scrape off her eyes: scraped palms catching the bumper, knees folding small as if a body could save itself by becoming less.

Her phone vibrated in her fist. *Kearns: Units crossing the bridge. Airship not up. Stay put.*

Another beat. *We've got intersections flagged. We're on them.*

On them wasn't *with* them. On them wasn't *inside.* The street smelled like wet dust and brake pads; her throat tasted like pennies. The words she'd carved under her sleeve pulsed against her wrist—**I belong to me**—but the letters didn't stop her from seeing how easy it would be to become air.

She drifted to the corner and stopped on the curb because stopping was the only thing that felt like choosing. A horn spat at her when her toe hovered over paint; a man rolled down his window and said something she didn't catch, his mouth a hard line that didn't know how close it was to breaking skin. She stepped back. The slush at her heels made a sucking sound like the street wanted to keep her.

Don't move. The text boxed her in. *Keep eyes.* The other one pulled her forward by the face. She compromised: chin up, boots planted, mind running, cataloging. White panel vans ghosted past in her skull; this city had a thousand. She could list the dent, the crease, the way the panel waved under light. She could list the smell—old bleach, wet concrete. She could list the voices—rasp and lazy. Nothing on the corner asked for a list. Everything asked for faith.

A siren yelped somewhere to her left and died. She turned her head too fast, and the world lagged a second behind, like glass catching. The window of the locksmith across the street threw back her reflection; for a breath it didn't move. The mouth stayed shut while hers opened. The eyes slid past her like she wasn't worth looking at. She lifted her hand on instinct to touch the glass; inside, nobody glanced up. The seconds stretched thin. Then the pane caught up and gave her back herself, delayed, like a bad feed. Her stomach tipped. Rejection didn't need a body to stand next to her. It only needed a surface.

"Not now," she said, and the words hit the wet air and broke.

Footsteps scuffed behind her; she turned so fast her neck popped. Just a guy hauling a dolly stacked with boxes, hoodie up, head down, the tired trudge of someone whose day didn't care about vans. He passed within arm's reach and didn't tuck his chin or square his shoulders or look at her at all. Loneliness wasn't an empty street. It was this—bodies within breathing distance that never turned.

Her phone buzzed again. *Kearns: Unit at 9th lost visual at the overpass. Checking cameras.*

Another line: *Stay at Pierce. I'm sending a car to you.*

The word *lost* carved something low. She typed without thinking: *They put her in quiet—she folds small, scraped palms.*

Three dots. *Copy. Keep your head down.*

A gull screamed above the river like it had opinions, then went silent. The wind took a new direction and dragged the smell of menthol through the block. Her skin prickled. Somewhere, a door banged deep. Somewhere else, a laugh snapped short. She tried to fit the sounds into a map. The city wouldn't hold still.

A set of headlights turned the corner too fast. A cruiser. It braked hard in the crosswalk and shouldered itself half onto the curb, lightbar spitting. The officer in the passenger seat motioned her back with two fingers as he talked into his radio without breathing between words. The driver looked at her long enough to see all the way through; his gaze landed on the mud at her hem and the way her jaw had locked and moved on. Nobody asked if she was okay. Good. Okay didn't matter.

The radio chatter leaking from the open window wasn't television clean. It came garbled, and she had to assemble it like a puzzle with pieces missing unit at the bridge, unit at the spur, a white van that wasn't the van, a plate that almost matched until it didn't. Snowmelt dripped steady from the bay door she'd watched slide shut—count, count, count—and landed in a dark flower on the concrete. She counted anyway because numbers didn't make promises they couldn't keep. *One, two, three, four...* If she hit sixty, she'd start again. If she hit sixty enough, the sirens would bend back.

Pain slid in under her sleeve the way cold does—no knock, no hello. Not a mark this time, not yet. A tightening around bone. A reminder. *Stay with us and you won't have to stand here alone.* She pressed her palm hard over the ink until the skin ached and repeated in her head what she'd said at dawn: *You were wrong. I'm not yours.* The ache didn't leave. It moved over to make room.

The cruiser lurched out. Another took its place. The strobe rolled slow and sick across her knuckles. A woman with a stroller paused at the corner, the wheels gummed with slush and stared at the lights without getting closer. The baby's face was buried in a blanket, only a pink hat visible—small, undeniable. Brynlee's throat closed without warning, and she swallowed it down because this was not the time to cry over hats.

Her phone vibrated hard enough to jump in her hand. *Kearns: Possible stop at Riverbend and 14th. No confirmation.*

Her thumb hovered. She typed *I'm coming* and erased it and wrote *I can see the river* and erased that too and finally sent nothing.

The wind swung again, colder now, needling through her hoodie. The sky had that March color—white with the blue wrung out of it, like someone had soaked the day and hung it up wrong. She rubbed her hands together and felt grit grind into her lifelines. When she looked down, the black marker had smudged where her sleeve had dragged it. **I belon—** The last letters blurred into a bruise of ink. She pulled the cuff lower as if that could fix anything.

A memory knifed in the moment her voice broke on *I'm yours*, the way the world went out like a switch. She let it in, all the way. The shame, the cold, the absolute. Then she flipped it over, the way you turn a blade in your hand, so it faces the thing in the dark. *You needed that. You needed me afraid enough to obey.* The thought steadied her knees.

Across the street, a security camera on a rusted bracket blinked its red LED at nothing. She lifted her phone and snapped it anyway. If Kearns needed footage, he'd know which door to bang on. If the men circled back, the timestamp would know she hadn't left.

A white smear of exhaust clung to the warehouse wall, trembling in the cold. The taillights had left their echo in a puddle near the curb, two red ghosts rippling, the water smoothing them flat. Gone wasn't abstract. Gone had shape, color, heat already fading in the air.

The sirens forked and thinned. She stacked the minutes at her feet like bricks—*one, two, three, four*—until the pile felt high enough to hide behind. Cold had crawled into her calves, numbing them through denim. Slush gripped her boots like the street wanted to root her there. Her fingers had gone stiff around the phone, plastic biting bone, every vibration a shock she almost dropped. Her pulse thudded out of sync with the sirens, making her body believe the city itself was skipping.

The wind swung, dragging the faintest coil of siren back around the block, thin as thread. She closed her eyes, forced breath all the way down, and pulled that sound taut through her fists.

I'm here. Still here. If you have to come through something, come through me.

The Fallout Expands

By morning the city had teeth.

Lydia's face burned from every screen—phones propped against water bottles on desks, TVs in diners, even the marquee outside the gas station two blocks from Ashwood. The photo the anchors used was the same one Brynlee had seen over and over: a little too bright, Lydia's hair tucked wrong behind one ear, eyes wide enough that the years between then and now felt like a theft.

At school, whispers braided down the halls. *That's her. She saw her.* Brynlee didn't need names to know they meant her. Heads tilted, eyes caught and skittered away. A group of sophomores she didn't even know stopped mid-conversation when she passed, their silence heavier than if they'd shouted.

Her locker had never been so loud. Metal clanged under her hands; every hinge shrieked back. She kept her head down, but it didn't help. Her phone buzzed so hard against her thigh she thought it might bruise. Messages stacked, unread: *is it true? did you really see her?* Screenshots of news alerts, classmates demanding answers she couldn't give.

By third period, Harper had cornered her in the bathroom. "Why didn't you tell me?" The words cracked like she'd been holding them since the night of the vigil. Harper's breath hitched.

Her bracelets clattered as she pulled her arms tight against her chest. "You could've trusted me. I wouldn't have—" She bit it off.

The silence after stung worse than the accusation. For one second, memory twisted cruel: Harper in seventh grade, being the first one Brynlee told about a crush and swearing she'd never tell; Harper holding her hand under the bleachers after she bombed a test, laughing until Brynlee did too. Harper was always the one she told first. Until now.

Brynlee didn't answer. Her reflection in the mirror looked worse than silence—paler, eyes ringed with nights she hadn't slept, her sleeve pulled down like it might still hide the sting no one else could see.

By lunch she didn't even try to sit at the Williams' table. Mara and Jacob had their heads bent together, voices low, eyes darting toward her once, then away again. It wasn't cruelty. It was distance, stretched so tight it could snap.

And then the call came.

Her teacher appeared with the brittle look adults wore when they didn't want to spook anyone.

"Brynlee? Main office."

Her stomach dropped. This was what she'd wanted before—proof someone finally believed her—but the validation tasted like exposure. The whole school's eyes on her back as she stood felt less like vindication and more like a noose pulling tight.

Her parents were waiting, coats still damp from sleet, her mother's eyes wide like she'd run all the way here, her father's jaw locked so tight it could've cut glass.

The detective who'd texted her before stood with them. His badge flashed, but his eyes didn't. He flipped through a folder she couldn't see, set a small recorder on the counter, and left it switched off. His voice was even. "We'll need you at the station. Just a few clarifications."

Her mother's hand landed on her shoulder, warm, too warm. "Why didn't you tell us?" she whispered, and the hurt in it made Brynlee's chest ache worse than the welts ever had.

The detective was already moving. Her father nodded at him, then looked back at Brynlee with an expression she couldn't translate, not yet—something between fury and pride and fear. Like he was reading a language he hadn't practiced in years.

Brynlee followed them out, each step loud enough to sound like a verdict, pressing heavier and heavier on her chest. She couldn't tell if she was walking toward justice. Or her own sentencing.

Station Lights

The ceiling buzzed. Fluorescent light bled across metal, across her hands folded tight enough to blanch the knuckles. The room smelled like burned coffee and wet wool, every inch too loud.

Her mother sat to her left, posture perfect, both hands clasped around a Styrofoam cup she hadn't drunk from. Her father had claimed the seat to Brynlee's right, legs braced like he could shield her with his knees alone. His hand landed heavy on her shoulder—strong, steady. Protective. Restraining. The weight of it a message she couldn't translate. Both at once. She couldn't tell if it anchored her or pinned her down.

Kearns leaned on the other side of the table, badge catching the light, pen ticking against a notepad. "You said you saw her." No preamble, no softening. He adjusted his pen, the click too loud. His eyes narrowed, not cruel, but surgical. "Walk me through it again."

Her throat tried to close. She stared at the seam in the table, counting breaths. "At the mall. Weeks ago. I saw her. Lydia. She was—" The word jammed. Running. Taken. Gone. "She was with two men. They pulled her. I tried to—" She cut herself off. Tried to stop them. Tried to shout. Tried to matter.

Kearns waited. Pen stilled. Then started tapping again—too long this time, the rhythm uneven, a tell he didn't seem to notice. When the light above them flickered, his eyes flicked up and back down too fast, like he'd rather not have seen it at all.

Her mother's fingers tightened around the cup until it crumpled, Styrofoam squealing. "Brynlee," she whispered, low, raw. "Why didn't you come to us?"

The shame burned hotter than the overhead light. She pressed her hands flat against the table so no one could see them shake.

Kearns shifted. "You also took a photo." He slid a printout across the table. Blurred corner of the van. License plate caught in a flash. "How'd you think to catch this?"

Her father's gaze cut sideways, sharp, waiting.

"I don't know," she lied. The memory of her phone in her hand, the Spirits' hiss in her ear—*see, show, prove*—throbbed too close.

Kearns tapped the photo. "This helped. It puts pressure in the right place. But you understand, Brynlee, this makes you part of the case now. If those men know you saw them—"

"They do." The words slipped before she could stop them. Her chest squeezed. "They saw me."

Her mother sucked in a breath. Her father's hand pressed harder against her shoulder, the weight of it an anchor dragging.

Kearns nodded once, jaw tight. "Then we'll put a car outside your house. For now, don't walk alone. Don't post anything. If they make contact—anything at all—you call me first."

The buzzing overhead sharpened, a hitch like a throat clearing. The light flickered once, then steadied. Brynlee's skin prickled. No bruises. No welts. No mark. Just the silence of something watching, satisfied.

She dropped her gaze to the photo. The license plate numbers blurred where the ink bled. Her reflection in the glossy surface lagged again—the same wrongness as the window, the same off-timed mouth. For a breath, she wasn't looking at herself at all, but something using her shape.

Their Satisfaction

The house was too quiet. Not the good kind—no movie murmuring, no mismatched socks on the tile. Just the kind of quiet that pressed its hands flat against her ears until every creak of the furnace rattled her bones.

Her parents hovered like storm fronts—charged, waiting for the wrong word to strike. Her mom moved through the kitchen in restless circuits—opening the fridge, closing it again, rearranging cans that didn't need rearranging. Her dad sat at the table, unread newspaper stretched between his hands, the paper shaking just enough to give him away.

Every so often their eyes slid toward her, and then away, quick, like she'd grown a second face they couldn't read. The detective's words had followed them home, stitched into the walls: *If those men know you saw them—*

Brynlee sat on the couch, sleeves tugged low, the photo burned into the back of her eyes. The reflection that hadn't been hers. The plate numbers that seemed to swim when she looked too long. She kept waiting for the welt to rise, for the bruise to bloom, for her body to mark her again.

Nothing came.

No sting. No heat. No whispered threat in her ear. Only silence.

She should've been relieved. She wasn't. The absence pressed harder than pain ever had, a weight sinking deeper with every breath.

Upstairs, her phone buzzed on her nightstand. She hadn't left it there. She hadn't set a recording to play. The buzz cut off—then her voice spilled down the stairs, warped and wet at the edges, leaking through the walls:

"I'll go to the police. I don't care what you say."

The playback twisted, bled into itself.

"You'll take us to them."

Her mother clattered a dish too hard against the counter. "What was that?"

"Phone," Brynlee said, too fast, too tight. Her throat hurt.

Her father lowered the paper, eyes pinning her. "Then answer it."

She didn't move. Couldn't. The buzzing stopped on its own, leaving the house drowned in silence again.

The Spirits weren't punishing her tonight. They didn't have to. She'd done what they wanted. The silence was their version of approval.

And it was worse than bruises, worse than welts, worse than rejection. Because it felt like she'd agreed to something she hadn't meant to.

Her father's voice broke through, rough at the edges. "Brynlee—look at me."

She lifted her head. He searched her face again, like the language was still there somewhere if he just tried hard enough.

The words rose unbidden in her chest, sour and sharp: *I belong to me.*

But the silence upstairs hummed louder. A reminder: *she wasn't sure anymore.*

The Fallout Continues

Phones lit halls before first bell, more blinding than fluorescents. Every swipe brought Brynlee's name tangled with Lydia's— threads stacked with theories, cropped screenshots of news clips, blurry photos of her walking between classes as if she were already evidence. Someone had made a TikTok splicing Lydia's missing poster over Brynlee's yearbook picture with the caption: *She saw her. She knows.*

Every look in the hall carried weight. Some hungry, like she was holding secrets they wanted. Some hungry. Some suspicious. Some pitying. All of them burned.

By lunch, the whispers had bodies. Two girls at the soda machine fell silent mid-sentence when Brynlee passed. A sophomore she barely knew asked if she'd *really talked to the FBI.* Even Jacob and Mara sat smaller at their table, voices tight, like being seen with her might snap their already-thin safety net.

Her tray clattered when she set it down, the sound cracking the hush around her. Heads turned. She chewed and swallowed without tasting anything, wishing she could shrink small enough to vanish.

Halfway through the period, Mrs. Jamison, the secretary, appeared in the doorway. Her voice wavered with the weight of it: "Brynlee? The office again."

Heat rushed her skin. She could already feel the verdict before she stood.

This time, her parents weren't waiting. The Turners were.

Lydia's mother's face looked carved from grief—hollow cheeks, eyes ringed dark. Her father's posture was straighter, but brittle, like a man bracing for impact. Mrs. Turner reached for her, then stopped halfway, fingers hovering. Her hand trembled in the space between them, close enough that Brynlee could feel the air move. "You saw her," she whispered. The words trembled. "You *saw* our girl."

Brynlee's throat locked. No one had ever said it so plain.

Behind them, near the far wall, Vivienne stood with her parents. The room's hum seemed to still around her—polished, distant, but her gaze was locked on Brynlee, sharp and unreadable. A tether pulled between them, too taut to ignore.

Brynlee swallowed hard. Everyone wanted something. The school wanted her story. The police wanted her memory. The Spirits wanted her obedience. And now the Turners wanted their daughter back.

The weight of it bent her spine until she thought she might snap.

Vivienne tilted her head, just enough for Brynlee to catch. No smile. No pity. Just recognition, cold and absolute, like someone else who knew the language of ghosts.

Collision Glass

The gym didn't smell like sweat tonight. Banners were stripped down, tables draped in white cloth, centerpieces flickering with cheap tea lights. A banner across the stage read: **COMMUNITY THANK-YOU DINNER.**

It was supposed to be about closure. About gratitude. But Brynlee felt every eye tip toward her family as they stepped inside. Her parents leaned close, guiding her with smiles that strained at the corners.

She spotted the Turners near the front. Mrs. Turner sat stiff, eyes rimmed red but not hollow anymore. Mr. Turner's hand rested on hers, still and steady. They looked smaller than Brynlee remembered from news photos, as if grief had pared them down.

Across the room, the LeClairs moved like they belonged to the lights themselves. Mrs. LeClair's laugh rang too bright, her husband pressing hands like checks in envelopes. Vivienne trailed a half-step behind, posture perfect, but her eyes—those caught Brynlee and held.

Then Mrs. LeClair stopped. Her gaze snagged on Mrs. Turner—one heartbeat of hesitation before she crossed the room.

"Marjorie," Mrs. LeClair said softly, hand trembling just enough that Brynlee noticed.

Mrs. Turner rose. For a heartbeat the whole gym seemed to brace, waiting for rejection.

Instead, Mrs. Turner caught her old friend's hand in both of hers. Her voice cracked but held: "You don't know how many times I wished you were there."

Tears burned sudden at Brynlee's eyes. Around the table, people exhaled all at once, the sound like glass unbreaking.

Mr. Turner stood, clasping Mr. LeClair's hand. The two men didn't speak long, but their shoulders eased fractionally. Not forgiveness, not yet. But something that made the air less brittle.

Vivienne's eyes hadn't left Brynlee. The tether between them felt heavier now, sharper. Recognition, and something like relief.

Her dad's hand pressed her shoulder. Protective. Restraining. Both at once. "We don't have to stay long," he murmured.

But Brynlee stayed rooted. Not while Vivienne's gaze pinned hers, and the two families across the room tried, awkwardly, to stitch something broken back together.

The Daughter Left Behind

That night Brynlee slept shallow—dragged under, hauled back like waves. Her room blurred, then slipped—the edges thinning. She knew the taste of it now: the Spirits' grip.

But when the dark folded open, it wasn't her own house.

She stood in the high-lit foyer of the LeClair estate. Marble floors, chandelier dripping gold light. She shouldn't be there. Her feet weren't on anything solid; she knew it.

Vivienne's voice cut the air: sharp, trembling.

"Do you even know what you did to me?"

Her parents froze. Her mother still held a heel in one hand. Her father's phone hovered midair.

Brynlee's pulse stuttered. She didn't move. She wasn't meant to be seen.

Vivienne's words came hard, each one cracking against the chandelier glow. "When Lydia was taken, you buried yourselves in work. You pulled away from everyone. From me. She was gone, and suddenly it felt like I was too."

Her father set his phone down slow. Her mother's lips parted, no sound.

"I was twelve," Vivienne's voice shook now, "and I lost my best friend, my whole world. And I lost my parents too. You thought building the business was strength. But I was already falling."

The words throbbed in Brynlee's chest like they were hers. The Spirits' presence pressed in—silent, watching, like hands braced against her ribs. See, they whispered without sound. *See how it scars.*

Vivienne's voice cracked again: "I don't hate you. I forgive you. But you left me alone when I needed you most. I don't want to disappear while I'm still here."

Her mother crossed the space in two strides, heels clattering, arms wrapping her daughter. Her father's hand touched Vivienne's shoulder, tentative, as if afraid she'd shatter.

The chandelier flickered once—light breaking like breath held too long.

Brynlee staggered back, shaking. The last thing she heard was Vivienne's voice, raw and small: *"I was still here."*

And then the floor gave out.

She jolted awake in her own bed, sweat damp at her hairline, her wrist burning as if she'd been the one to say it.

This time, the Spirits hadn't punished her—they'd shown her truth.

Held Too Close

The kitchen smelled of cinnamon rolls from a tube—over-sweet, heavy in the air. Her mom had woken early to bake, claiming "you've been through enough stress lately, you deserve something warm." Her dad hovered at the table with the paper open but unread, glancing over it every few seconds like she might vanish if he didn't keep eyes on her.

Brynlee sat between them, fork idle, stomach knotted. The night still clung to her—Vivienne's voice, raw and breaking, her words about being left behind. And now here sat her parents, close enough to touch, watching every breath.

"You didn't eat much yesterday," her mom said softly, pushing the plate closer. "Please try. Just one bite."

Her dad folded the paper. "We're proud of you, Bryn. You've done so much more than most kids could handle. He hesitated, paper edges soft in his hands. "But it's time to let us help now. No more secrets. No more trying to carry this alone."

The words should have steadied her. Instead, they pressed down. Protective. Restraining. Both.

If she let them too close, they'd cage her. If she kept them out, she'd shatter. There was no middle.

Her fork scraped porcelain. "I'm not hungry."

Her mom reached across, fingers brushing her sleeve. "You're pale. Maybe you should stay home today. I'll call the school—"

"No." The word shot out too sharp, her own voice startling her. "I'm going."

They blinked, her dad frowning, her mom pulling her hand back like she'd been burned.

The silence rang louder than the clink of dishes.

She wanted to say she loved them. She wanted to say thank you. But the words caught under the weight of last night, Vivienne's confession looping in her skull. *I lost my parents too.*

And all Brynlee could think, trapped between her mother's worry and her father's steady stare, was that being loved this hard pressed the air out of her lungs.

Unspoken Mirrors

Ashwood's halls smelled of pencil shavings and reheated pizza—a Monday smell that should've been ordinary. Brynlee kept her head low, weaving through the current of students, her backpack straps digging into her shoulders. She hadn't slept right since the Spirits dragged her into the LeClairs' foyer.

Vivienne's voice still rang in her head. *I lost my parents too.*

By the time she reached the cafeteria, her chest was already tight. Mara and Jacob were laughing softly over something at their table, but she didn't move toward them. Not yet. She couldn't—not with the weight pressing her ribs. Instead, she slid into a table near the windows. Alone.

Her tray sat untouched. She wasn't sure if she'd forgotten hunger or outgrown it. The fork tapped against the tray's edge until the sound grated her teeth. She tapped the plastic fork against the edge until the rhythm made her teeth ache.

A shadow fell across the table. She looked up. Vivienne.

"Everyone's staring at you," Vivienne said quietly. Her tone wasn't sharp, but it wasn't gentle either. Guarded.

Brynlee almost laughed. "Story of my life lately."

Vivienne slid into the seat across from her without asking. The cafeteria noise dulled—not gone, but muted, like her body only cared about the space between them.

For a minute neither of them spoke. Then Vivienne's eyes flicked to Brynlee's wrist, where she'd been unconsciously rubbing. "Still hurts?" she asked.

Brynlee froze. "What?"

"You flinch like it does," Vivienne said, almost clinical, like she was stating a fact about the weather. Her gaze softened just a fraction. "Whatever it is, you don't have to pretend it isn't there."

Brynlee's breath caught. She wanted to blurt it all—the Spirits, the bruises no one else could see, the way her reflection betrayed her. But Vivienne's expression was unreadable, carved from years of silence. So, she swallowed it.

Instead, she said, "You ever feel like everyone's watching you, but nobody really sees?"

For the first time, something cracked in Vivienne's face. A twitch at her mouth, not quite a smile, not quite pain. "All the time."

Their eyes held. In that moment Brynlee didn't need the Spirits whispering to tell her they weren't strangers, not really.

The bell shrieked overhead, snapping the world back. Chairs scraped, trays clattered. Vivienne stood first, smoothing her sweater like armor.

Before she walked away, she said, almost too quiet: "You're not the only one they notice."

And then she was gone, leaving Brynlee staring at her reflection in the cafeteria window, wondering if Vivienne had seen the same thing she did—the reflection that sometimes looked back wrong.

Ghost Silence

The quiet stretched too long. Brynlee lay on her back, staring at the hairline crack in her ceiling, the fan ticking at its highest speed just to keep her tethered.

Brynlee lay on her back, eyes fixed on the hairline crack across her ceiling. The fan ticked at the highest speed, the sound barely keeping her tethered. She hadn't woken sweating, hadn't jolted from a nightmare in weeks. No bruises, no welts, no warped reflections clawing out of the glass.

At first she called it mercy. Now it felt like abandonment.

The air felt heavy, like it had weight but no warmth. Her phone screen glared pale blue against the dark. Nothing from Mara, nothing from Jacob. Harper's name sat buried under unanswered texts, the ones she still didn't know how to touch.

Are you done with me? The thought pressed so loud she almost whispered it, like they might still hear through the walls.

The mirror on her dresser gave nothing back but her own tired face. No delay. No twitch. Just her.

It should've been a relief. It wasn't. The silence pressed against her ears like cotton stuffed too deep, until she thought she could hear her pulse in her teeth.

If they were finished, what did that mean? That she'd done enough? That Lydia's rescue was all they wanted? Or worse—that she'd been discarded, just like Vivienne had been before her?

She turned her face into the pillow and clawed at the sheets until her knuckles ached.

You don't get to vanish. Not like this.

The house groaned around her—her father clearing his throat in the hall, her mother's footfall pacing between their room and the kitchen. Too close. Too alive. They thought they were keeping her safe, but safety felt like walls closing.

For the first time, she wanted the shadows back. Not because she missed the punishments, but because silence made her wonder if she had imagined all of it. If she had screamed "I'm yours" to nothing. If she had nearly broken herself for a dream that dissolved when the world turned ordinary again.

Her phone buzzed once. She lunged for it.

Only a weather alert: Wind advisory.

The laugh that tore out of her was too sharp, too thin. She slapped the phone face down and lay there, eyes wide, waiting for something—anything—to break the quiet.

The house exhaled—pipes cooling, a shutter shifting—but no voice followed.

Nothing did.

And that was worse than their voices ever had been.

Empty Halls

Ashwood hummed like a beehive half-dead of bees. Fluorescents stuttered, lockers clanged then settled, hand sanitizer stung the air. Brynlee moved through it the way you wade a cold river—careful, numb from the knees down. No texts chirped her pocket. No sting under her sleeve. The Spirits had gone quiet and left her with the noise of everyone else.

Second-period hall pass in her fist, she drifted past the trophy case. Her face floated in the glass between old wins and dust, ordinary, unwarped. For a second she missed the wrongness—at least you knew what to push against when the mirror hated you back.

At the end of the corridor, the twins sat on the radiator under the big window that didn't open right. Jacob talked with his hands, palms nicked, making Mara laugh in that soft, private way she didn't waste on anyone else. Vivienne stood with them, posture straight as always, but leaning in—close enough to be counted, not close enough to be held. She handed Mara a paper napkin without comment when the girl coughed hard, then tucked a loose curl behind her own ear like she hadn't done anything at all. It was nothing. It was everything. It was the little gravity they were building that worked without her.

Brynlee made herself keep walking. If they looked up now, she wouldn't know what to do with her face. If they didn't look up, she'd hear that hollow ring that came after metal slammed shut. The hallway swallowed her footsteps whole.

The cafeteria smelled like reheated pizza and bleach. She chose a window table and pretended to eat until the fork's scrape got on her nerves. Across the room, a freshman dropped a milk, and it burst, white spreading toward sneakers that hopped back too late. Someone clapped like a joke had landed. The sound rolled and died before it reached her.

Harper appeared in the doorway, hair yanked into a high knot, bracelets bright at her wrists. She paused like she'd walked into a room she didn't mean to enter. Their eyes caught and both of them flinched. Harper's gaze slid past in the next breath, not mean—just survival—and she aimed herself at a table of theater kids she didn't even like. They made room. Brynlee watched the empty space Harper didn't cross and felt it press into her ribs.

Sixth period, a teacher asked for group work and desks scraped into islands that didn't invite her. She bent over the worksheet and wrote answers she didn't believe, pen digging grooves into paper until the tip threatened to tear through. At the bell, she took longer than necessary to cap the pen and line the edges of her notebook with the desk, as if straight corners could hold a day together.

After school, the air outside had that late-March bite, wet and metallic. The bus yard yowled. She walked home because her legs needed a job and because the house would be loud with love when she got there. Her mother always started talking as if the silence between school and front door meant something terrible had happened in the car. Her father stood straighter when she came in, a guard dog pretending to be a man reading a paper. The sound of them used to mean safe. Lately it meant nowhere to place your hands.

Upstairs, she shut her door soft and sat on the floor with her back against it like she could hold the day out with her spine. Her phone lit her face. *Harper* at the top of the screen, the thread piled with ghosts. Photos: two pairs of feet in creek water last summer; a screenshot of a dorm Pinterest board with neon sticky notes and ugly rugs; a video of them singing badly while the dog howled. The more she scrolled the more her throat tightened, like memory had corners she kept hitting with the same bruise.

Thumb over the keyboard. The word balloon blinked empty, patient. Her mind ran drafts—*I'm sorry, I was scared, please*—and shredded each one before it formed. She could hear Harper's laugh under the swings. She could hear the way it hadn't come back since.

She locked the phone. Unlocked it. Opened the thread again because pretending she wouldn't didn't change anything.

Can we talk?

She typed it and didn't send it. The cursor blinked like a pulse she couldn't regulate. Downstairs, a drawer shut too hard; a pan hit a stovetop; her mother called her name with warmth that felt like a hand over her mouth. She almost answered, just to make it sound normal. Brynlee closed her eyes against the ceiling and the fan's steady tick and the smooth, untouched glass of the dresser mirror. The Spirits' silence pushed from one side. The world's noise pressed from the other. Her thumb hovered.

Not yet.

She set the phone face down on the carpet and listened to it vibrate with nothing at all.

Olive Branch

The message sat in her sent folder like it might rot there—Can we talk?

This time she hadn't deleted it. She'd pressed send and felt the air in her chest collapse when it went through. The screen stayed blank for so long she started counting heartbeats. At eighty-nine, it buzzed.

Fine.

One word. No emoji. No warmth. Just permission.

—

The park was all wind and rust. Chains groaned on the swings, bare branches scraped the gray sky. Harper waited by the slide, arms crossed, bracelets clinking soft with each shift of her weight. She didn't smile when Brynlee walked up. The wind shoved her hair against her cheek; she didn't move it.

"You wanted to talk," Harper said. Her tone wasn't cruel. It was worse—flat.

Brynlee swallowed. "Yeah."

"You cut me out." Harper's eyes held hers this time, sharp. "You let me think I was crazy for caring. You made me feel like I didn't matter. And then you just…show up."

The words hit harder than any bruise the Spirits had left. Brynlee's throat worked. "I didn't know how else to keep you safe."

"Safe?" Harper's laugh cracked. "You're the one I'm supposed to keep safe. That's how it's always been."

Brynlee's chest seized. She stepped closer, words scraping raw: "We were supposed to do everything together. College. Same dorm. A double wedding." Her voice faltered, but she forced it through anyway. "Kids who'd call each other cousins. We said that, Harper. We planned it."

Harper flinched. For a second her face almost broke—eyes bright, mouth trembling like memory had sucker-punched her. Then the wall slammed back up.

"That was before," she said.

Brynlee's hand twitched like she might reach out, but she shoved it into her pocket instead. "It's still what I want. I just—" Her voice cracked. "I don't know how to get back there without losing you in the process."

The silence between them roared. Wind pushed a swing until it squealed. Harper blinked hard, looked away, and muttered, "You don't get to say that and make it easy."

"I'm not asking for easy," Brynlee whispered. "I'm asking for a chance."

Harper turned then, really looked at her. A thousand things flickered through her eyes—hurt, loyalty, suspicion, love. The corner of her mouth jerked like she almost wanted to answer, but she didn't.

She just said, "Don't make promises you can't keep."

And walked past her, slow enough that Brynlee felt the space tear open again, but not slam shut.

It wasn't forgiveness. Not even close. But it wasn't the end. The wind pushed the swings again, slow, like something listening.

The Request

The text came in the middle of nothing. No Spirits breathing down her neck, no shadows bending wrong—just her on the comforter, trying not to scroll herself hollow. Just her in her room, sprawled across the comforter, trying not to scroll herself hollow.

Vivienne: *She wants to see you.*

For a second Brynlee thought she'd read it wrong. The words blurred, doubled, rearranged. She blinked hard. Still there. *She wants to see you.*

Lydia.

Her chest cinched so tight her ribs forgot how to work. She sat up too fast; the phone slipped from her hand and smacked the carpet.

Not her parents, not a detective, not Harper—her.

Of course, Lydia knew her name. Everyone did now—the girl who saw her, who wouldn't let it go, who forced people to look when they wanted to look away. The one who made it impossible to bury her story under silence.

But knowing her name wasn't the same as wanting to see her. Wanting meant Lydia remembered. That in the middle of whatever hell had been carved into her, she'd held on to the thought of someone out here pulling threads until they tangled enough to bring her back.

It meant Brynlee wasn't just a stranger. She was the girl Lydia connected to her survival.

And that was heavier than any bruise the Spirits had left.

Her mom's voice floated up the stairs just then—warm, ordinary, carrying her name with the rise-and-fall cadence of dinner. Plates clinking. Silverware set. Normal life threading the air while Vivienne's words still burned her screen.

Brynlee's stomach flipped. How could both exist in the same world—homework and meatloaf downstairs, Lydia Turner alive somewhere else?

Her thumbs hovered useless. She typed and erased: *Are you sure? Why? Where?* None of it sounded right.

Vivienne sent another: *She asked for you by name. And she won't see anyone else until she sees you.*

Brynlee pressed her palm flat to her sternum, as if she could keep herself from shaking apart. She wanted to throw up. She wanted to run. She wanted to already be outside Lydia Turner's door, knocking until her knuckles split.

Her mom called again, closer now. Brynlee shoved her feet into shoes, grabbed her hoodie, phone still clutched like proof. The hallway stretched ahead, each step louder than the last.

She reached the front door.

The knob was cold under her hand. This wasn't the Turners' house yet. Not Lydia's threshold. Just her own. But opening it meant leaving behind warm dinner plates and the illusion of safety. It meant stepping toward the girl who had lived inside her nightmares and outlasted them.

She blinked once, and for a heartbeat the glass panel beside the knob wasn't empty at all. It was Lydia's face behind it—eyes wide, mouth forming the same word it had in the mall, in the van, in the dream: *help.*

Vivienne's text burned against her palm. *She asked for you by name.*

Brynlee swallowed hard.

Then she opened the door. The wind met her like it had been waiting.

Threshold

The ride blurred. Brynlee couldn't have said what streets they took, or whether the light was green or red. Her dad's voice tried once or twice—safe questions, small talk—but she couldn't climb high enough to answer them. Every word in her throat was Lydia's name, and it burned too hot to let out.

Her mom sat angled toward her, hand brushing Brynlee's sleeve as if smoothing out tension could help. "You don't have to, sweetheart," she said once. Soft. Careful.

Yes I do. The words snapped through her head, jagged. This wasn't something she could step back from. Lydia had asked. Lydia wanted her. And that meant showing up even if she unraveled on the doorstep.

The houses grew bigger, older, the kind with porches that remembered whole families. Brynlee's breath shortened the closer they drew. The glass of the car window showed her own reflection, eyes wide, jaw locked—until for half a blink the mouth didn't move with hers. She shut her eyes hard. Not now. Not them.

Her dad pulled to the curb. The Turners' house was smaller than she imagined, quiet and plain. A wreath sagged on the door though Christmas had been months gone, the bow faded, like it didn't know how to stop waiting.

She couldn't make her fingers move. Her nails dug crescents into her palms, but her hands stayed frozen in her lap.

Her mom touched her arm again. "We'll come in with you."

"No." Her own voice startled her, scraped raw. "Just... let me."

Her parents glanced at each other, a conversation in silence, but didn't argue.

The air bit colder than March should've been when she opened the door. She stepped out, legs stiff, shoes crunching against the leftover grit of salt in the driveway. Every step up the walk felt like stepping into a verdict.

At the porch her vision doubled. She blinked fast until the boards steadied. The door had glass panels; shadows moved faint behind them. One was her mother's shape, slight, hair pulled back. Another—smaller, narrower.

Brynlee's pulse slammed so hard she thought it might shake the porch rail. She curled her fingers around the doorknob. It was warm, as if someone had just touched it from the other side.

She breathed once, twice, acid thick in her throat. The world outside went quiet—cars gone, wind stalled. Just her heartbeat, hammering her ribs.

Something on the other side breathed in. The knob turned under her hand.

Lydia

The door cracked, then opened wide enough for the air inside to rush out—warm, sharp with detergent and something faintly sweet, like a candle burned too long.

And there she was.

Lydia Turner.

Not a nightmare shadow, not a news photo, not a blur in a van. Real. Alive.

Her hair was shorter now, uneven at the ends like it had been cut in anger. Her face was thinner, cheeks hollow, but her eyes—God, her eyes—were the same. Wide and brown and full of things Brynlee couldn't name.

For a second neither of them moved. Brynlee's lungs locked. This was it—the girl she'd screamed for, fought for, bled for. The girl who'd haunted every hour since Christmas.

"Brynlee." Lydia's voice cracked on the first syllable, then steadied, quiet but sure. "You're the reason I'm here."

The words hit harder than any scar she carried. Brynlee's throat closed. Her body tilted forward—then stopped. A flicker of fear spiked hot: *What if she blames me? What if she doesn't remember me the way I remember her?*

But Lydia's gaze didn't falter.

Her hand lifted, trembled, then dropped to clutch the edge of her sleeve. Her palms were raw, still healing—the same hands Brynlee had seen scraping at the bumper, folding small. They weren't symbols anymore. They were scars.

Brynlee stepped forward before the fear could take root. Lydia met her halfway, arms sudden and desperate, and they collided—awkward, too tight, almost painful. Lydia's breath shuddered against her shoulder.

"You saw me," Lydia whispered. "You didn't let them erase me."

Brynlee's own breath tore out in a sob she hadn't meant to give. She held on tighter, squeezing like she could anchor Lydia here with force alone. "I almost gave up," she choked. "I almost—"

"But you didn't." Lydia leaned back enough to look at her, eyes wet but fierce. "You didn't."

Something inside Brynlee cracked then, but not the way it had before. Not hollow. Not breaking. It was release—the weight of months sliding off her chest all at once, leaving her raw and shaking but still standing.

Mrs. Turner appeared in the hall behind her daughter, eyes rimmed red but smiling like it hurt. She reached to steady Lydia but didn't pull her away. She just mouthed *thank you* over her shoulder, and Brynlee had to look away before she drowned in it.

Lydia's fingers curled into her sleeve, holding her like proof. "Stay a little," she said softly. Not a plea. A request. A tether.

And for the first time since the Spirits came, Brynlee didn't feel like she was drowning.

For once, silence didn't mean absence. It meant peace.

She felt chosen.

The Weight in the Room

The couch swallowed her edge-first, cushion sinking under her like it wanted her gone. Too soft, too loud in its sigh when she shifted. Nails pressed half-moons into denim, grounding or proof she still existed. Stay still. Stay small.

Lydia. Alive.

Hair hacked uneven, scars raw across her palms. Her mother's hand never leaving her back. Her father holding the wall like it might break without him.

Every sound carried miles. A floorboard groan. The hitch of a breath. Too much for walls this thin.

"I kept thinking nobody saw me."

Words cut her open. The voice she'd chased through nightmares.

"I saw you." The sound ripped out fragile, like glass set down too hard.

"And you didn't look away."

Lydia's fingers knotted into her sleeve, the same hands she'd seen clawing at a bumper. Not symbols anymore. Flesh. Scars.

Nod. Quick. Can't speak or the sound will split her chest.

The couch pulled deeper. A seat that wasn't hers, hollowing under her weight, ready to erase her shape the second she stood. Witness. Intruder. Both.

The knock at the door jarred her ribs. The sound didn't belong here.

Vivienne. Pale, eyes already wet. She didn't glance at anyone else. Straight to Lydia, like gravity had finally snapped into place.

"Viv." One syllable, cracked.

They collided in the center of the room, arms wrapping so tight their bones might fuse. Lydia's face pressed to Vivienne's neck, a sound ripped from her that didn't belong to relief or grief alone but something sharper between. It was everything she wanted—and none of it was hers.

Anchor against anchor. Two halves locking back in.

Denim bit into her palms. The hollow under her legs sank deeper, swallowing the shape of her. The Spirits had promised this mattered. Lydia mattered. Vivienne mattered. And now they had each other. A circle already whole before she'd even arrived.

Invisible.

The hollow seat held her in place. If she stood, nothing would miss her shape.

Perimeter

Porch light in her eyes, gravel under her soles, throat raw from holding everything down. The car door thunked shut; the house opened its mouth—warm air, lemon cleaner, the hum of the fridge a steady line under it all. Keys landed in the ceramic bowl by the door. A sound that meant home. A sound that pressed on the places still shaking.

Mom hovered close enough to be heat. Dad did that slow scan of her face again, the one that used to make her roll her eyes—like he was trying to read a language he'd forgotten. Questions sat behind both sets of teeth. Don't ask. Not yet. If one of them said *Lydia* out loud, the room would tear.

Cans hissed open—Cokes because coffee would be too loaded with meaning. The fizz snapped in the quiet. Her fingers wrapped cold metal and didn't trust themselves. Table edge under her hip, familiar gouge from the time she'd knocked a chair into it and lied about the dog. A thousand stupid, safe memories crowding shoulder to shoulder with the new ones that had knives.

"We're proud of you," Dad said, and the words went heavy, not the cheery kind. His hand landed on her shoulder, warm, wider than it used to be when she was small. Protective. Maybe restraining. Couldn't tell. "And we're... we're going to keep you close for a while." He tried for a smile that didn't quite make it. "Okay?"

Close. The word shrank the kitchen two sizes.

Mom slid a printed form onto the table like a peace offering. Numbers circled. Names highlighted. "Kearns sent these. Victim services. A counselor who works with... with girls who've witnessed things." Her voice stayed soft even when it hit the word that made air freeze. "You don't have to go, but we'll go with you if you want. Or sit in the car. Or... bake in the parking lot." Her mouth twitched. The joke landed crooked and brave.

Every cell in her body wanted to crawl out of its skin. Therapy meant strangers digging where even she didn't want to go. But Mom's fingers were shredding a napkin to threads, and Dad's jaw had that tight line that showed up when he was trying not to beg. *Okay doesn't mean okay. It means shut up before they crack further.*

"Okay," she said out loud, flat.

Mom's shoulders dropped a fraction. Dad exhaled like he'd been sent back from a cliff.

"We're also turning on location sharing," Dad added, gentler than any rule had a right to be. "Not to spy. We just... the world feels different tonight. Humor your old man."

Her phone dragged at her hoodie pocket, heavy. When she shifted, it buzzed against her thigh—Harper. She didn't look. Couldn't. The unopened text pulsed through denim while her parents closed the circle tighter, two worlds tugging her in opposite directions.

"Fine," she said. "Share it."

Mom reached across and smoothed a strand of hair behind her ear the way she used to before fourth-grade photos. The touch landed like a benediction and a leash. "We'll give you space," she promised in the same breath she was closing the circle.

The fridge hummed louder, lights stayed steady, the hall mirror showed her reflection synced for once—no lag, no distortion. The Spirits were gone. Or quiet. Somehow that was worse.

Dad tapped the form. "We can say no to interviews. We can say yes to nothing. Nobody owns your voice. Not the school, not the news." His eyes flicked to the hall closet like he knew exactly where the boxes slept. "Not even Christmas."

Christmas. The three gifts. Waiting. Watching. Still sealed.

The house held its breath with them. She nodded into her mother's shoulder, gave Dad the smallest smile she could keep from shaking, and let the circle close—for tonight. The fridge kept humming, steady as a held breath.

The Offer

After curfew tasted like toothpaste and Coke gone flat. Bedroom door cracked, hall night-light making the carpet a thin river of gold. Her phone pulsed in her palm—Harper's bubble at the top like a heartbeat she refused to check. Below it: Vivienne—*Can you meet me tomorrow after school. Community center. 4:30. Not about you.*

Not about you. Relief and sting in the same breath. *Okay,* she typed and watched the word sit there like a small obedient thing she didn't recognize.

Ashwood bled its last bell into cold air. March hadn't decided what it wanted—sun on the sidewalk, wind like a hand closing. She walked the two blocks to the community center with her hands jammed into her pockets, counting the cracks in the concrete so she wouldn't count the ways the day could go wrong. No Spirits. No lag in the glass of the front doors. Just a bulletin board with curling flyers and a paper chain someone hadn't taken down after Valentine's.

Vivienne waited in the foyer. Not the statue version from the vigil, not the polished mannequin from the first week. Sweater sleeves pushed to her elbows, hair slightly wrong at the part like she'd gotten impatient with it. Her eyes slid once toward

Brynlee's wrist—habit now—then back to her face. "Thanks for coming," she said, and the words didn't bounce off. They landed.

"Is Lydia—" The question jumped out before she could stop it.

"She's resting." A small smile, careful. "This is... something else."

They crossed a hall that smelled like floor cleaner and old crayons. The office door stood open. Inside: two chairs already taken, two more empty. Mara's braid. Jacob's jacket patched at the shoulder with a square of denim darker than the rest. Mrs. Williams stood behind them like a wall you could lean on; Mr. Williams scrubbed grease from his knuckles with a paper towel that gave up immediately. They all looked at Brynlee at once and then pretended they hadn't.

Vivienne cleared her throat. "My parents are parking." A beat, and then, softer, to the twins, "I know this is weird. I asked them to come here instead of the office downtown."

Weird didn't cover it. Money had a smell—leather, cologne, a whisper of new paper—and it ghosted through the doorway two minutes later when Mr. and Mrs. LeClair stepped in. The mother's face had retaught itself how to make warm; the father's suit wore him like an apology. This could go wrong in a dozen ways. Brynlee's stomach tightened and held.

"Thank you for making time," Mrs. LeClair said, palms open like she was arriving at a friend's sink, not a negotiation. She didn't look at Brynlee first. Good. "Mr. and Mrs. Williams, I'm Elise. This is Marc. We own LeClair Fabrication out off the bypass."

Mr. Williams nodded once, wary quiet. "I know the place," he said, voice sanded down by long days. "Big floor. Good welders."

Marc's mouth twitched like a man trying not to advertise. "We try." He glanced at his daughter—Vivienne's chin lifted a hair in answer—and then he took a breath that moved his shoulders. "We heard you've been taking jobs wherever you can find them. The kind that don't pay on time." A pause. "I made that kind of mistake when I was twenty. It cost me months I didn't have."

Mrs. Williams's hand settled on the back of her husband's chair. "We get by," she said, and the quiet pride in it made Brynlee's throat pull tight.

"This isn't charity," Elise said, stepping in before the word could sour the air. "It's a job. A real one. With training, benefits, and a schedule that doesn't break bones. Entry wage is twenty-eight an hour; reviews at six months and a year. We need a floor lead who can learn the CNC line and then teach it right. Your references say you teach with your hands."

Color climbed Mr. Williams's cheeks, not embarrassment—recognition. The way a man sits up when someone names the thing he knows how to do. "I can learn your line," he said. No brag. Fact. "CNC's a language. Once you get the verbs, the rest follows."

Marc smiled for the first time, quick and real. "That's exactly how I think about it."

Papers slid from a folder like careful weather. Contracts. Start date in May. Health insurance. PTO that didn't feel like an insult. And then a smaller envelope, unsealed. Elise set it on the table but didn't push it across like a tip. "An advance," she said. "On salary. So, you can breathe while you catch up. Month-to-month shouldn't be a cliff edge."

Brynlee's lungs forgot the second half of the breath they were taking and had to go back for it. Advance. The word flickered a picture: a kitchen not counting quarters, a grocery cart that didn't have to be navigated like a minefield. The twins' eyes locked on the envelope the way kids look at rain when the roof stops leaking.

Mr. Williams didn't touch it. He looked at his wife first. She looked back, no flinch, all the conversation they needed passing without sound. He picked up the envelope then, like it was fragile, like it might break into light.

"What do you want in return?" he asked, and the question landed clean, not suspicious—just a man who knew the price of favors.

"Your work," Marc said simply. "Your time. Your brain. If you decide it's not a fit, we part ways like adults. If you decide to stay, we build something." His eyes flicked to Vivienne and back.

"We should have done more, sooner, for more people. We're... trying to start here."

Vivienne hadn't moved from her place by the door. Shoulders squared like she'd hold the frame up if it buckled. When her parents finished, she met Mrs. Williams's gaze. "I asked them," she said. No apology. No shine. Just the truth.

Mrs. Williams's hand rose halfway like she might reach across the space and touch that squared shoulder, then fell. "Thank you," she said, and the words weren't small. "But only if it's right for us."

"Only if it's right for you," Elise echoed, and the room loosened one notch.

Something unknotted in Brynlee's chest she hadn't known was tied. Not a savior scene. Not pity dressed in a suit. An offer that let a man stand up in it.

Mara's hand found Jacob's under the table and squeezed. He let it happen, stoic face cracking just enough to show relief's first light. Brynlee looked away to give it privacy and caught her own reflection in the office window—no lag, no second set of eyes layered wrong. The quiet held.

"May I show you the benefits page?" Elise asked. "And the training schedule? We can adjust the hours until school lets out so you're home evenings."

Home evenings. Small words that could change the shape of a family.

Mr. Williams nodded. "Show me where to sign," he said, and then, louder to the twins without looking at them, like he was telling the room who they were going to be now, "We're doing this right."

Pens scratched. Paper took ink. The envelope disappeared into Mrs. Williams's bag like a promise you didn't say aloud for fear it would run.

When it was done, the room exhaled. Vivienne stepped back like she'd been holding a door open with her whole body and could finally let it swing. Her eyes found Brynlee's then—one second, two. Not triumph. Not debt. Solidarity, clean and without perfume.

"Thank you," Mrs. Williams said, this time to the LeClairs, and then to Vivienne, and then her gaze slid to Brynlee at the last like she hadn't decided how to parcel gratitude to a girl and all her ghosts. "For bringing what you could."

What she could. The words slid into place like a key.

Outside, the air had gone colder while they'd been changing the future in a fluorescent office. The light over the side entrance hummed steady. No shadows lengthened when they shouldn't. No breath where breath shouldn't be. On the sidewalk, Jacob bumped Brynlee's shoulder with his once, pretending it was an accident. Mara linked an arm through hers for three steps and let go like she was practicing the feel of a world that didn't require clinging.

Vivienne fell into step a pace behind, then beside. "They'll move before summer," she said, voice low. "My parents already started looking at rentals near the bus line. Something with a real kitchen."

A picture flared—pinto beans simmering, potatoes popping in oil, cornbread split with butter running. A table where bills weren't wolves. "Good," Brynlee said, and the word didn't scrape on the way out for once. "Good."

Her phone buzzed against her thigh. Harper's name bright on the screen. A short message—five words and a space. *I read everything. Come over?*

Two worlds tugging again. The old one, the new one. Her parents' perimeter, the street she'd chosen anyway. She breathed until the air actually reached the bottom of her lungs and texted back a time that wasn't brave or cowardly—just real. *I'm here. Still here.*

By the corner, the office window held four reflections walking where there had only been three before. All synced. No delay. No refusal to meet her eyes. She kept moving.

Tremor

Harper's room pressed close, candle-sweet and familiar in all the wrong ways. The posters, the bracelets, the chaos-bedspread she used to collapse into—it was all the same, but none of it was hers anymore.

She stayed near the door too long, hands cold. Then words ripped out, rawer than she meant:

"You remember when you covered for me? Seventh grade. I forgot the essay, and you shoved yours under my name. Said you didn't care about the grade, you just didn't want me looking stupid."

Harper's bracelets jangled as she pushed up on her elbows. Eyes sharp, not soft. "Yeah. I remember."

"You always had my back." Brynlee's throat ached. "Even when I didn't deserve it."

Silence sprawled between them.

Harper sat all the way up now, hair falling forward, arms crossed. "That's the point, isn't it? You didn't let me have your back this time. You shut me out. Left me standing there like an idiot while you…" Her voice snapped off, teeth on the rest.

Brynlee's chest tightened. *Say you'll forgive me. Say we can start over.*

The phone buzzed in her pocket—sharp, insistent. Heat pooled in her stomach. She didn't move. Harper's eyes flicked down, then away, like the silence around the buzzing said more than words ever could.

"Okay," Brynlee said. Too steady. A lie dressed as surrender. Not okay at all.

The lamp on Harper's nightstand flickered once. Twice. No storm outside. Just the air bending wrong.

Brynlee's head jerked toward the mirror above the desk. Harper sat behind her in the glass—but those eyes slid right past. Not looking at her. Not seeing her.

Cold dug under her ribs. *Not here. Not now.*

The air pulsed once—heartbeat, hum, warning—and then stilled.

The light steadied. The reflection snapped back in place.

Harper didn't notice. She was still watching, jaw set. "You can't just throw one memory at me and expect it fixes everything."

Brynlee's pulse rattled in her ears. She wanted to scream *I know. I'm trying. Please let that be enough.*

She only managed, "I'm trying."

Harper didn't answer.

The silence between them thickened, heavy enough to feel like something alive. Brynlee stayed on the edge of the chair, pulse thudding through her wrists, every second stretching like it meant to snap.

Not safety. Just the inhale. Before the next strike.

Interference

The house smelled like pot roast and soap, safe things, normal things. Her mom's voice floated from the kitchen, soft and coaxing, calling her to the table. The TV in the living room mumbled at low volume, some sitcom laugh track hiccupping too loud against the walls.

Her feet dragged anyway. Every step into this house felt like stepping under water. Heavy. Slow.

She sat where she always sat. Her dad's hand brushed her shoulder in that way he thought was grounding. Too warm. Too steady. A weight disguised as comfort.

"You look tired," her mom said, spooning potatoes onto her plate like she could fix anything with starch and salt.

"I'm fine." The words came out flat, an automatic setting. Not fine. Not even close.

Her phone buzzed once against her thigh. She palmed it under the table. No number. No contact. Just a gray square where a name should've been, the notification bar reading: *Still watching.*

Her chest tightened. She slipped the phone face-down before either of them could ask.

The TV snapped louder—no warning, no reason. A reporter's voice cut clear: "...the van seen near—" before the sound fuzzed to static, then smoothed back into canned laughter. Her dad frowned at the remote like maybe the batteries were dying.

Her fork scraped her plate. The noise shivered in her teeth.

The kitchen light hummed. Just a hum. Just electricity. But it crawled in her ears until it became a wordless drone, a reminder that even here, surrounded by love that pressed too close, she wasn't free.

Her reflection in the darkened window over the sink lagged half a beat behind, mouth still chewing when she had already swallowed.

She dropped her gaze. "May I be excused?" Her voice sounded polite enough to hide the shaking.

Her parents traded a look she didn't decode, then nodded.

Upstairs, she shut the door, pressed her back to it, and breathed hard enough that her ribs ached.

The phone lit up on its own. Blank screen. No text. Just a low vibration that didn't stop until she set it facedown again.

The hum from downstairs seeped through the floorboards. Or maybe it was inside her chest.

She pulled her blanket tight, whispering to herself, a secret no one else got to hear:

"I know. I know you're not gone."

The house stayed quiet. Not empty. Never empty.

The Hollow Applause

The gym reeked of sweat, floor polish, and old popcorn.
Bleachers groaned under half the school's weight. Banners hung
crooked, letters peeling from tape too weak for cinderblock. A
podium waited at center court with a microphone that hissed like
it had a secret.

Applause cracked sharp against the walls. Not for her, not
officially, but every hand clapping made her skin sting like it was.
Community effort. Vigilance. A young life returned. Words like a script
read off the paper in the principal's hand.

Harper wasn't beside her. She hadn't been for weeks.
Brynlee's thighs stuck to the varnished bench alone, the space at
her side a wound the clapping couldn't drown.

Vivienne sat two rows down with her perfect hair and her
perfect posture, her face marble-smooth. But when she turned,
just a fraction, Brynlee caught it: the tiniest flicker in her eyes. She
knew the sound was empty too.

The microphone popped. Her name leaked out—not in full,
just the *Bryn*— warped, swallowed, cut. She stiffened, blood
rushing too fast to her face. No one else reacted. The principal
kept droning, students kept clapping, the sound filling every
hollow of her skull.

Her hands clenched on her knees until her nails left half-moons through denim. The applause should've been warm. It wasn't. The hum rose beneath it—low, familiar. It was hollow, tin beating tin. Every strike landed like dirt being shoveled onto a coffin.

The speech wound down. More clapping. Louder. Her chest tightened like it might split. She imagined standing, screaming over the mic, telling them this wasn't finished, that Lydia was home, but the nightmare wasn't over, that the silence meant nothing was safe yet.

Instead, she sat, spine locked, eyes burning.

When the noise finally broke apart into chatter and scraping shoes, she felt bruised all over. Not touched but pounded by hands that didn't know they were applauding. A funeral no one else could see.

Residual Noise

The noise didn't leave the gym. It followed her out—palms slapping, shoes squeaking, hollow thunder. In the hall it just changed shape. Lockers slammed open. Laughter ricocheted off tile. None of it touched her, but every sound landed anyway. Somebody shoved someone else for fun.

She walked through it like she wasn't there. Eyes slid past her. Voices curved around her without touching. A minute ago, they'd all been clapping hard enough to split skin. Now? Nothing. Invisible.

Her ears still rang. Each footstep hit too sharp, too loud. Like she was walking on top of the applause instead of floor tile.

She dug her phone out just to anchor her hands. No new texts from Harper. No new anything. She almost shoved it back when the screen blinked awake on its own.

Unknown number.

Three words.

She still waits.

Her throat clamped. The message burned brighter than the screen. Lydia wasn't gone. Not finished. Not free. The applause in the gym had been for a half-truth.

A door banged shut somewhere down the hall. She flinched and jammed the phone back in her pocket like it might bite her.

Keep walking. That's all she could do. Keep walking even if each step pulled her deeper into something that had no exits.

The hallway stretched longer than it ever had before, lockers repeating like a bad dream. If she turned back, the gym would still be clapping.

Under Their Roof

Onions hit oil; the pan answered with a hiss that filled the kitchen. Radio low, some talk show pretending to be harmless. Dad's keys clinked in the bowl by the door like always. The house tucked itself around all of it, the way a coat does—heavy on the shoulders, warm in places that made it hard to breathe.

A plate set in front of her, fork bright against the rim. Steam ghosted up and kissed her face. Mom's smile held in place with pins. "Eat while it's hot."

Chew. Swallow. The motion worked even when nothing else did. Salt sat on her tongue and didn't dissolve.

Phone in her pocket pressed a rectangle against her thigh. Three words seared behind her eyes: *She still waits.* The screen had gone dark, but the message hadn't. It lived under her skin now, a splinter you couldn't tweeze out.

Dad tried for casual. "How was the assembly?"

"Loud." One word that didn't invite the next. He nodded like that answered anything.

Mom slid a folded paper across the table the way nurses slide forms to people who are already dizzy. "I called. Dr. Medina has a Tuesday after school. If you'd rather mornings, there's a cancellation list." Her voice carried careful. "You won't have to talk if you don't want to the first time. You can just... sit in the room. See if it fits."

The fork weighed more than it should. If she said *The Spirits texted me,* if she said *They're still here,* the room would crack right down the middle. Mom would clutch the counter; Dad would go hard around the mouth and start making lists, calling names, building walls with his hands. Lockdown would stop being a chapter title and become the air. She swallowed the truth, and it scraped on the way down.

"Okay." Flat. The kind of okay that meant *don't push or I'll bolt.* Mom's shoulders dropped by inches. A win pressed into the margin.

Dad took a breath that smelled faintly of coffee and work. "We should talk summer," he said, too light. "Your mom's schedule landed. I can move some shifts. We could get to the lake a weekend or two. Or—" He glanced toward the hallway without meaning to. "—do something bigger."

Bigger. The hall closet breathed dust at the edge of her vision. Top shelf. Three shapes tucked into shadow, their corners sharp even through cardboard. Sleepers. Watchers. She pictured tearing into them and finding them empty, confetti and air where promises should be, and almost laughed. The sound died before it reached her throat.

"School's not done," she said, because it sounded like a reason even if it wasn't the point. The point was: time didn't belong to them. Not really. The Spirits had been keeping a ledger since December, and she didn't know when they'd stop tallying.

"The counselor can wait until after midterms," Mom offered, mistaking the silence for schedule math. "We don't have to rush anything."

Everything had already been rushed by a clock they couldn't see. *She still waits.* The words pulsed with her wrist. She set her fork down before metal scraped plate again and made Dad flinch.

He changed lanes. "Kearns called," he said, careful. "He said you were helpful. He also said you don't have to answer anyone else's calls. Reporters, kids with podcasts, whoever. We'll field those. Your mother will turn into a dragon if she has to." He tried a smile. It stuck better than most. "Pretty sure she's been waiting her whole life to burn a blogger."

Mom's mouth twitched. "Watch me."

The joke should have landed. It hovered and then fell, soft as a paper plane that didn't catch air.

She reached for her water. The glass sweated in her hand. Condensation ran over her knuckles and made everything slick. The radio clicked to an ad. Words she didn't ask for pushed through: ...*travel documents processed in as little as...* She set the glass down too fast. It thudded. Dad's eyes flicked up and away like he'd learned to watch her like a skittish animal—no sudden moves.

"We should renew your passport," he said, like creeping up on a skunk. "It's expired. You know how slow those offices are."

Heat climbed her neck. *You bought something. You planned without me.* Or maybe they hadn't. Maybe it was just a sentence dropped into a room to see how it rang. Either way, the word tilted the floor. Passport. A door with rules stamped across it. A kind of leaving that required permission.

"Sure," she said, and her mouth tasted like metal. "Whatever."

The light over the sink hummed. Just a hum. No flicker. No lag in the window glass. The empty spaces where the Spirits usually breathed stayed empty and somehow that was worse. Quiet wasn't peace; it was a hand lowered and waiting. She'd learned the difference.

Mom stood, scooped plates with the speed of somebody who'd been a waitress once and remembered. "Laundry's in the dryer. If you bring your basket down, I'll help." She aimed it casual; it landed like a plea. *Let me touch your life. Let me fold the parts you won't.*

"After I finish homework." Lie smooth enough to pass. Dad pretended not to hear the wobble in it.

He touched the paper again, his nail tracing an appointment time without meaning to. "We can... we can make a plan," he said. The word kept showing up, stubborn. "Summer. Therapy. School. We can build it out, so it doesn't all feel like it's happening at you."

At you. Nails bit into her palm where the phone lay. The message pressed back: *She still waits.* Plans stacked up like Lego towers, impressive until a careless foot took them down. She breathed slow through her teeth and nodded so they would stop looking at her like she might evaporate.

Upstairs, the hallway thinned. Her door eased shut on its old squeak. She leaned her forehead against the wood and counted to ten because numbers obeyed when feelings didn't. The room smelled like shampoo and old paper and the ghost of winter. She pulled the phone out and opened the text again, like staring would change the words. No number. No thread above it, no thread below. Just the line itself, floating.

She typed *Who?* and didn't send it. The question wasn't for them. It was for her. Lydia was home; the girl in the box still lived in every shadow. The Williams kids had a door cracked open. Vivienne had a spine made of quiet steel and a family learning how to hold it. *She still waits.* Maybe the pronoun wasn't singular at all. Maybe it was the world the Spirits kept showing her—every empty chair, every unopened door, every girl who folded small and waited for someone to count to sixty and then start again.

The hall mirror stayed true when she checked it—mouth moving when her mouth moved, eyes lining up without slipping. No punishment. No reward. Just the eerie mercy of being left alone with her own head.

She slid the phone under her pillow anyway, like a kid hiding a talisman. The house breathed around her—the dryer thumping, the television laughing at something that wasn't funny, her parents talking low enough that love sounded like a secret they didn't want to scare. The three boxes on the top shelf exhaled dust, patient.

Tomorrow had edges already. School. A text to Kearns she'd write and erase twice before sending. A stop by the Turners' if Lydia wanted company that didn't ask questions. Maybe Harper's message finally opened and answered with a time that didn't lie.

Under their roof, she could borrow quiet. Not keep it. Borrow.

She closed her eyes and tried to pretend the weight pressing on her chest was a blanket and not a hand. She pretended anyway.

Public Scrutiny

The air at Ashwood buzzed wrong. Not the usual Monday drag, not even the leftover nerves from exams. This was sharper, faster. It hissed under breath when she passed, snapped shut when she turned her head too quick.

Her name lived in their mouths—Brynlee Hall, over and over.

Some kids said it flat, some like it tasted sour, some like they wanted to believe it but didn't.

By second period, her chest felt thin. The whispers weren't just noise anymore—they were a tide, rising high enough to drown. Lydia's picture had been plastered across the morning announcements. A teacher said "miraculously found" with too much smile. Someone in the back muttered, *Ask Brynlee, she saw her first.*

Laughter cracked open. Not cruel, not kind. Just there.

She gripped her desk until her knuckles blanched. Don't look up. Don't give them more.

The bell jarred. Kids spilled into the hallway. Phones glowed everywhere—screen after screen of Lydia's face, the Turner family outside their house, the headline: **SURVIVOR FOUND**

AFTER ELEVEN YEARS. Beneath it: rumors stacked like teeth. *Local teen tipped police. Local teen knew all along.*

"Hey, Brynlee—" a boy swung his phone around, half-grin feral. "You psychic or something?"

She kept walking. His laugh chased her anyway.

In the bathroom, the noise muffled but didn't vanish. Two girls at the sinks didn't lower their voices.

"Can you imagine? If I'd seen her, I would've told someone immediately."

"Maybe she didn't because she wanted the attention now."

Their reflections caught hers in the mirror. Both turned away fast, like she wasn't worth looking at.

Her phone vibrated. She yanked it out like it might explain everything.

Another text. Same unknown number.

Truth always rots when left in silence.

Heat pooled in her stomach. The stall door loomed too close. Her lungs worked too hard for too little air.

Her reflection didn't lag this time; it just looked tired of being recognized.

Someone knocked at the bathroom door, impatient. A teacher's voice called through, sharp. "Hall pass?"

Brynlee shoved the phone deep in her pocket. Wiped her eyes on her sleeve. Straightened.

Walk out. Walk like you don't hear them. Walk like the words aren't carving you hollow.

The hallway greeted her again—phones up, voices curving, all of them watching without watching.

And for the first time, she wondered maybe this was the point all along—not silence, but exposure.

The Quiet Offer

Cafeteria air always ran warm, like it had been breathed too many times. Trays clacked, ice machines coughed, somebody's laugh chopped the room into pieces. The table near the back corner held its usual noise—jokes ricocheting, rumors wearing new hats. She picked the edge seat that kept her back to cinderblock and made the fork scrape against plastic until the sound steadied her hands.

A shadow crossed the table and didn't keep moving.

Vivienne slid her tray down without the ceremonial pause girls used when they were choosing sides. Just sat. Sweater sleeves pushed to mid-forearm, hair a little wrong where the wind had insisted. No glance at the door. No scan for better company. A metal water bottle thunked soft on laminate, and that ordinary sound landed like a verdict.

Conversation at the nearest table hiccupped, adjusted, went on louder. The room always got louder when it pretended not to look.

"Your seat?" Vivienne, quiet. Not small. Just calibrated so the question didn't carry.

"It's a seat." The answer came too flat. The fork had grooves now.

Vivienne's gaze flicked, quick as a reflex, to the cuff over Brynlee's wrist—habit she couldn't break—and away before it turned into a stare. "They'll get bored," she said, picking up her apple like this was just food and not triage. "Not because they understand. Because attention has the lifespan of a fruit fly."

"Comforting." The word scraped on the way out.

"It's not meant to be." Bite. Chew. She set the apple down with care, as if noise had rules today. "They want your version to be a performance. Something with applause at the right places. They don't know what it costs to carry a thing when no one claps."

The fork stopped grinding. That sentence carried the weight of someone who'd learned it the expensive way. The room's hum pressed against both ears at once, like headphones on the wrong setting. "Do you?" It slipped out before pride could choke it.

A small lift of one shoulder. Not coy. Not confession. Agreement with a ghost. "Enough to know there's a difference between being seen and being looked at."

The table across the aisle turned a phone so the camera could drink her in. She kept her eyes here, on the safe square of laminate between them. "Library would be quieter," she said, because retreat sounded weak and she needed the option anyway.

"They'll follow you with their eyes, not their feet," Vivienne said. "It's louder there when it's supposed to be silent." She nudged the water bottle with a knuckle, a tiny orbiting of nervous energy that gave her away. "This is fine."

The word fine landed like a card face-down. Brynlee breathed around it. Soup cooled without ever being hot enough to taste. The rumor-rattle behind her spine tried on new endings to her story; each one fit wrong and got worn anyway. Every version wore her face wrong.

"Do you want me to sit," Vivienne asked after a beat, "and not talk?"

The question loosened something that had calcified since morning. "Yes," she said, and then, because the truth needed more breath than that, "and no." The stupid honesty of it flushed heat up her neck. "Just... not questions you already know the answers to."

"Then no questions." Vivienne unscrewed the bottle cap and took a long drink like patience could be swallowed. When she set it down, she didn't look at Brynlee; she watched the room past her shoulder with the steadiness of someone who'd learned how to guard a door without making it a scene.

Minutes stacked. The hum of the soda fountain, the squeak of sneakers, the clatter of a tray dropped and rescued before it shattered. No performance. No pity. Presence, clean.

A boy at the next table said her name too loud and laughed into his palm when his friend elbowed him. Vivienne didn't flinch. "They'll move on to a new story by Friday," she said, pitched for just two people. "It won't mean less. It'll just be quieter." A pause, thinner than paper. "Quieter is survivable."

The fork found the seam where tray met table and pressed until plastic bowed and held. "You talk like you've rehearsed this."

"I talk like I've lived in rooms where everyone has an opinion and none of them help." The corner of her mouth lifted, not quite a smile. "You can borrow that line if you want. It shuts down the amateurs."

Borrow. The word made the air easier in the lungs for a second. "Thanks," Brynlee said, and acceptance didn't choke this time.

They ate nothing and pretended it counted. A custodian's cart squealed by wheels protesting tile. Over at the doors, Jacob's profile cut against light; Mara's braid flashed red as she turned. They clocked Brynlee in the corner, weighed the room, gave her the grace of not making her wave from a drowning place. Later.

Vivienne slid a folded napkin across without looking. Not a note. Just the offer to catch anything that fell apart. "If you need to leave before the bell, I'll make a distraction."

"What kind?"

"The kind that looks expensive, breaks into exactly three pieces, and buys us forty-five seconds." A beat. "I've had practice."

The laugh surprised both of them. It didn't fix anything. It kept something from breaking.

The bell didn't rescue. It just shuffled the pieces. Chairs scraped. Voices surged. The phone turned toward her blinked away. Vivienne didn't rush to stand; she waited until the aisle had thinned and then rose in a way that made space where there hadn't been any.

"Walk you out?" Not a question with teeth. An umbrella offered in a rain that might not start for five minutes.

"Yes," she said, and hate flared quick that yes belonged here and not in the text thread still unopened with Harper's name at the top. The hate burned out as fast as it lit. A handrail to grab is still a handrail, even if it isn't the one you reached for first.

They moved through the noise shoulder-to-shoulder. No miracle. No speech. Just two girls cutting a path that didn't ask permission. In the glass of the trophy case, their reflections kept pace—no lag, no slide of eyes away. For the first time all day, the image gave her back what she knew to be true: still here. Still moving. Not erased.

The Weight of Moving

Hallways churned with backpacks slamming lockers, voices pitched too high from soda and gossip. The kind of noise that usually swallowed her whole. Today it scraped instead—too bright, too sharp, like tinfoil on teeth.

Brynlee let the crowd move around her. The Williams twins drifted ahead with their usual orbit, Mara laughing at something Jacob muttered low. A laugh that came from safety, not joy. It tugged at her anyway.

She kept her distance. Close enough to see they were okay. Far enough that she didn't have to prove she was. A week ago, she would've trailed their steps, matched their pace. Today she watched the gap widen until the crowd swallowed them. The ache that flared didn't surprise her—it had been waiting, patient, since the office, since Harper's eyes had gone glassy with betrayal.

A text buzzed under her palm. Harper's name. She didn't open it.

The lockers blurred, the faces blurred, and for a moment she thought the world might blink her out again. Not vanishing this time—just thinning, like smoke. The temptation to let it was sharp.

But then—Vivienne, at the end of the hall, pivoted toward a stairwell with that clean, deliberate walk that didn't ask if anyone was watching. She caught Brynlee's eye as if she'd expected her to look. No smile, no wave, just acknowledgment.

Something like a tether pulled tight between them.

Not friendship yet. Not safety. But not nothing.

She swallowed, adjusted her strap, and stepped into the current of bodies. Backpack weight, hallway heat, real things that didn't vanish.

The hum of the crowd pressed close, pressing like hands that weren't there. Her mind whispered the same thing it had whispered in alleys, in dreamscapes, in front of glass that refused to look back: *Still here. Still moving.*

And for the first time in days, it didn't sound like a lie.

The Gifts

The cicadas had started their summer chant, a shrill buzz that clung to the air like heat itself. Brynlee sat cross-legged on the living room rug, the three boxes still parked under the tree that wasn't there anymore. Her mom had tucked them against the wall after Christmas, never moving them farther, like they belonged to a season that hadn't ended.

Now it was May, the AC humming against the windows, and her parents stood across from her like a jury. Her dad's arms folded, his mouth twitching like he wanted to smile but didn't want to push. Her mom, gentler, just said, "It's time, B."

She wanted to say no. She wanted to say she didn't need them. But the boxes had sat there so long they felt less like presents and more like unfinished business.

Her fingers tore the first ribbon loose. Cardboard split. Inside—luggage, gleaming blue, tags dangling. A whole set, sturdy zippers and wheels that begged for distance. The new-plastic smell hit her first—sharp, clean, unghosted.

The second box: vouchers, tickets, a tidy folder stamped with the name of a tour company. Paris. Rome. Prague. A summer of countries she'd only seen on Pinterest boards and glossy travel vlogs.

The third: an envelope fat with prepaid cards, her mom's handwriting scrawled across the flap. For clothes. For whatever you need.

Her throat locked. Three. Just three. Not scraps. Not proof she wasn't enough. Three doors flung open.

Her dad knelt beside her, voice low. "We wanted you to have more than stuff this year. We wanted you to have…room."

She blinked hard, heat stinging her lashes. Once, three had felt like betrayal. Now it felt like exactly enough.

Her palms pressed the tickets flat against her knees, the paper cool under her skin. Not boxes anymore. A way forward.

The Why

The dream took her without warning. Not the falling-into kind.
The *dragged-under* kind.

The world around her tilted into static until only the three of
them remained—Pain's skin pulled too thin, Loneliness with his
hollow eyes, Rejection blurred at the edges like she was already
gone.

"Why me?" Brynlee's voice cracked. It was the only question
that had ever mattered. "Why all of this? Why *me?*"

Silence stretched, thick as frost.

Pain spoke first, voice scraped raw. *Because you bend*

Loneliness followed, a grin that cut wrong. *Because you break*

Rejection last, her words like glass sliding over glass. *And
because breaking you was the only way to keep them whole*

Her chest burned. "I don't understand."

The dream shifted. The ground beneath her fractured into
panes of glass, each one catching a flicker of future.

Mara, standing at a podium too tall, speaking into a
microphone, her voice steady even as her hands shook. Jacob,
older, leading others through smoke and wreckage, his arm
pulling someone smaller into light. Vivienne, her wealth poured

into foundations and schools, her signature curling across checks that rewrote laws.

And Lydia—Lydia's face on a screen, her voice filling a room of thousands. Not begging, not broken. Commanding. And being *heard*.

The glass shuddered, as if the visions cost the world too much to hold.

"If they had shattered now," Pain rasped, "none of it would come."

Loneliness leaned close, the echo of his grin dragging cold over her ribs. *One child vanishes, and the silence spreads. Four vanish, and the silence devours a generation*

Rejection's outline sharpened for a heartbeat, her voice low and final: *You were the hinge. You were the fracture point. Through you, they live*

Brynlee's knees buckled. She pressed her palms into the glass. The reflections blurred under her touch, but the futures remained.

"You could've chosen anyone." The whisper cracked. Pain's ruined face tilted. *We did*

Loneliness's voice tangled hers. *And they would not have held.*

Rejection bent close enough for her absence to press into Brynlee's skin. *You broke, and in breaking, you bound them.*

Loneliness leaned close. *You're not erased from it. You're the spark. We did not call you chosen because you were perfect. We called you chosen because you were breakable enough to bend without snapping*

The visions winked out, one by one.

Still here," she thought. But it wasn't defiance now. It was truth. She fell through silence.

The Repair

Her phone sat heavy in her hand like it knew what she owed. Harper's name glowed on the screen, unopened threads stacked like bricks, each one left to rot. She scrolled until she hit the first one—back before the silence, before the fight, before she'd chosen everyone but the girl who had been there from birth.

Thumb hovering. Heart hammering. If she pressed, the whole world might collapse.

Do it.

Her fingers stuttered over the keys. *Can we talk?* Delete. *I miss you.* Delete. Finally, one word: *Please.* Sent before she could stop herself.

The dots blinked, vanished. Blinked again. Vanished again. The kind of hesitation that hurt worse than silence.

Hours later, Harper showed. No dramatic knock, no explosion of anger. Just her in the doorway, hair tangled from wind, bracelets quiet for once.

Brynlee's throat closed. "We had plans," she said before she could lose courage. You haven't forgotten, right? You're not going to let my selfishness erase us?

Harper's eyes flashed, wet but sharp. "I remember everything. That's the problem. Every good thing I had—every laugh, every stupid inside joke—had your face on it. And when you shut me out, it all broke. Do you get that? You didn't just drop me, Bryn. You took everything with you."

Her knees nearly buckled under the weight. "I thought I was protecting you."

"From what? From being my best friend? From caring about you?" Harper's voice cracked, but she didn't look away. "You can't call that protection. You call that selfish."

The word lodged in her ribs like glass. She nodded fast, too fast. "I know. I was selfish. I was wrong. But I'm here. I'm trying now."

For a long moment, Harper said nothing. Just stood there, arms crossed, jaw tight. Then she sighed, bracelets clinking faintly. One hand pushed her hair back, and for half a second her mouth twitched like it wanted to smile—old muscle memory trying to resurface. She smothered it, but the flicker stayed.

"I'm not promising you forever again. But I'll sit down."

Brynlee nearly sobbed with relief. She bit it back and slid over, leaving space on the bed.

Harper sat, not touching, not smiling, but not leaving either. The bed dipped under her weight. The air smelled like rain on metal.

It wasn't a bow. It wasn't perfect. It was a splintered thing, taped together. But it was theirs again, for now.

New Walls

The house didn't sag. That was the first thing Brynlee noticed as the car pulled up. The rooflines were straight, shutters fresh-painted. A wide porch stretched across the front, not showy, just steady, like it had been waiting for someone to sit there and drink sweet tea on summer nights.

Mara stood frozen at the curb, grocery bag still dangling from her hand, staring like the place might dissolve if she blinked. Jacob finally nudged her shoulder. "Told you," he muttered, but the crack in his voice betrayed him.

Inside, sunlight slanted through windows that actually opened. The living room smelled faintly of new carpet and lemon polish. Not mildew. Not dust. Just clean air. The kitchen had counters that gleamed instead of peeling laminate. Cabinets with hinges that didn't shriek. Mrs. Williams pressed a palm flat against the sink edge, whispering something Brynlee couldn't hear, then turned her face away fast when her eyes filled.

Upstairs, Mara claimed the corner bedroom and squealed over a built-in desk, already laying invisible plans for notebooks and nail polish. Jacob wandered into his own room, bigger than he'd ever had, and tested the door twice—open, close, open— like he didn't trust it wouldn't jam halfway.

Mr. Williams stood in the hallway, shoulders straighter than Brynlee had ever seen them. "Feels like…" He stopped, voice thick. "Feels like starting over."

Brynlee trailed her hand along the smooth banister, her chest heavy in a way she didn't have words for. The Williams family had been surviving in splinters. Now the pieces fit together again.

No chandeliers, no marble floors—none of that. Just enough. More than enough. A place with room for laughter, room for sleep that wasn't haunted by the drip of pipes or the threat of a landlord's notice.

When Mara tugged Brynlee into her room to bounce on the bed and test the springs, Brynlee laughed, really laughed, until her stomach hurt.

Borrowed Day

The mall smelled like pretzels and perfume—too sweet, too sharp. Brynlee let herself breathe it in anyway, like this was what a seventeen-year-old was supposed to do. Not haunt police stations. Not bruise under invisible hands. Just…wander from store to store, her friends orbiting beside her, shopping bags bumping against knees.

Mara shoved a pair of sunglasses onto Brynlee's face, oversized and glittering, the kind made for beach trips. "Perfect," she said, grinning. "Very European movie star."

"Very bug-eyed alien," Jacob countered. Mara snorted soda through her nose and nearly dropped the fries. Vivienne only arched a brow like she'd seen the same glasses on three magazine covers already.

"Try this one," Mara said, dropping a hoodie over Brynlee's arm like she had money to burn. Jacob made a face and mimed a model pose that cracked Vivienne's guarded smile into something real.

For a while, it worked. They were loud enough to echo off glass storefronts, close enough that shoulders brushed, easy enough to forget how brittle winter had felt. Lydia's laugh kept sneaking out, small and unsure, but each time it grew steadier.

Normal. Almost.

The sound tugged at Brynlee's chest. For months she'd only heard Lydia's voice in nightmares, in whispers of help she couldn't answer. Now here she was, arguing about sunglasses. Alive.

They collapsed in the food court, trays crowding into the sticky space between them. Grease pooled in the paper boats, soda fizzed loud enough to drown the mall's piped-in music. Lydia leaned against Brynlee's shoulder, warm, alive, fries dusting salt across her sleeve. Vivienne rolled her eyes when Jacob tried to balance a fry on his lip, but she didn't move away.

Brynlee chewed and nodded in the right places, but her phone stayed faceup on the table, screen lighting in intervals that never came from the number she wanted.

Harper.

She typed once—*Not the same without you.* Typed again—*We used to own this mall, remember?* The empty bubble blinked like it was laughing at her.

Her chest tightened. Maybe healing didn't mean the hole disappeared—just that she could walk around it. And maybe they could. Maybe this was proof: new laughter, new warmth, new weight leaning against her arm.

But when the group finally rose, bags bumping, voices bouncing off skylights, the ache tagged along.

She smiled with them. She let herself be pulled forward. She even meant some of it.

But when your person isn't there, it hits different.

Brynlee tilted the frames down her nose. "You're all jealous."

And in her head, the comeback landed the way it always had—Harper tugging the glasses off and jamming them on her own face. *"Jealous of how I look better in them? Absolutely."*

Ridiculous. Petty. Loud. Exactly the kind of moment Brynlee thought she'd lost forever.

Later, in the bathroom, she rinsed soda salt from her fingers and lifted her eyes to the mirror. She braced for lag, for the sick twist of a reflection that didn't obey. Instead, she saw herself, unbroken, unblurred. Just a girl with damp hands and tired eyes. She touched the glass—cool, flat, ordinary—and her throat tightened. No hum. No shadow. Just light.

But under the laughter, Brynlee kept catching herself staring too long—at Mara's shoulders finally loose, at Jacob joking without glancing over his shoulder, at Vivienne allowing herself to smile like she wasn't afraid it would be taken away, all while missing Harper's bracelets clattering back into her space like she'd never left it. Even at Lydia, quiet but steady, sipping her smoothie until it was gone and the straw scraped.

This could have been erased.

She would have come back to Harper tossing her a shopping bag. *"Don't freak—it's just nail polish. You need color in your life."*

Brynlee would catch it, almost laughing. Almost crying.

For one afternoon, the weight lifted. For one afternoon, they were just teenagers again, standing under the mall skylight, laughter bouncing off tile and glass.

A day on loan from the silence.

Chorus

Mara

I prayed the day I met her. Not the way you're supposed to, with folded hands and quiet words. Just in my head—don't let her see how hungry we are, don't let her see we don't fit.

But she did. She saw everything. And instead of running, she stayed.

I think about that a lot now. About how she sat down at our table when everyone else walked by like we were invisible. About how she looked at me and Jacob like we weren't charity, like we weren't shame.

Sometimes I wonder if she knows what that means—to be noticed. To be chosen.

✦

Jacob

She doesn't know it, but she's loud. Even when she's silent, she's loud. A room changes when she walks in.

For months, I hated it. I thought it was arrogance, like she thought she was better than the rest of us. Maybe part of her did. But now I think it's something else.

Hope's loud, too. It grates when you're used to quiet. It pushes in where you didn't ask for it. That's her. Loud hope.

I don't know what that makes me, needing it. But I do.

✦

Harper

Every secret I ever had, she carried. My crushes. My failures. My stupid fears I couldn't tell anyone else. I thought that was love. Maybe it was.

Turns out it was also armor.

Because when she pulled away, every bad thing I'd buried came crawling back. All the nights she patched me together without even knowing—it all came undone. I hated her for that. Still do, a little.

But here's the thing: she's still the first person I want to tell everything to. Even now. Even when it hurts.

✦

Vivienne

I told myself she was just another girl with loud shoes and louder opinions. Someone who didn't know the rules of orbiting people like us. Someone I could ignore.

But I couldn't.

The first time she looked at me, really looked, I wanted to hate her for it. Because she saw something I'd worked so hard to hide. Because she didn't flinch.

And because for one second, I felt seen in a way money never bought.

I hated it. I needed it. I still do.

✦

Lydia

I used to think being forgotten was worse than being taken. That maybe if no one remembered me, the hurt wouldn't either.

But she remembered. She saw me in the glass when no one else did. She screamed my name when I couldn't scream my own.

I still don't know why it was me she fought for. I was gone so long I stopped counting. I stopped believing anyone would come.

But when I close my eyes, I hear her anyway. That voice cutting through the dark. That promise she never made out loud but kept anyway.

She's the reason I'm here. Breathing. Standing. Saying my own name.

The Departure

The airport felt like a place made of goodbyes, even when it was supposed to be beginnings. Announcements bled from the intercom, the same handful of syllables twisted in too many accents. Kids dragged suitcases with wheels that squeaked. A couple argued quietly over boarding passes.

Brynlee kept her grip tight on her own ticket, like it might vanish if she let it breathe. The others were ahead—Vivienne gliding as if she'd always belonged in terminals like this, Mara and Jacob trying to hide their wide-eyed excitement behind sarcasm, Lydia hugging her jacket tighter, still learning how to be alive in crowded spaces. They were hers now, all of them. But there was still a hollow place beside her.

She checked her phone again. The last text to Harper glared back—*Not the same without you.* No reply.

Her parents had cried at security, their arms too much, their goodbyes too careful. They wanted her safe. They didn't understand that safety had been torn open long ago. This trip wasn't escape; it was what came after surviving.

A chime split the air. Final boarding call. The group moved toward the gate, pulling her with them.

And then—

A voice—sharp as glass, cutting through the terminal.

"You thought you could do this without me?"

Brynlee spun before she even let herself hope.

Harper.

Messy braid, crooked eyeliner, carry-on slung like she owned the world. Her chest heaving, her eyes burning, her mouth set in that familiar half-dare, half-demand.

Not a question. A verdict.

Brynlee's throat closed around every apology she'd rehearsed and lost. Harper was already moving—fast, hard, the kind of collision you couldn't brace for. Arms clamped around her, crushing, desperate, shaking. Brynlee's feet left the floor for half a breath. Relief hit like a bruise.

She buried her face in Harper's shoulder and let it out—the sob she'd held back for months. Harper only squeezed tighter, her own voice breaking against her ear:

"You're stuck with me, Hall. Always were."

Something inside Brynlee unknotted.

They pulled apart just enough to look at each other. Harper's grin wobbled but didn't fall. Brynlee laughed through tears, ridiculous and alive, because there was no other way to hold all of it.

The gate attendant glanced up, impatient, but Brynlee didn't care. She had what she needed.

Together, they crossed the jetway.

The metal groaned beneath their steps, the air different on the other side—sharper, cleaner, sinking deeper into her lungs like she hadn't breathed right until now. The floor didn't echo anymore. It carried. Like the world had finally stopped holding its breath.

She looked once at the window as the plane waited, engines humming low. Reflections wavered in the glass, three shadows fading at last—Pain, Loneliness, Rejection—watching, then dissolving like mist. Not gone. Just done.

Brynlee's hand brushed Harper's, her anchor and her proof.

Every step forward steadied. She was still here. And this time, she was not alone.

Epilogue

Florence was softer than she imagined. The kind of city that didn't need to shout to be seen.

Sunlight climbed the stone roofs in slow gold, catching on windows and domes, turning everything warm enough to hurt a little.

Brynlee stood at the overlook above Piazzale Michelangelo, suitcase at her side, the wind brushing her sleeves. Below, the Arno glimmered between bridges like a long-held breath finally let go. Bells chimed somewhere behind her—low, steady, older than anything she could name.

The others had drifted ahead—Mara and Jacob arguing about gelato flavors, Vivienne pretending not to listen, Harper tugging at her sleeve with a grin that meant *come on, you'll miss it*. Even Lydia, quiet as ever, had color in her cheeks again.

They had all found a way forward. So had she. Maybe that was the point.

She glanced down at her hands, tracing the faint lines the Spirits had left behind. They weren't marks anymore—just memory, folded into skin that had learned how to hold the world without flinching.

Her phone buzzed once. A text from her mom:

You seeing the light yet?

Brynlee typed back: *Yeah. It's different here.*

The reply came almost immediately. *Good. Let it in.*

She smiled, tucking the phone away. For a moment she caught her reflection in the brass of the railing, just herself—no flicker, no lag. The absence felt like mercy.

The plane tickets rustled in her pocket when the wind shifted, paper against fabric, ready for whatever came next. She'd spent so long waiting for her life to start again that she hadn't realized it already had.

"Bryn!" Harper called, waving from the steps below. The sound carried easily now, through clean air.

Brynlee turned, her pulse steady, her steps sure.

The sun broke through the clouds then—hard and brilliant—and the whole city glowed like it had been holding its breath for her.

She didn't look back.

There was no need to anymore.

Author's Note

If You Look Away didn't begin as a book.

It began as an English paper my daughter, Jessica, wrote in high school—a modern take on *A Christmas Carol*, where the Spirits weren't Past, Present, and Future, but Pain, Loneliness, and Rejection.

Something about that idea stayed with me—the way those emotions can haunt and shape us just as deeply as any ghost.

I wanted to know what would happen if those Spirits walked into a modern life, into a girl who had everything and still felt unseen.

That question became this story.

I thought I was writing about loss—what happens when the world cracks and no one notices.

But somewhere between the drafts and the silence, it became a story about survival, and about the quiet, persistent ways love and light find their way back in.

Brynlee's journey isn't neat. It isn't tied with a bow. Neither is healing.

Sometimes it's just the choice to wake up, to keep moving, to reach for one more light in a world still learning how to hold you.

If you've ever felt unseen, unheard, or unsure of where you belong—this one's for you.

You're still here. You're still moving. That's enough.

Thank you for reading, for feeling, for not looking away.

With love,

Devona Burgess

ABOUT THE AUTHOR

 Devona Burgess is an author, publisher, and creative visionary whose stories walk the line between light and shadow—between beauty and brutality, faith and fear, truth and obsession.

She is founder of Devona Burgess Publishing Group, home to three imprints that reflect her range: *Hollow Mark Press* for psychological thrillers, *Little Lumen Books* for children's titles, and *Salt & Sparrow Press* for faith-based works.

Devona lives in the Appalachian foothills, where the mountains often find their way into her stories. She shares her life with her husband, Quincy, their four children, and a close-knit family that remains at the heart of everything she creates.

www.ingramcontent.com/pod-product-compliance
Lightning Source LLC
Chambersburg PA
CBHW021406110726
47901CB00008B/2081